Totally Bound Publishing books by Alexa Milne:

Sporting Chance

I0681386

SPORTING CHANCE

ALEXA MILNE

Sporting Chance
ISBN # 978-1-78430-303-7
©Copyright Alexa Milne 2014
Cover Art by Posh Gosh ©Copyright October 2014
Interior text design by Claire Siemaszkiewicz
Totally Bound Publishing

Published in 2014 by Totally Bound Publishing, Newland House, The Point, Weaver Road, Lincoln, LN6 3QN, United Kingdom.

SPORTING
CHANCE

Dedication

This is my first novel and many people helped me get it to completion. To begin with, I'd like to thank Julia, who read it through and made suggestions, and Sue, who wants me to tell you Iestyn is pronounced Yest-in. Next, I'd like to thank Faith, my editor, for all her encouragement and advice. Lastly, I'd like to thank Cath, who helped me at every stage of the process, listened to my grumbling and taught me practically everything I know about correct punctuation.

Chapter One

Oh hell!

His arse hit the ice.

This was going to be so embarrassing.

He really should have looked where he was going and taken more care. It wasn't that he meant to show off in front of the kids when they'd goaded him into demonstrating how he could skate backward. But that was how he found himself crashing into another body, a rather large male body, then scrabbling, unsuccessfully, to try to get himself up as he apologized. Iestyn heard the kids laughing. How the hell was he going to get up and retain some sort of dignity? Whose bloody idea had it been to come on this skating trip from school, and why had he volunteered to go? He heard a voice—a rather gorgeous lyrical voice—say something, but he wasn't sure what. He found himself looking up into the face of the most handsome man he'd ever seen.

"Would you like some help getting up?" the vision said, holding out a hand.

Iestyn took the help offered and let the good-looking stranger pull him to his feet. He was shocked to find, when he'd stood up, that the man appeared to be significantly taller than his own nearly six feet.

"Thanks," he said, brushing the ice from his trousers. He glanced over to find the kids staring at him. "What? You've seen a man fall over before, haven't you? Even a teacher."

But they just kept on staring at the man who had helped him up.

"Sorry about that lot. Honestly, you can't take them anywhere, and thanks for hauling me up. I'm not very good at this lark, really." He didn't want to stare but he couldn't resist looking the man up and down. His rescuer was impressively built with blue eyes and blond hair that seemed determined to defy any sort of styling.

"Yeah, that much is obvious but don't worry. I can cope with men falling at my feet. I get it a lot, though usually it's because they've just missed tackling me. The blond, godlike creature held out his hand. "Sorry. It's not often that I have to introduce myself. My name is Dan Morgan."

"Ah, judging from the reaction of the kids, I should have heard of you."

A smaller man, who was standing behind them, sniggered at his comment.

One of the boys rushed forward. "Can I have your autograph, Dan?" he asked.

The other kids came forward too, offering whatever they could find for him to sign.

"You don't have any idea who I am, do you?" the younger man said as he signed the autographs.

"No, sorry. I don't, but obviously the kids do, so you're either some sort of pop star or, from what you've said, a sportsman. I'm guessing rugby."

Josh, a character in Iestyn's form, stepped forward. "Take no notice of Mr Jones. The only game he plays is chess. He wouldn't know one end of a rugby ball from the other."

"Well, to be fair, they are actually pretty similar," Dan replied.

Iestyn frowned at Josh, not for the first time, then looked back at Dan. "So you play rugby then, and I should know this because?"

"Bloody hell, sir. Sorry, but he's Dan Morgan." Now it was Josh's turn to frown. "He plays for Glamorgan Giants and Wales. Most experts reckon that he's going to be Welsh captain for the Six Nations. Call yourself Welsh, sir!"

"Actually, that's rather a moot point. I may be called Jones but I wasn't born in Wales, despite my father's best efforts. I was born in the Highlands of Scotland, because we were on holiday and I came earlier than expected. My dad was gutted, I can tell you."

"Sounds like an interesting story," Dan said. "Perhaps you'd like to tell it to me sometime soon, maybe over dinner."

Iestyn Jones blinked a few times and wondered if he'd heard right. Had this guy just asked him out? Dan had to be at least ten years younger than him, not to mention six inches taller.

Dan passed him a card that said "Ring me" and gave a number. He smiled and walked back to greet his friend who had been standing some distance away. Watching him go, Iestyn held onto the card and twirled it in his fingers, not sure how to react to this strange development.

"You're in there, sir," he heard a familiar voice say.

"Shut up, Josh. Come on. I see Miss Jenkins over there tapping her watch. It's time we weren't here."

"But, sir, he's gay and you're gay," Josh persisted.

"Really?" He shouldn't have been surprised. His gaydar was normally useless. "Never mind that. I don't need a matchmaker, thank you." That he was gay was no secret to the kids or to any of the other staff.

His best friend Julie Jenkins came toward him. "Is it right what the kids have just told me? Have you just been asked out by Dan Morgan? My God, he's gorgeous. I can't tell you how many women would like a piece of him."

"Well," Iestyn said, grinning widely. "It seems that Dan Morgan wants a piece of me."

Chapter Two

"So are you going to ring him, then?" Julie asked that night.

Julie was Iestyn's oldest friend. They'd lived on the same street and gone to the same schools. However, their choice of university had parted them and Julie had gone off and gotten married. It had lasted all of three years before she had returned home. Now Julie taught music at two schools on a part-time basis.

It was Friday, so tradition had it that their group went out, had a few drinks, then went to one home or another for takeaway curry, pizza, or Chinese. There were six of them in their little group — Iestyn and Julie, along with Matt who taught PE, Sian who taught art, and Gareth, who had claimed to teach science — however, not everyone had been convinced of that. He'd since trained as a plumber, having found that teaching was not for him. These days they were lucky to get him out on a Friday as 'time was money'. Still, it was nice to have a tame plumber on call.

Lastly, there was Kate, who taught a variety of subjects that ended in 'ology'. Most people who saw them all together assumed that they were three couples, which wasn't the case.

Except for Julie, they had all started teaching at the school at the same time and had become friends. As they were all sad and single, as Gareth often described them, they had developed the habit of going out on Friday nights. Of course, nothing was ever that simple about the group dynamic. Julie fancied Matt, who was completely oblivious — or appeared to be. Sian fancied Kate but said nothing. Iestyn thought both the other men were handsome but as both appeared to be straight — other than the occasional drunken snog — he kept on looking elsewhere. Now he had Dan's phone number.

As soon as he'd gotten home that night, he'd Googled Dan Morgan. Iestyn had to admit that the guy looked great in shorts. Those thighs and shoulders were impressive, and he even looked good in a suit. There were several photos of him receiving prizes for being the young Welsh player of the year. The stories mentioned Dan's apparently now exboyfriend Aron Roberts. Iestyn noted that they'd been together since high school, but there was no official announcement of why they were no longer a couple.

He disliked uncertainties and he wasn't about to step on anyone's toes. He knew he was an old-fashioned romantic but he didn't like to share and he'd never really been into one-night stands. Well, not often, especially after the embarrassing incident in the bus shelter all those years ago. He'd managed to get to the age of thirty-four and had slept with fewer than ten people, although 'slept with' was pushing it for some of them. He'd had two long-term boyfriends but no one else since he'd had his heart broken by Steve.

He couldn't understand why the handsome rugby international star should have given him his phone number.

"Are you ever going to answer me, or are you already imagining what he could be doing with you?" Julie continued.

"Sorry," Iestyn replied. "I was just thinking."

"Yeah, we can imagine," Gareth commented. "He's a big lad. Are you sure you can handle him?" He laughed at his own innuendo.

"God, he wishes," Matt added. "He really is a fantastic player and he should be Welsh captain soon. Some people think he might be made captain for the Six Nations. Hey, if you get to shag him, d'you think you could get him to come to the school to talk to my boys? A local lad who made good always helps inspire them."

"Hmm, I haven't even decided if I'm going to ring him yet. From what I've read, he had a long-term boyfriend. They could get back together again. Perhaps this Dan is trying to make him jealous, and I'm not that sort of bloke."

"Looked him up, then," Sian said, smiling.

"Well, yeah, it's not every day that a bloke ten years younger and six inches taller, with more than enough muscles to spare and a great arse, gives you his number. I'm knackered, not bloody dead. Well, not quite."

"Him and his boyfriend split up a while back, according to the gossip columns," Sian continued. "The boyfriend went to America to work and there's no rugby there so…"

"Therefore, I repeat my question," said Julie. "Are you going to ring him? He obviously wants you to. Otherwise, he wouldn't have given you his number."

"But why would he give Iestyn his number? Sorry, I know you're my friend, but let's face it—you're a nerd and a geek. You're hardly love's young dream, are you?" Gareth, as always, said what others just thought. "And the man is fit. Whereas you consider table tennis to be active. I don't get it. What could he possibly have in common with you?"

"Yeah, I suppose you've got the advantage of height, but you're out of condition and you could do with losing a few pounds," Matt added.

"Not to mention your hair is beginning to recede and you're as blind as a bat without those glasses. Why you don't wear contacts, I don't know," Julie finished.

"Okay, anything else before I go home and put a bag over my head? So far I'm fat, geeky and myopic, but I am six foot so that makes up for it."

"Actually, you do scrub up well, when you try. I'll give you some exercises that'll tone you up. Perhaps you can start coming to the gym with me. Tell you what, why don't you join me tomorrow?" Matt said.

"Suddenly, I'm really hungry. Think we can forgo the karaoke tonight? So what are we having and where are we going to eat?" Iestyn said.

"It's my turn," Kate replied. "So let's have Chinese and pick up some more to drink. You'll have something to work off in the morning, then."

"Sounds good to me. Chinese is always better when there are lots of us as we can eat each other's. Drink up and we can get going."

Chapter Three

Iestyn strolled into the staffroom at seven forty-five on Monday morning. He still hadn't made that phone call. He'd gone to the gym with Matt on Saturday morning but felt so useless that he'd found he couldn't face ringing anyone, let alone someone whom he'd watched play rugby on TV that afternoon. The man really was sex on a stick. So, instead of picking up the phone, he'd spent Saturday night in, playing chess against someone in Australia. Thankfully he'd managed to win a few games, which had propped up his fragile ego and made him feel slightly less useless.

He'd spent Sunday at his parents. At least these days he didn't have to explain to his nan that he was gay and so hadn't found a nice girl to settle down with yet. Strangely, he missed his nan a lot. She'd been forthright and took no prisoners, his nan. It had been six months since she'd died at ninety-three. Somehow, every other Sunday, when he returned to his parents for lunch, he expected to be greeted by her usual opening gambit of "Not lost any weight then I see!" And so Sunday had passed without the call being made. Having sorted out things for the day in his room, he returned to the staffroom, taking the seat opposite Matt and Kate. At first, everything seemed the same as usual then Vicky, the school secretary, had come in, sat next to him and got her pen out, ready to take the briefing notes. She leaned toward him conspiratorially.

"So, I believe you met Dan Morgan on Friday afternoon."

Iestyn wondered for a moment then remembered that her son Adrian had been on the trip.

"Yes, he managed to break my fall very successfully and was still able to play on Saturday," he explained.

"I'm surprised they let him skate, you know, just in case he got injured," Vicky continued. "Perhaps he'd just sneaked out. He's gay, you know."

"Yes, so I'm told." Iestyn was really trying not to sound irritated by her obvious insinuation. Why was it that some people seemed to believe that if two gay men met each other they would want to get into each other's pants?

"So did you give him your number?" she asked, oblivious to Iestyn's growing annoyance.

Matt leaned across the table. "No, he didn't, but Dan Morgan gave Iestyn his number, didn't he? So have you rung him yet?"

Vicky stared at him. "Really? Dan Morgan gave you his number? Bloody hell!"

Iestyn said nothing when Vicky got up and took a seat at another table. He saw Kate glare at Matt.

"Why did you say that?" she snapped at Matt. "Now everyone will know. You're as thick as pig shit sometimes and have the emotional intelligence of a gnat."

He watched the news cross the staffroom like a Mexican wave until he could stand it no more and walked out, almost knocking over the senior leadership team as they came in.

* * * *

A little while later, Iestyn was sitting in his room. Now he was going to be the center of speculation. He decided to stay there for the whole day. At least this way the gossips would have to come and find him if they were that bothered. The bell rang and his form began to troop in.

"Sir, Ady says that you fell on Dan Morgan last Friday. Did you, really? God, he's fit, sir. Such a pity he's gay. Still, that wouldn't bother you, would it, sir? So did he say anything to you? Did you get his autograph? Ady says Mr Morgan signed his shirt."

"That's enough, Megan. Yes, I did meet Mr Morgan, but only for a few minutes."

"Long enough for him to give you his number, though, sir!" Josh Richards shouted as he came in the door.

"Thank you, Josh. Late again, I see."

A clamoring of questions followed about whether what Josh had said was true, about how lucky Iestyn was and when was he going out with the rugby player, and where were they going to go on their date. Iestyn wanted the floor to open up and swallow him. It continued in the same way for the rest of the day from all the older pupils as the rumor went round.

He finally made a decision. He would ring Dan that night when he got home, after a couple of beers. He would. He really would, wouldn't he?

Chapter Four

Iestyn stared at the phone then at the number on the card. He traced the number again and again until he could have tapped it out from memory. Then the phone rang and he jumped a mile. He half expected it to be Dan Morgan but no, it was Julie.

"Have you called him yet? What did he say? Was he nice? I bet he was lovely, wasn't he? Come on, spill, Jones." She stopped abruptly. "You haven't called him, have you?"

Staying silent, Iestyn didn't know whether to nod or shake his head.

"Well?" Julie asked.

Iestyn heard her tapping her pen on something.

"No, not really." He paused. "Okay, not at all. I just keep thinking that he was only being polite. Come on, Julie. He's an international rugby player and I'm a history teacher who thinks that chess is a sport. I hate getting a fleck of mud on my suit and he loves wallowing in the stuff. We have nothing in common. We'd just sit there. It would be embarrassing and well...you know." He suddenly realized he was talking to himself. She'd put the phone down on him. She *really* had.

A couple of minutes later the doorbell sounded. Once he opened the door, Julie pushed past him into the living room. She picked up the card Iestyn had left on the arm of the sofa, grabbed his discarded phone and dialed the number before he could stop her. Then it connected and he heard the words "Dan Morgan" spoken in those deep Welsh tones.

"Is anyone there?" Dan continued.

Iestyn grabbed the receiver. "Yes, sorry. It's me," he began.

"Me who?" Dan asked. "Come on, who is this and how did you get this number?"

"You gave it to me," Iestyn said. "My name's Iestyn Jones. We bumped into each other skating last Friday."

"Oh, yeah, so we did." Dan suddenly sounded a lot more interested. "You decided to call after all, Mr Jones. I'd begun to think you weren't going to, but here you are. So, how shall we do this?"

Iestyn could almost hear a purr in Dan's voice, which would definitely be affecting a certain part of his anatomy if Julie weren't right next to him.

"I don't know," he said. "You asked me to call and now the ball, to coin a phrase, is in your hands."

"Okay, what about dinner Saturday night? The restaurant in St David's Hotel is good. Let's meet in the bar at seven, shall we?"

Iestyn swallowed and tried not to wince as Julie was holding his thigh so hard it would leave finger marks.

"Yeah, that would be good. I've never eaten there. It's a pity it's too cold for eating on the terrace. I believe the view is lovely. Even better, I'll be on holiday by then. But haven't you got a game on Saturday?"

"Yes, we've a cup match against the Ospreys but we're at home. I'm sure I can get ready in time. So it's a date, then. I'm looking forward to finding out all about you, Iestyn Jones."

A shiver traveled down his spine. "I'll meet you at seven then, Dan." He put the phone down and looked at Julie, who finally removed her hand.

"See, I told you," she said. "It sounds like he's dying to get into your pants."

"What? You think I'm going to sleep with him on our first date? Not a chance of that. I don't even know what the situation is with his old boyfriend yet. No matter how good-looking and famous he is, I'm not just going to have sex with him, even if he asks nicely."

Julie looked at him with a glint in her eye. "Well, you are having dinner with him in a hotel. You haven't considered that he might book a room just in case?" she teased.

"Oh, God, d'you think so?" He fell back against the sofa.

Julie got up and came back with a glass of wine.

"Here, drink this," she said, "and tell Aunty Julie."

"It's just… Well, I haven't…"

"Ah, yes, it's been a while, hasn't it? I never like to ask. Everyone seems to imagine that gay men are out cruising every night."

Iestyn made a noise something like a cross between a harrumph and a snort. "Oh, yeah. That's me—out every night with my tight T-shirt and jeans, finding men who'll give me a hard time." He laughed when he saw Julie's face, "Oh, all right, poor choice of words."

"I would have thought an accurate one," she said. "So I gather it has been a while. Since Steve?" she questioned.

"Yep, since that bastard told me that we were over and buggered off to Nottingham to be an assistant head. He didn't even tell me about the interview. Six months we'd been together."

"But you didn't love him, did you? He wasn't the one."

"No, I suppose not." He put down the wine and placed his head in Julie's lap.

"Oh God, Julie, do you still believe in *the* one? We're not getting any younger, are we? You thought you'd found him and we both know how that turned out."

"No, you're right. He wasn't. In the end, leaving him was easy—easier than it should have been. But what did I do? I just scurried back to you, my gay best friend, and safety." Her phone sang out *I Will Survive*.

"I must change that." She looked at the screen. "It's Matt. Hi," she said.

Iestyn got up and poured another glass. He looked at the pile of Year Twelve essays only half marked on his desk and knew he'd have to get up at five am to try to finish them.

"Yes, Matt, he did ring your rugby player, and no, he didn't start by asking him if he fancied coming to coach your under fourteens rugby team. I think he had other things on his mind. Yes, they are going out to dinner on Saturday. I'll mention it to him or you can tomorrow. Perhaps you'd like to announce it in assembly that they're having dinner together, just to be certain that everyone knows. Yes, true, but sometimes you are an unthinking arsehole, who believes that everything revolves around you and sport. Oh, don't give me the hurt voice. You know it doesn't work on me. I'm not one of those women who only want to squeeze your pecs or look at your six-pack. You forget that I've seen them too often. We'll see you tomorrow, so go and lift some weights, or drink a protein shake, or whatever it is that you do." She pressed the *Off* button and sighed.

"You like him, don't you?" Iestyn said.

"Is it that obvious?" she replied.

"Only to me. You always get cross with men you like. When we were little, you used to shout at me all the time then try to kiss me."

"And you used to run away and hide. I should have known then that you didn't like girls."

"To be fair, most ten-year-old boys don't like girls," he said, defending himself.

"Yeah, but you used to look goggle-eyed at Mark Davey when you were ten. You even bought football cards so you could swap them with him and pretended to know who played for City because he supported them."

"Then he broke my little heart by moving to Cirencester and I didn't understand why I cried every night for a week."

Julie hugged him. "But there was always me," she said, "and there always will be."

"Perhaps we should get married," he said.

"Marry you? Ye gods, I'd have to put up with a sci-fi fan who plays chess and talks about history. Not a chance, Iestyn. Not a bloody chance in hell!"

Chapter Five

He picked Julie up at six thirty for the annual staff Christmas party held at a local hotel. He usually hated these evenings and only went to them because the others called him names if he didn't.

"You look stunning," he said, as Julie teetered down the path from her house. Luckily, the ice and snow had abated for a while and it was merely cold. Her tight-fitting, green dress accentuated every curve and set off the red hair cascading around her shoulders.

"Thank goodness," she said, getting into the car. "I feel like I can't breathe wearing the complete Gok Wan collection needed to smooth everything off, and these shoes are a bit of a challenge. You're not so bad yourself but then you always do look good in a suit. Have you decided what you're going to wear for your date yet?"

Iestyn put the car into gear and set off. "I thought I'd wear the dark gray three-piece," he said. "I can't decide whether to go for a white shirt or something with color. I have a purple one that goes well with the suit."

"Oh, go for the purple one. Although you look good in the red one you've got on tonight as well. Are you going to wear your glasses?" she asked.

"You know I'm blind as a bat without them. I'd never be able to read the menu. Anyway, I had them on when I nearly knocked him over. Perhaps he likes the geeky look."

The streets of Cardiff, decorated with strings of colorful Christmas lights, were filled with traffic and idiots who seemed determined to get themselves killed crossing the road as they dashed from shop to shop in search of presents. Iestyn had been forced to stop more than once as he negotiated his way through the throng of people. They arrived just in time to get some drinks and take their seats opposite Kate, who was telling Sian about an event at St David's Hall in the New Year.

"I'll come with you," Sian offered.

"Really?" Kate said. "I wasn't sure it was your thing. The music is a bit modern. We could have dinner in the restaurant before if you want."

Iestyn noticed the hopeful smile that crossed Sian's lips and wondered if Kate really was oblivious to how Sian felt about her. He looked up when Matt arrived at the table, saw Julie's face and realized that some people obviously just couldn't see for looking.

"You're all looking gorgeous, ladies," Matt said as he sat down next to Iestyn. "It should be a good night," he continued, looking around at all the other groups there for the dinner and disco. "These office girls are often up for a bit of extra-curricular activity."

Julie sighed.

He smiled wanly. *Yep, people can be oblivious to the obvious.*

The meal was nothing special, just a typical Christmas dinner. The conversation was all about plans for the holidays. He was going to his parents, as usual. Julie was having dinner with her sister's family, and the others were much the same, planning to spend time with various family members.

"What's Gareth doing?" Iestyn asked Matt.

"He says he's on call, because he can charge triple time over Christmas, so he doesn't really care. He's going away over New Year's to the Barbados on his own," Matt explained. "You know what he's like. I think he's hoping to meet some rich woman while he's there."

The meal over, the tables were cleared and the dancing began. It didn't take long for the drink to set in and for people's inhibitions to begin diminishing. He watched with Julie as Matt danced his way around the floor. He really was incredible. The woman crowded around him like moths to a flame as he wriggled his bottom with his hands above his head, spinning to face all of those around him in turn. Iestyn hugged her, knowing how she'd be feeling as Matt performed.

"He really does have a great arse, doesn't he?" Iestyn observed. "He always reminds me of that bit in the film *In and Out* when Kevin Kline tries not to dance then goes for it. I don't think Matt knows how *not* to go for it on the dance floor. Anyone who moves like that really *should* be gay."

He put his chin on Julie's shoulder and observed for a while as a woman allowed Matt to grind against her. They moved as one. The floor pulsated with people allowing little room to maneuver. The woman turned and whispered into Matt's ear. He smiled at her and watched her leave the floor. Iestyn half expected him to follow. Instead, Matt pushed his way through the crowd and came back to the table, falling down into the seat next to Iestyn.

"Having a good time?" Iestyn asked.

"You know me," Matt replied. "I'm always willing to keep women happy."

Iestyn sensed Julie tensing beside him.

"You should try it, Iestyn, rather than sitting here nursing your mineral water. I don't know why you chose to drive. Anyway, I hear Dan Morgan likes to move his body." He rose and pulled Iestyn up with him. "Come on. I'll show you how."

Matt spooned against his back and Iestyn let him for a moment. "For fuck's sake, Matt, you know it's not really me," he said, sitting again. It wasn't that he couldn't dance but he always carefully chose *where* and *when* he let himself go.

"Oh, well," Matt said as *Relax* started to play. "Time to shake my arse again and please all the ladies."

"Why don't you go out there with him, Julie?" Iestyn asked her.

"Look at them, Iestyn. They're all size eight with perfect hair and teeth, and willing to put out. I feel like an old woman next to them. Why the hell would he want me?"

"Because you're beautiful. You've just lost your confidence. Some women would kill for those curves and your hair color. Come on, dance with me."

She looked confused. "But you hate dancing. I've hardly ever seen you dance."

Iestyn smiled. "Well, we all have our secrets. I can move but I've always felt a bit embarrassed about it. Mum made me do ballroom dancing when I was little. I have a bronze medal, you know. I can still do a decent foxtrot or tango. I'll risk looking like an idiot so you'll look good next to me." He hadn't told her about what had happened in Ibiza. He'd gotten completely drunk when Steve had gone off with another bloke to have sex on the beach. Iestyn had danced himself stupid and allowed a complete stranger to rut against him on the crowded dance floor. When the guy had put his hand down Iestyn's jeans and made him come, he hadn't given a damn. He supposed that had been the beginning of the end for him and Steve. A few weeks later, Steve had told him that he was leaving.

Within minutes, Julie and Iestyn were on the floor dancing to *Crazy Right Now,* shaking their arses and not caring. Iestyn glanced over at Matt, who had to pick his chin up. Matt stared even more at them when some bloke started paying attention to Julie, swinging her around the floor.

Iestyn made a discreet exit and sat down. He watched Sian on the floor with Kate. He thought they looked comfortable whispering to each other. Perhaps Sian wasn't completely barking up the wrong tree. Kate was pretty cagey about her love life. Julie was thoroughly enjoying the attention from the few people around her when suddenly Matt appeared and took her by the hand. The others melted into the crowd as she spun around in front of him. Matt followed suit. To Iestyn, it was like staring at an astonishing mating dance on a natural history program. They moved together then apart, both teasing the other. Julie shamelessly pushed back against Matt. The lights flashed different colors and the music blared.

Iestyn found his mind wandering to his dinner plans with Dan on Saturday. He wondered what the other man wanted from him. It had been a while since he'd been intimate with anyone. Since Steve had left, Iestyn had put on some weight, whereas the rugby player appeared perfect. Still, at least he'd get a dinner out of it. He looked up to find that Matt and Julie had disappeared. As he scanned the room for them, his phone beeped for an incoming text.

Had an offer I couldn't refuse. Love you. Julie xx

Iestyn wanted to be pleased for his friends. He loved both of them and he wanted them to be happy, but he read the message with mixed feelings. *Maybe it'll all work out. Bugger.* But although he'd sort of encouraged her, he thought there would be pieces to pick up in the morning. It would probably end in tears—mostly Julie's.

The clock struck midnight. Kate and Sian were still dancing. Sitting by himself, a sense of total loneliness swept over him. He really didn't want to stay there anymore. He found his car and drove home. He needed some sleep to rest his shoulder. He suspected that one way or another it was going to get some use in the morning.

Chapter Six

Iestyn opened one eye when his phone buzzed at three the following morning. His head didn't appreciate the movement. Perhaps having those few solitary drinks when he'd got home hadn't been a good idea after all. He picked up the glass of water next to his bed and swallowed a couple of mouthfuls. He looked at the message and realized it was Julie.

It read simply—

Shit!

His phone buzzed again an hour later. This time the voice message was male and somewhat more eloquent.

"Bugger! You're to blame for this, Jones. I need to get out of this. Never sleep with people you work with. Look what happened to you. Shit! Fuck!"

Two hours later, his alarm went off and he wished that Chris Evans wasn't quite so full of himself in the morning. He groped his way to the shower and just stood there for several minutes letting the water wash over him. He shampooed his hair and lathered himself until he felt almost human. His mouth tasted like a rusty tin can and he guessed that his breath could drop a moose. Back in his bedroom, he picked out one of his school suits, a white shirt and navy tie, then carefully went downstairs.

Still a little delicate from the night before, he made himself a large mug of tea and decided on toast. He sat chewing each mouthful slowly and wondered about his two friends. They'd obviously ended up sleeping together and were now regretting it. Perhaps even now they were awkwardly greeting the morning, one of them making a quick exit from the home of the other. Iestyn thought back to when Steve had announced that they were over.

"You're going where?" he'd shouted.

"Nottingham. I've got a new job as deputy head."

"Since when? When did you go to an interview?"

"You know that two-day course before half term. I didn't want to tell you it was an interview just in case I didn't get it, but I got the job."

Iestyn shuddered, remembering the pitying look Steve had given him before Steve had finally said, "Look, this isn't really working for me, Iestyn. I think it's best if we make a clean break."

But, of course, it hadn't quite been a clean break. They hadn't moved in together so that made things easier but they'd had another four weeks of being together at work to cope with. What had made things worse was that everyone knew and everyone had tried to console him.

"He's just a complete arsehole, Iessie," Julie had said, using his family's pet name for him. "You deserve better. You never know what, or who, is just over the horizon."

And she'd been right, because tomorrow he had a date with probably the most famous rugby player in Wales.

When he pulled into the school car park, Julie's Mini was already there. He breathed in then sighed. *Best to get on with it.*

Julie wasn't in the staffroom so he climbed the stairs to the second floor and found her nursing a coffee in the music room.

"I got your text," he said to announce his presence. He had to admit that she looked terrible. Dark circles lurked under her eyes.

"Shit, Iessie, I've blown it. Now what am I going to do?"

He desperately tried to smother a snigger.

"Bloody hell, how old are you?" she said. "I like him, Iessie, and now, well, he just thinks I'm some sort of desperate lush."

"So I guess you and he…"

"Yes, Iestyn, we had sex. At least, I *think* we did."

"You think? Aren't you sure?" he asked.

Julie shrugged. "I was pretty drunk. I remember some kissing, then I woke up in very little clothing with him snoring next to me. And that's another thing. I had on that Gok Wan stuff that pulls you in. I can't remember taking it off and he'll have seen it. I wanted to get out of there so quickly I just stuffed it into my handbag."

"I assume there might have been signs of sexual activity, a used condom or, well… Do I have to spell it out? Did you take precautions?"

"I'm not sure that we got as far as full sex. He probably got bored taking off my underwear. We were both pretty far gone. Will you ask him for me?

Oh God, Iestyn. Please, never, ever let me do something like this again."

"Come on, Julie, it might not be as bad as you think. Do you want to see him again? I mean properly, like on a date? Should I try to find out how the land lies?"

"Oh, I don't know. I just want to get through today and try to forget that last night happened."

Iestyn moved behind her and gave her a big hug. "Come on, it could be worse. At least it doesn't look like you had unprotected sex, so you won't be pregnant."

She jerked her head up and hit him.

"Look, you said it didn't seem like you'd had sex, so don't worry. I'm sure you'll be okay," he tried consoling her.

"I can't believe I've been so stupid. I feel like I don't know anything about him really. Fuck! Fuck! Fuck!" Tears welled in her eyes. "I'm bloody thirty-three, not sixteen."

"I'll talk to him," Iestyn said, really not wanting to do any such thing.

He left her sniveling into a tissue and walked down the corridor to the stairwell at the other end of the building. He knew he could go faster but somehow he dreaded talking to Matt more than Julie did. He got on well with Matt. Male PE teachers were notorious for taking themselves too seriously, but Matt had a decent sense of humor and could laugh at himself. He was the sort of person lucky enough to feel comfortable in his own skin and gave the impression that he regretted nothing, so the voice message had come as a bit of a surprise to Iestyn.

He made his way to the PE office. As he approached, the pounding bass hit him. Heavy rock didn't augur well. Matt played this sort of music when he wanted to shake himself out of a mood.

Iestyn stood in the doorway, watching Matt play air guitar for a while until his friend caught sight of him mid-move, stopped abruptly and turned off the music.

"That good, eh?" Iestyn said. "I assume you scared everyone else off. I'm surprised you can stand the noise, considering how much you drank."

"You know me, Iestyn. I can handle my drink and I never get hangovers."

"So you planned last night, then?" Iestyn questioned. "I've just left Julie upstairs." He didn't want to tell Matt how upset she'd been.

"How is she? Sorry about the message— But bloody hell, Iestyn—why did you let me go off with her? You're supposed to be her best friend and protect her from the likes of me!"

"Pardon? Since when did I become her father *and* your minder? You're both adults and can make your own decisions and anyway, you slipped away before I could stop you. I assume you think that you made a mistake. Is there no chance that this is the beginning of something special? You did look good together."

"Oh, come on, Iestyn. Julie's been married before and that didn't work."

"Hang on. Are you saying she's soiled goods and not worthy of you, because if you are, I may have to explain to her why I've punched you. I know you can be a shit at times, but that's low, even for you."

"No, I'm not saying that, but you know what I mean," he continued.

"To be honest, I don't think I do. Julie married a complete arsehole. He cheated on her every chance he got. Now, I'm beginning to think you're an even bigger arsehole. Did you fuck her?" he added, feeling the need to be brutal.

"Did she say I did?" he asked.

"I'm asking you. Surely you must know."

"I remember some kissing and we got to the bedroom and removed some clothes, but after that it's a bit fuzzy."

"I think you both fell asleep," Iestyn said. "You two need to talk. Sort this out, please. I've got other things to worry about."

"Oh, yes," Matt said. "Your date with Dan Morgan. Don't forget to ask him about the rugby visit."

"Of course, Matt. 'Can you come and coach our Year Ten rugby team?' will be the first words out of my mouth," Iestyn said. "Sort it, Matt. Will you? Do you have any feelings for her?"

"I like her but she's Julie. D'you think I should ask her out properly?"

"Well, it might be that you find out you like each other. Oh, and I'm not coming out tonight, because I want to be fresh for tomorrow." He moved toward the door. "Speak to her like an adult, Matt, and do it today. Why don't you take her to the pub and see how things go?"

Matt nodded. "I'll ring you Sunday and let you know what happened."

The rest of the day was filled with Christmas activities and the end of term assembly. He had no time to speak to either of them alone again. As he left that afternoon, his phone beeped with a message.

We're going to talk tonight. Love you. Have fun tomorrow.

Iestyn smiled to himself then panicked. It would be tomorrow in twenty-four hours. Tomorrow he had a date with a gorgeous sportsman quite a bit younger than himself. The wait for Saturday evening was going to be tense.

Chapter Seven

It seemed to take ages to put a Windsor knot in his tie. He'd finally chosen the dark gray suit with a pale blue shirt and lighter gray tie. His black brogues shined after several treatments with polish and brushes. He popped his pocket watch into his waistcoat. The watch had been a present from his father, a family heirloom, and he loved to wear it with his three-piece suits. He turned in every direction, looking at himself in the mirror. Yes, there was a slight bulge around his middle, but he told himself that with his height, he could get away with it, and a waistcoat covered a myriad of sins. He pushed down his hair, put his wallet in his pocket and pulled on his black overcoat. The taxi arrived right on time.

During the drive to the hotel, his nervousness grew. He still had no idea why Dan Morgan should want to go out with him. Panic-stricken that they'd have nothing to talk about, he knew there would be lots of awkward silences filled by too much eating and drinking. Still, at least the rugby player would be in a good mood as he'd captained the Giants to victory that afternoon.

The driver announced that they were there. Iestyn paid him and stood for a moment in front of the hotel. How should he do this? If Dan was there that would make it easier, but if he wasn't…

Come on, Jones, stop being such a wimp and get in there. He found the bar and realized, as he looked around, that he had arrived first. Should he order or should he wait? How did one do this? And what did he do with his coat?

"Drink, sir?" the bartender asked.

"Yes, a beer, please."

The young man asked him to make a choice.

"That one," he said, pointing only because he liked the label. He was no connoisseur of alcohol.

He sensed a presence behind him and saw the bartender smile.

"I'll get that and another for me, please," the voice said.

Iestyn turned around on the stool to find Dan Morgan standing behind him. He swallowed and a whole host of butterflies released themselves into his stomach. The man looked like most people's idea of a Greek god in human form. Dan's shoulders filled his black suit perfectly. Iestyn found it impossible not to scan downward to Dan's narrower hips. He couldn't help feeling pleased that Dan had obviously taken care about his appearance for their date, even making an effort to control his unruly mop of blond hair. He noted that the suit would have cost the average teacher several months' wages but boy, was it beautiful, and Iestyn couldn't help feeling envious.

"Wow, that's an Armani, isn't it?" He had to stop himself from reaching out to feel the material between his fingers.

Dan smiled at him. "Yep, I did a bit of modeling a while back for a photo shoot and they gave me this. You look good in yours as well."

"Can I take your coat, sir?" The girl already had one coat over her arm and Iestyn realized that it must be Dan's.

"Yes, thank you," Iestyn croaked, his mouth suddenly dry. He took off the coat then swallowed some of his beer.

"Shall we sit over there?" Dan asked. "The waiters will bring us menus."

"You've been here before?" Iestyn asked.

Dan smiled as if the question was stupid. "Yes, a few times. I like it because it's relatively private and you don't get people demanding photos or autographs."

"I suppose you must get that a lot," Iestyn said, as they settled adjacent to each other on the brown leather sofas at one side of the bar.

Menus appeared, as if by magic.

"I can't really complain," Dan said. "Sometimes it's great to get the recognition and I love talking to the fans, but there are times when, you know, it's just a newspaper reporter trying to get a scoop on the gay rugby player."

"Shit, I hadn't really thought about that," Iestyn said. He realized that getting involved with a celebrity might have complications.

Dan saw the look of concern cross Iestyn's face and changed the subject. He didn't want to give Iestyn any reason to think that seeing him wasn't a good idea. He wasn't sure why but instinctively, he was comfortable with the other man and it had been a while since he'd felt that with anyone.

"Let's choose what to eat then we can find out about each other." He hoped that Iestyn wasn't having second thoughts already. Dan couldn't identify why he'd given this man his card. Of course, the glasses had helped. He'd always had a thing for men with glasses. Then there were the man's eyes. He wondered if his date knew that he had eyes Dan simply wanted to drown in. They were blue, but not bright blue. They twinkled like the Bristol Channel on a better day, when the sun shone brightly and the water was a blue-gray shade with little lights flickering across the surface. He had a kind face that looked lived in and slightly world-weary, and Iestyn's body appeared to have the same qualities. Dan had to maintain his shape for his sport, not to mention the advertising contracts he had. His muscular form was kept that way by several training sessions a week and many hours in the gym, so he had no interest in finding someone exactly like himself. He didn't usually hand out his number to strangers he'd just met, but there was something about the man next to him that had caught his attention.

He knew he shouldn't but he briefly compared him to Az. He smiled to himself. He still thought of his ex by his childhood nickname, even though he now insisted on being called Aron. Az had insisted that it was part of his way of moving on. Iestyn was quite a bit taller and carried significantly more weight, and Az's eyes had been brown, not blue. Their hair appeared similar in color, although Dan could see odd flecks of gray at Iestyn's temples. However, Dan had to admit that Iestyn dressed better. Az had always preferred his T-shirt and jeans to formal wear, not to mention his work overalls. The color of the suit and shirt really complemented Iestyn's eyes.

"So, have you decided what you're going to have?" he asked, coming back to the present. "I'm going to have the scallops and beef."

"Okay," Iestyn replied, putting the menu back on the table. "I'm going to have the terrine and the chicken. The dishes all appear to be rather complicated. I have to admit I'm more used to Chinese or curry when I go out."

"Well, perhaps we can do that next time," Dan said, lifting his hand to summon the waiter. "Now, all I know is that you teach and can't skate very well. I want to learn everything about you by the end of this meal."

The waiter took their orders, and Dan sat farther back in the armchair.

"All right," said Iestyn, seemingly taken aback by the question. "I teach history to eleven to eighteen-year-olds. I've been teaching for twelve years."

"And do you like teaching? I guess it's not the easiest of jobs?" Dan asked, his curiosity growing.

"Yes, I've never wanted to do anything else. Some days I wonder why I bother, but not often. I love my subject, and I love all the little stories there are to tell. It's nice to get to do the local history as well."

"Yeah, I loved doing Welsh history, especially Owain Glyn Dwr," Dan said. "His attempted rebellion was fascinating. I'm sure there's a film in there someone hasn't done—like a Welsh *Braveheart*."

Iestyn looked at him, astonished for a moment. "You did history?" he asked, blushing. "Sorry, I didn't mean that to sound insulting."

"No, offense taken and yes, I did. Sorry, were you expecting that as a sportsman I'd have no interest in anything other than lifting weights and running around a pitch?"

Iestyn looked embarrassed. He held up his hands in surrender. "Okay, you're right and I'm stupid. I should have known better. I know not all sportsmen are ignorant and I agree with you about Owain Glyn Dwr. So what A levels did you do then?"

"I did history, religious studies, sociology and PE. History was always my favorite, along with PE. I had some great teachers. I think teachers are amazing. Without mine, I wouldn't be here today doing this, I can tell you. I was a confused and angry teenager, but a few of my teachers saw potential in me and sorted me out. They helped me deal with being gay and my mother's illness."

Before Dan could say more, the waiter appeared to announce that their table was ready.

Their starters were served as soon as they took their seats. Dan realized that so far they'd only talked about him. "Enough about me. Tell me about you, Mr Jones. I assume you're local."

"Yep, except for that hiccough of being born in Scotland, I'm pretty much Welsh, back a few generations. I did history at Birmingham but decided to come back here. I'm the youngest of three kids. I have a brother and a sister who are ten and five years older than me and both are married with kids. I have three nephews and a niece, whom I adore. My parents are still alive and, although my dad isn't well these days, my mam is remarkable for her age. They live in Sully and my siblings live locally as well. We'll all be together for Christmas and it will be bedlam."

Iestyn picked up his fork and began to eat before his food got too cold.

"You have quite a large family, then," Dan said.

"I suppose so. You said your mother was ill when you were at school. That must have been hard."

Dan put his cutlery down for a moment.

"You don't have to talk about it," Iestyn said between mouthfuls.

Dan hesitated. He usually didn't talk about his family. The papers had all tried to get him to spill the beans about his tragic past, but it was too personal to share. One reason he found dating difficult was the problem of people who might kiss and tell for the odd thousand pounds, but Iestyn didn't strike him as that sort of person.

"It's a bit of a cliché. I never knew my father but I had my mum and my grandparents, then my mum got breast cancer when I was twelve. I didn't know much about it then, as she kept things from me. It came back a few years later and, despite the treatment, she'd left it too long. She died just after my seventeenth birthday. My nan and my teachers got me through it. Nan was amazing and I wasn't always as good to her as I should have been. She's insisting on making Christmas lunch for us again this year, despite her arthritis. I know I won't be able to move afterward and will fall asleep in front of the TV until *Doctor Who* comes on."

"Sounds tough. My nan died last year. She was an old battleax but I loved her dearly. I must admit I was her favorite, being the youngest. This will be our first Christmas without her. It's going to be strange." Iestyn paused for a moment as the plates were cleared and their main courses were set out before them. "Look, I need to ask about Aron. He's your ex-boyfriend, isn't he? You were together for a long time."

"Been looking me up, then?" Dan said, laughing.

"Well, I believe in doing my homework," Iestyn countered. "And every photo I found has him next to you. You were quite the celebrity couple for a while but now he's in the US, yes?"

"What you actually want to know is if we're really over, and that's understandable, I guess. The answer is yes, we are. I'll admit it wasn't my decision and I went off the rails a bit at the time, but he was right. We'd been together eight years and hadn't been with anyone else. He needed to go and do the job he'd always dreamed of. He's an aeronautical engineer and in this job, he gets to build planes and fly them. Me, I get dizzy jumping up for throw-ins. I love to travel but I can't stand flying, and he lives and breathes it. I couldn't go to America, as that would have meant leaving my job. There's no rugby over there and I have a chance to be captain of Wales, so I'm told. Az has someone else now, and I'm young, free and single." He picked up his knife and cut off some more beef. "This meat is wonderful," he said. "How's your chicken?"

"It's very good, but I think I'd prefer a decent madras, to be honest. I think good food may be wasted on me. This wine is nice, though."

Dan thought that it should be, considering the likely mark-up. "Next time we'll just do takeaway if you want," he ventured.

"So there's going to be a next time?" Iestyn asked tentatively.

Dan leaned forward and put his hand on Iestyn's arm. "If you want there to be," he whispered. "I've enjoyed this evening and I can't believe how quickly it's gone by. Would you give me your number?" Of course, he already had Iestyn's number logged in his mobile from when he'd phoned him but he didn't want to take anything for granted. He'd been so nervous. He'd never had a first date before. Iestyn smiled at him and his heart began to melt just a little. He *really* wanted that number.

"Here," Iestyn said, handing over his mobile. "Put the number into your memory. I'm going to my parents on Christmas Eve until the twenty-seventh but after that, I'm free. The next few days are going to be manic. I've got to go shopping tomorrow. I haven't bought a thing for anyone. Julie and I are going to blitz Queen Street."

"Julie?" Dan asked.

"Julie's my best friend and a fellow teacher. We're going shopping and having lunch tomorrow. She's experiencing a few relationship problems, which reminds me, I said I'd ask if you'd be able to come and coach the school's rugby teams. Matt, our head of PE, asked me. As for Julie, I've known her forever. We grew up on the same street."

"That must be nice," Dan replied wistfully. "And sure, me and a few of the guys could come to your school. The Giants have a school's outreach program. I'll see if I can sort out some possible dates."

Iestyn looked at him. "I guess when you split up with Aron, you lost your best friend as well?"

Dan fixed him with a serious look, impressed that Iestyn had worked this out. "Yeah, that's true, and in some ways that was the worst of it. I missed being able to talk to him more than anything else. I missed how he'd be doing a Sudoku and half listening to me rant about some decision made in the game that day. I was left with a big empty house we used to live in together. In the end, I moved into a new flat with great views. At least I've got something to look at, even if there's no one around to talk to." He knew he was pushing things when he said, "Look, I'm having a New Year's Eve party there. Would you like to come? You could bring a few friends and family. It'll only be some of the team and a few friends from school I haven't seen for a while."

"I don't know," Iestyn said. "It may be a bit soon for that."

Dan tried to hide his disappointment, but Iestyn obviously caught it anyway.

"I'm not saying no," Iestyn said in a rush. "Perhaps if we go out before then and see how that goes?" He swallowed the last of his coffee, his gaze following the waiters clearing tables around them. "I think it may be time to go," he observed.

Dan spoke to the waiter and ordered a taxi for them both. "I use the same firm all the time," he explained. "They keep their mouths shut about who uses the cars—they have a contract with the Giants they don't want to lose."

* * * *

Iestyn couldn't help but smile to himself on the journey home. Whatever he'd expected Dan to be like, it wasn't the rather reticent man he'd discovered this evening. Apparently, Dan had been through some things that had caused him to doubt those around him. And Iestyn had to admit he'd enjoyed the evening too. Dan had turned out to be more interesting company than Iestyn had thought he'd be and Iestyn found that he wanted to discover more about Dan, as well as what was under that fabulous suit. Even though he'd never really been a rugby fan, Iestyn found himself listening with interest as Dan talked about his hopes to be named as the Welsh team captain.

The street was quiet when the taxi pulled up outside Iestyn's house.

"No, this evening is on me," Dan said when Iestyn tried to give him some money to pay for his share of the fare. It surprised Iestyn when Dan told the taxi driver to wait and accompanied him to his door.

"Can I come in for a moment?" Dan asked.

"Sure. If you want," Iestyn replied.

Once inside, Dan reached into his jacket and pulled out a small box, his hand trembling. "Look, I know this is presumptuous of me, but I saw these and wanted you to have something for Christmas. I hope you like them."

Iestyn's own hand shook as he opened the box to find silver cufflinks in the shape of rugby balls. A little overwhelmed by their simple beauty, he said, "These are lovely, but—"

Suddenly he found Dan's lips pressed softly against his. There was something different, though, something he tried to work out. He'd been kissed before but never quite like this. Then it hit him—he was looking up. Dan was substantially taller than him. He let himself sink further into the kiss, enjoying the sensation of Dan's muscular body pressed against him. Dan pulled Iestyn closer, allowing Iestyn to breathe in the lingering scent of the other man's earthy aftershave, combined with what Iestyn imagined was just Dan's personal aroma.

A wave of lust swept through his body as he angled his head to maintain the contact with Dan's kiss. It was weird how Dan made him feel both safe and horny at the same time. It was an exhilarating mix that made his head swim. The sheer physicality of the man threatened to overwhelm his senses. He sank a little further into the kiss. He gently probed with his tongue, needing to go deeper into Dan's mouth. When Dan pulled away, it took all Iestyn's strength not to press forward again.

"I'll ring you," Dan said, somewhat breathily.

Still rooted to the spot, Iestyn watched him hurry down the path then he closed the door. He raised his hand and touched his still tingling lips. He closed his eyes and leaned against the wall in an effort to recall every touch. Reluctantly, after removing his coat, he walked into the living room and sat on the sofa. He picked up the photo of his nan from the table.

"I think I've found someone, Nan. I know you'd like him. Well, you'd fancy him for certain, as he's a bit like Granddad. And I think he likes me as well." He reached for his laptop and found what he was looking for. He thought he'd seen that there was a new biography of Owain Glyn Dwr. He ordered it, thinking he could send it to the rugby club or give it to Dan after Christmas.

That night he dreamed of rugby players and romantic walks along the beach and for the first time in ages, he smiled as he drifted off to sleep.

Chapter Eight

Christmas Eve arrived at last. Iestyn watched his mother move constantly between living room and kitchen. Unlike his brother and sister, he'd inherited their mum's dark hair instead of his father's ginger— now sandy—hair, although Iestyn did have his dad's blue eyes. His mother whirled like a dervish as she made sure that everything was ready for the next day. She'd insisted that he come the night before and stay there. The others would arrive on Christmas Day.

"You can keep your father amused while I get everything sorted, unless you want to peel the potatoes, or the carrots, or the swede." She reeled off a list of other jobs that he could carry out.

"Get over here, son," his father said. "You know you're better off staying out of her way."

Iestyn got the chessboard from the cupboard and set it up on the table next to his dad. He knew that his father found it hard to accept his physical condition. His dad was a proud man but arthritis had taken its toll over the years since he'd been forced to give up work. Now he needed a stick to cross the room, a stairlift to get upstairs and a wheelchair to go anywhere outside.

Iestyn had been damn lucky with his parents. Both of them had taken his announcement about his sexuality in their stride. His mother had simply said, "Thank goodness you've told us at last. Now we don't have to pretend we don't know anymore."

"Come on, Iessie," his dad had said. "Who did you think you were fooling? Have you ever taken a good look at the pictures on your wall? You don't like football and yet there are footballers. You should also hide your sketchbook. I'm just hoping you don't hand those in to your art teacher, although they do appear to be very accurate."

Iestyn remembered having turned several shades of red, finally bordering on puce. After that, his brother and sister informed him that they already knew, because he was always making cow eyes at the best-looking boys in the sixth form. Yes, he knew he'd been bloody lucky.

"Right, Dad, white or black?" He didn't know why he asked, as his dad always chose black.

His mother mouthed a "Thank you" and disappeared into the kitchen once more.

They played several games, each winning more than once. His mother provided tea and biscuits at some point as they continued. After six games, they were three all.

"Last game," his mother said. "Tea's ready soon. We're having sausage and mash as the next few days will be full of turkey and stuffing galore, until we all get very bored of thinking what to do with it."

Iestyn won the last game of the day. His dad was getting tired.

"So four–three to me then, Dad. Perhaps we'll get in a couple of games tomorrow."

"Fat chance," his dad retorted. "It'll be bedlam in here tomorrow."

He tried to frown, but Iestyn knew that he loved having his children and grandchildren around him. His father especially loved his new granddaughter who, at age two, would be the star of the day. He would listen to her sing and watch her dance then read her stories until he was hoarse. Megs would love him and pull his beard as she always did, practically since she'd been born. If Iestyn had been his nan's favorite, Megs was undoubtedly going to be her granddad's chosen grandchild. Megs' conception had been a bit of a surprise for his brother and sister-in-law. Huw was ten years older than Iestyn, and Meg's brother Ben had already reached double figures when his mother, Sue, had found that she was pregnant. Megs ran rings round her parents but they all doted on her and she appeared to be completely fearless.

"There you go," his mam said, handing over the plate. "I want to see it all gone," she added.

"Mam, I'm thirty-four, not ten," Iestyn protested. "And I could do with losing a few pounds. After being here over Christmas, I'll have to join Matt at the gym every day."

"That boy is ridiculously thin," his mother said. "He could do with eating a few pies to put some flesh on those bones. Any woman sleeping with him would be able to amuse herself during the boring bits counting his ribs."

"Mam! Do you have to?"

"What, you think only the young can talk about sex? You, your brother and sister weren't created through Immaculate Conception, you know. Anyway, it's time you got out there again. How long has it been since that bastard left you high and dry?"

"Six months, Mam, and could we please not have a conversation about this son of a friend of yours, or her nephew, or someone else you have met who works in the supermarket?"

His mother ruffled his hair and gave his father a look that Iestyn had seen too many times. "Leave him alone, Mary. He's a good-looking boy, taking after you as he does, and I'm sure he won't be single for long."

Just then, Iestyn's phone chose to beep. He ignored it.

"Aren't you going to check on that?" his mother asked.

"I will when I've finished eating," he replied. "It won't be anything important." He checked the message when his mother left the room to make tea. He caught his dad's smile out of the corner of his eye.

Thanks for the book. Have a great Christmas. Dan xx.

His stomach flipped over and he couldn't help letting the corners of his mouth turn upward.

Grinning, his dad leaned over and whispered, "It's all right, son. I won't tell your mam. I know what she's like."

"Thanks, Dad. It's early days yet and I don't want to say anything in case nothing comes of it."

* * * *

They spent the rest of the evening watching the usual television fare for Christmas Eve. His parents went up to bed at ten thirty. He gave them time to use the bathroom then went upstairs as well. Since he'd left home permanently, his bedroom hadn't changed much in the last twelve years. The posters had been removed and replaced with a few tasteful pictures of local landmarks. He got out his phone and texted a quick message back to Dan.

Have a happy Christmas too. I hope you've been good. Iestyn xx

Chapter Nine

The next day, pandemonium descended. His mother got up at six to put the turkey in the oven. She believed in slow and low as far as turkeys were concerned. Iestyn heard her moving around downstairs and wondered if he should get up. He lay looking at the ceiling. His parents had lived in this house all his life. His father had helped to build it all those years ago when they were just married. Now, Huw ran the building firm his grandfather had started. Things weren't easy in the recession but they were surviving.

Unlike his father, whose condition had forced him to give up work, his mother had never quite got the hang of being retired. She still gave the occasional lecture and her opinion was often sought when new Welsh poets appeared on the scene. She still wrote and currently was researching for her new book about the Welsh poet, R.S. Thomas. A builder father and a lecturer mother might seem an unusual combination, but for nearly fifty years it had worked. Iestyn was grateful that he'd been given his parents and this house out of the millions available.

He decided to put on the cufflinks Dan had given him. He'd brought a dress shirt especially.

At eight, he knocked on his dad's door and asked if he needed anything. To his surprise, his dad was already dressed and draining his cup of morning tea.

"Is that you up, love?" his mam called up the stairs.

"Yes, Mam. I was just looking in on Dad. I'll be down now," he shouted back.

He found her in the kitchen cutting up the last of the vegetables to go with the dinner. "Just give me a minute, Iessie, and I'll do you some breakfast."

"It's fine, Mam. I'll do myself some tea and toast and get out of your way. Is there anything you want me to do?" he asked.

"Yes. I need the big table extension so all the adults can sit around. We'll bring in the small table from the front room for the children, although I guess Megs will use the high chair. I did remind them to bring it."

"Stop panicking, Mam. Everything will be fine. I assume we're opening presents before eating, as usual."

"That's the plan. Ah, that's your father on his way down. Make him another cup, will you? And pour him some cereal."

By the time Iestyn had finished, his father had taken his place in his normal seat. Iestyn put the tea and cereal in front of him and sat, too.

"Mind you don't get crumbs on the floor," his mother said sternly. "Or you'll be Hoovering again!"

"Yes, Mam," he replied, carefully ensuring that none of the toast crumbs left the plate.

He got the bags of presents from the front room and set them around the Christmas tree in the bay window. He'd helped his brother, Huw bring in the tree the week before and as usual, they and the children had decorated it on the Sunday before Christmas. Once again, the Scooby-Doo angel adorned the top. He'd put out the last present when the front door opened and the first of his siblings and their families arrived. His sister Rhian had inherited their father's red hair and this had transferred to the twins, who were now five years old. The boys, Lloyd and Lewis, threw themselves at Iestyn.

"Uncle Iessie, we've brought our Legos. Will you help us make the castle later? Daddy said you'd be better as you know about history."

His brother–in-law Gareth made a silent whistling motion and wiped his hand across his brow, thankful that he'd escaped that task.

Iestyn mouthed a silent "Thanks for that" toward him as he put the presents they'd brought around the tree.

"Beer?" Iestyn asked.

"Please," Gareth replied. "Rhian is driving tonight. She only rolled a two to my six. Come on, boys. I'm sure Uncle Iestyn will help you this afternoon, at least to begin the castle."

"Dad, d'you want one?" Iestyn asked.

His father nodded just as the third part of the family arrived. Rhian disappeared into the kitchen to be thrown out, as usual, after she'd made her customary offer to help. Huw came through the door carrying Megs, who demanded to be let down, as she'd probably demanded to be picked up just before that. She immediately went to her granddad, who reached to pick her up and took the book she proffered for him to read.

"Let us know when she gets too much," Huw said. "Beer for us, too, would be nice."

Ben looked up from his phone briefly before taking his favorite position in the other armchair.

Mary came into the living room. "Lunch will be ready in two hours, so it's time to open the presents. Everything is in hand in there."

It took over an hour to get through them all, as each person took one at a time, including the children. As was the norm for any family, there were socks aplenty. Iestyn had bought books, CDs or DVDs for everyone. If it was square and therefore easy to wrap, he bought it. He opened his present from his parents. They knew him well and he smiled when he saw it was a complete history of science fiction. It would be a great toilet read.

They started getting the table ready at one thirty, laying out the mats and coasters along with the cutlery and glasses. Iestyn put out the crackers so they could pull them and all wear the paper hats throughout the meal. Like always, Ben whinged about, sitting with the children again now that he was eleven.

"Next year you can sit here, when you're in secondary school but for now, you can keep an eye on the twins," his mother said.

Finally, they all sat at the tables. They piled their plates up with meat and vegetables, and everyone filled their glasses with wine or soft drinks. They toasted the family, pulled the crackers and each put on their hat and read the terrible puns until they began to eat.

The family chatter continued over lunch until Ben, bored with eating and dealing with his cousins, spoke.

"Uncle Iestyn, is it true that you're going out with Dan Morgan, the rugby player?"

Iestyn spluttered and everyone else stopped eating.

"Don't be silly, Ben! How could Uncle Iestyn have met him?" his uncle Gareth said.

"But you have met him, haven't you, Uncle Iestyn? And he gave you his phone number," Ben continued.

Iestyn looked pleadingly at his father, who obviously saw that Iestyn didn't want to talk about this.

His father said, "I think that's enough, Ben. Come on, everyone. Let's eat before the food your mother has made gets cold." But his pleas fell on deaf ears.

"My friend Jamie, from judo class, said his brother Josh saw him give you his card, Uncle Iestyn. So did you phone him? He must have liked you, and you're gay and he's gay, isn't he, so..."

Iestyn put his knife and fork down, knowing he needed to say something. He didn't want to lie—not to his family—not when his friends already knew that he'd been out with the rugby player. "All right! What Ben says is true. I met Dan Morgan while I was on a school trip and he did give me his card and told me to ring him. We had dinner at St David's Hotel a few days ago and that's it so far."

"Bloody hell, my little brother is going out with the most eligible gay man in Wales. Who'd have thought it?" Huw said, slapping him on the back. "So what's he like, then? And that explains the cufflinks. I did wonder about them, as you've never shown the slightest interest in rugby."

"He's nice, interesting, totally not what I expected him to be, and yes, he did buy me these and we are going to go out again."

His sister whispered in his ear. "So was he good?"

Iestyn blushed.

"We've only been out once, Rhian."

His mother caught on very quickly. "That's enough of that, I think. Let's finish this dinner before, as your father says, it goes cold."

Through the rest of the meal, Iestyn sensed a tidal wave of questions growing. He knew that as soon as they'd finished eating, he would face a huge barrage of interest and concern and the usual lecture from his mother about being safe. Huw would want to know about the rugby and Rhian would want to know if he really was as good-looking in the flesh. He swallowed more wine in the hope that it might help.

When everyone had completed the meal, and to get away from the questions he knew would come, he helped his mam take the stuff into the kitchen and volunteered to do the washing up. Out of the murmurings from the next room, he heard his father's voice in command mode.

"That's enough from all of you. Leave him alone. If anything comes of it, I'm sure we'll meet him, but they've only been out once and you lot can wait."

"I wonder if he'll get to go to his apartment. There were pictures of it in some magazine I read at the dentist's office a few months back. It has the most fabulous roof garden and views over to the Bay."

Shit! He nearly dropped the plate he was holding. *Trust Rhian to read the gossip magazines!* Iestyn thought. *I'm going out with someone whose home has been in a magazine. Somehow I can't see my little terraced house featuring in the same way, packed as it is with books and DVDs.* He passed the plate to his mother to dry.

"You will be careful, won't you, dear?" his mother began.

"Yes, Mam, I'm always careful, but we've only been out together once," he explained.

"That's often enough," she said.

"Well, not for me," Iestyn replied emphatically.

"Didn't he have a boyfriend? I'm sure I saw something about that when he was on that awards program, you know, when he was made captain of the Giants."

"They split up a while back. He told me all about him, so I'm not being stupid here, Mam. I thought he'd be a bit of a meathead, but he isn't. He's nice, and it's been a while. I like him, Mam. I like him a lot."

His mam kissed his cheek. "Then you go for it, son. He is very good-looking and you deserve some happiness."

Tears formed in the corners of her eyes.

"Come on," she added. "Just because you're going out with a famous sportsman doesn't mean you can't help me put everything away."

As he picked up the plates and put them in the cupboard, he thought once again how blessed he was to have these two people as his parents.

Chapter Ten

With Christmas over for another year and when Iestyn was back in his own house, Iestyn began his annual 'big sort', as he liked to call it. He took out the huge box file in which he put all the documents he'd accumulated over the year and sorted them into piles. He was just putting his bank statements in order when the phone rang. Happy to be relieved from the sheer monotony of the task, he rushed into the main room and grabbed the receiver before the ringing stopped.

"Hi, it's Dan," the sleepy voice on the end of the line declared.

"Hello, you. You sound as if you've just got out of bed."

"Still there," Dan said.

Iestyn had to stop himself from picturing the sight. He looked at the clock on his mantelpiece that told him it was after eleven.

"Late night?" he asked.

"Mmm, some of the boys came round. You know how it is."

They talked for a little while until Dan reminded him about his offer.

"So, come round tomorrow night," Iestyn said, "and I'll make you my world famous madras curry."

"You cook? I thought we were just going to get a takeaway," Dan replied enthusiastically.

"Yeah, I cook. I like to cook. I find it takes my mind off other things."

"Okay, then. I'd love to come round to yours and eat a home-cooked meal for a change. What time do you want me?"

Iestyn resisted the temptation to rise to the innuendo he swore he could hear in Dan's voice. "About seven and I'll have everything ready. Are you a rice man or half and half? I'll do some chapattis as well."

"Sounds fantastic and I'll eat whatever I'm given and be grateful. I'm hopeless in the kitchen, except for the basics," he admitted sheepishly.

"And I bet you have one of these huge kitchens that looks good but is never used. My sister said your flat featured in some magazine a few months back. I don't think my house will be up to those standards," Iestyn explained.

"Well, next time you can come to mine and I'll let you cook me something in it, if you want."

Iestyn could hear the hint of something more in Dan's voice and shivered with… What? Anticipation?

"I look forward to that," Iestyn said. "I'll see you tomorrow."

He spent the rest of the morning shopping. He had most of the things he needed already but he wanted fresh chilies, coriander, ginger and curry leaves, as well as the chicken. Back home and unpacking everything, he noticed that the light on his answer phone was flashing.

"Iestyn, it's Kate. Are you busy? Can I come round tonight? I need some advice about something. Tell me if I'm imposing. Sorry, I'm rambling. Ring me."

He made cheese on toast and settled down on the sofa to catch up with programs he'd recorded whilst at his parents. Once he'd finished eating, he picked up the phone and dialed Kate's number.

"Hi, Kate, I got your message. What's up?"

"I just need some advice about something. Could I just come round to yours tonight?"

Iestyn didn't push for any further information. "Okay, I'll see you later."

"I'll pick up something for us to eat on the way."

"Sure, bring pizza if you want. I've got some beers, or we can have wine. I'll see you at six-thirty." He wondered what was up. She'd sounded more than a little worried about something. Somehow over the years, he'd become the person whom the others confided in amongst their little group.

Kate, however, was difficult to fathom. He knew almost nothing about her past. She was single and had never been married, as far as he knew. She said very little about whom she found attractive. But she had other opinions that she wasn't afraid of speaking aloud. She was something of a feminist and rather left-wing—in fact, she was a bit of an old school sociologist. She made few demands as a friend. She was a good listener and had volunteered as a Samaritan for some years, so he was puzzled about this sudden need to talk to him.

He turned on the television and started to watch yet another game show that dominated afternoon programming but it didn't hold his attention for very long and he dozed off for a while. When he woke, the darkness shrouded the room. He got up, turned on the lights, ambled into the kitchen and made a mug of coffee, then he read the evening paper and finished the Sudokus, including the difficult one. The doorbell rang just after six thirty and he got up to answer it. Kate came straight in and headed into the living room with the pizzas. He collected the wine and joined her.

"It's Sian," she said simply. "We had dinner last night at her place and she kissed me and I kissed her back, then I panicked and walked out. I just left her standing there and now I don't know what to do. She's left several texts asking me to call, but I can't. It's all such a mess, Iestyn."

"Ah," he said and poured her a large glass. He was surprised that Sian hadn't phoned him as well. Perhaps she'd phoned Julie. He'd give her a ring later and find out.

"Ah? Is that it? What the hell have I done, Iestyn? I'm not gay but kissing her felt good. I know I shouldn't have walked out but I panicked. Did you know Sian was gay? I'm nearly thirty, for God's sake, and I've slept with a dozen or more men. I've never so much as looked at another woman—well, not in *that* way. At least, I don't think I have. See, now I'm questioning everything."

Iestyn raised an eyebrow. Even he'd glanced at women from time to time. Being gay didn't make you blind, after all. "Really? *Never*? Come on, Kate, everyone has thought 'what if?' at some point, haven't they? I know I have."

"What? You've thought about sleeping with a woman?" she replied.

"Well, not exactly, but just because I've only had sex with men there doesn't mean that I can't appreciate what the other half looks like. Strangely, I've always appreciated women with curves." He saw the hurt in her face and wanted to bite his tongue.

"Thanks, kick me while I'm down, why don't you? I can't help being like this. Are you trying to make me feel worse? Now I'm not a real woman and I'm also suddenly a lesbian? Great! I wish I had an hourglass figure too. I've always wanted breasts and hips. I even thought of getting fake breasts. My mum used to want to dress me up but I never had the figure for pretty party dresses."

"And yet most designers would love your figure," Iestyn observed, trying to make up for putting his foot in it. Sometimes he needed to think before he opened his mouth. "Magazines are full of beautiful women like you. Some people we work with would kill to be able to wear those jeans."

She sighed. "I know and it's bloody irritating sometimes when they go on about how fortunate I am to be able to eat anything. I don't feel lucky. I've never been able to put on weight, no matter how hard I try and other women hate me for it. I should have been born in the 1920s. I'd have been fine then. Is that why Sian fancies me? Because I look like a man? Isn't that a bit odd? If you fancy women, shouldn't you fancy the ones who are built like women and not like boys? I'm five foot three and seven stone wet through. I can still get into kids' clothes in some shops. I daren't wear navy in school as I get shouted at by other members of staff thinking I'm one of the pupils. You're a gay man—do you think I look like a boy?"

Iestyn wondered what to say. "Look, Kate. I'm in a no-win situation here. I don't think it matters what you look like. You need to talk to Sian. You kissed her then you walked out and left her. I imagine she's feeling pretty hurt and confused owing to your mixed messages. You said you liked kissing her?"

"Yes," Kate whispered. "How did you know you were gay, Iestyn? Did you find you fancied some other boy—or a celebrity or someone? Is there a moment when it hits you? Or do you always know somehow? Can you just fall in love with a person, regardless of what sex they are?"

"Come on, Kate. What do you *want* to do? You must have talked to people at Samaritans who were confused about their sexuality." He was desperate not to say the wrong thing again. "What did you tell them?"

"We don't give advice, Iestyn. We listen and try to get people to make their own decisions. It's not always that simple, but that's what we aim for."

"Well, it seems to me that you have two choices."

"I know—either tell Sian I'm not interested or find out if I am. But what do we do? Do we sleep together to see if I like it? And what if I do like it—or don't like it? It changes things, Iestyn. Suddenly I'm bisexual and what do we do then? We work together. I'd have to tell my parents. Oh, God!" She paused to gather her thoughts. "I know I like her. I've always liked her. We're good friends—or I thought we were. How did I miss that she liked me in a different way? Did you know? Does everyone else know? Is it me? Am I the only one who didn't see how she feels?"

"Yeah, I guessed she had some feelings for you but we've never spoken about it. I don't know about the others. Look, ring her, ask her to yours tomorrow and see how things go. You need to talk about it and perhaps experiment a little but be upfront with her, please. I remember the first time I slept with another man properly and it was...well, I just knew it was right. But there's more to it than just the sex, even for men. Well, for me, anyway. I've had sex without love and, though it's good, I know it's not what I want. As for the rest, you just have to take things one step at a time."

"You went out with that rugby player before Christmas, didn't you? Was he nice? He's a good-looking bloke, that's for sure."

Iestyn knew she was changing the subject but went with it. "Yes, he's nice and he's coming here tomorrow. I'm cooking my chicken madras."

"Lucky man! Don't overdo the chilies, though." She hesitated for a moment then smiled. The expression reached her eyes for the first time since she'd arrived. "You don't want too much hot stuff on his tongue or yours!"

Iestyn blushed. He just couldn't stop himself but he made a mental note not to put too many chilies in the curry, just in case. He had so many things to consider. Would they get to that? Was it all right to have sex on a second date, and why did he sound like a girl from a 1950s film? Shit! He'd had someone suck him off in a bus shelter before now, but he'd been pissed as a newt when that had happened, and now he was blushing at the thought of doing that in the privacy of his own home.

They finished off the pizza and the wine then sat back, slightly tipsy, on the sofa.

"You know, you're a really nice person, Iestyn. I've never heard anyone say a word against you, even when you were going out with that dick, Steve. You do know that none of us could stand him, don't you? We all breathed a sigh of relief when he left. He thought he was so much better than anyone else was and he was so far up his own arse that I'm surprised he didn't wave from between his own teeth. He was no good for you. Remember, you didn't go out with us for ages because he didn't approve of us. You need to find someone nice, so I hope this bloke treats you right. He'll have us to answer to if he doesn't." She leaned into him and put her head on his shoulder.

He was a little perturbed at her outburst. He'd known that his friends hadn't really liked Steve but her vehemence had surprised him. He wondered why Julie hadn't said anything, as she usually had a lot to say about his love life. Perhaps it was true that anyone might find it difficult to go out with him since they'd have to deal with his friends as well. But everyone had friends, didn't they? Dan would have friends and he'd have to get to know them, not to mention his teammates. There was so much to think about when one started a relationship.

He realized that Kate had fallen asleep. He gently moved off the sofa, laid her down then picked up his book and began to read.

Chapter Eleven

God, he was nervous—so nervous he'd nearly chopped off his finger whilst cutting up the root ginger to add to the mix. Finally, everything was put together and left to develop slowly on the top of the cooker. He made the chapattis and cooked the rice with added lemon flavoring. These he would warm up when Dan arrived.

Kate had left late the night before and he'd slept in that morning—well, until nine thirty, which was late for him. He liked mornings, finding it impossible to stay in bed beyond eight thirty unless he had a reason to, such as someone being there in bed with him. He liked sex in the morning. For some people sex was soporific, but most of the time he found sex invigorating, and it seemed to set him up to face the day.

As he stirred his tea, he found himself musing on whether Dan would be a morning person. He imagined that he'd be off for five-mile runs as the sun rose over the horizon or on some sort of exercise machine that he probably had in the corner of the room or perhaps in his spare bedroom that he'd have set out as a gym. He'd then have to take his sweaty body, with droplets rolling down between his strong shoulders, to the shower. He'd spread the shower gel all over himself and come out smelling of... Of what? What would Dan use in the shower? Perhaps he really used the range he endorsed in those adverts. Then he'd emerge all fresh smelling, wrapped in a small towel with those strong thighs and buff chest on display.

Iestyn looked down and realized his body had reacted to his imaginings. *Shit. Too much imagination is sometimes a curse.* He needed something to occupy the next couple of hours. He looked at the DVD collection on his shelves and pulled out *Raiders of the Lost Ark*. This would give the curry time to cook and him time to have a quick shower before Dan arrived.

* * * *

He was in the kitchen when the doorbell chimed. He brushed his hands on the tea towel and hurried to answer the door. He'd chosen a simple polo shirt and jeans to wear for the evening. He hadn't bothered with shoes or socks, as was his habit when he was in by himself. He gulped when he opened the door. Dan almost filled the doorway. He carried a bag and wore black jeans and a T-shirt, despite the cold, the sleeves of which only just covered his biceps. He looked magnificent, except for the woolen hat that was covering his hair.

"Well, do I have to stand here all night or are you going to let me in?" Dan enquired, his lips curving at both sides.

Iestyn blustered for a moment. "Sorry, sorry, you look great." *Am I supposed to say that?* "Come in."

Dan handed over the bag. "I brought some beers to go with the curry. It smells fantastic. I can't wait to taste it."

Iestyn watched him move down the hallway. He wasn't a small man himself but the space seemed to get smaller with Dan filling it. "The living room is to the left. I've set up the table. The food is ready if you want to eat straight away."

"That'd be great. I'm starving. We've been training all afternoon and that always builds up an appetite. D'you want me at the table now, or can I come in there and help?"

"No, sit. You're the guest here and I'll bring the stuff through. Open the beers with this." He threw the opener, which Dan caught easily in his large hands. Once again, Iestyn found his imagination working overtime with the thought of those hands wandering over his body. *Shit! Stop it. I'm going to have a hard-on that I can't hide in these jeans.*

Iestyn put the curry in a large bowl so they could help themselves. He warmed the rice and the chapattis in the microwave. He carried them out and set them on the table with the plates. "Help yourself," he said. "I decided against the chips. There's chutney if you want some. I eased up a bit on the chilies, as I didn't know how hot you liked it."

Dan filled his plate and began to tuck in. He groaned with pleasure, sending Iestyn's imagination spiraling out of control again.

"Wow! This is glorious," Dan exclaimed. "I could take it a bit hotter, though it's nice not to have to compete to see who can take it the hottest. Rugby players. Too much competition in all things."

"And you being the captain, I imagine you always have to go further than anyone else," Iestyn said.

Dan raised an eyebrow then winked. "Ah, that's where you're wrong. Being captain means that you have to know exactly when to stop and not take things too far. I'm the one who has to be the boring, sensible one. It's what they expect from me, so no getting too drunk or doing stupid things. No dwarf tossing for me. Wouldn't want to be compared to the England team, now would we?"

"I guess you try to stay out of the papers as well."

"If I can. Being one of only two *out* gay rugby players can be a bit intimidating. There are always people who want to know about my love life. After I split up with Aron, some papers even offered money for stories, but luckily I have a good agent and an even better lawyer. But enough about me. How was your Christmas? You spent it with your family, didn't you?"

"Yes, and, well… They know about you. I hope you don't mind."

"You told them?" Dan said, obviously surprised.

"Well, only when I had to. My nephew Ben does judo with the brother of one of the boys who was on the trip. He mentioned you'd given me your number so Ben asked if we were going out and I had to admit that we were."

"How did that news go down?"

"Same as always. Mam gave me the same safe-sex lecture, Dad warned everyone to shut up and leave me alone, my brother asked if you could get cheap seats for the internationals and my sister wanted to know if that was really your flat in the magazine article and where you got the kettle and toaster, as they were just the color she wanted in her kitchen.

Lewis and Lloyd, my sister's five-year-old twins, had no opinion and my niece was too busy dancing or annoying her granddad to give any thoughts on the matter."

"That sounds like fun," Dan said, thinking of his own quiet Christmas Day with his nan. He loved her dearly and he'd loved his mum, but a family like that sounded wonderful.

"Oh, it is, in small doses," Iestyn stated "I must admit it was lovely to get back to my own space. Sleeping in my old bedroom makes me feel like a teenager again. They all want to meet you, by the way."

Dan enjoyed talking about their families and being teenagers. He compared his experience of coming out with Iestyn's, knowing that in their own ways they'd been more fortunate than many others in the same situation.

"So you really didn't realize you fancied Aron until you saw him with that bloke and wanted to tear him apart?" Iestyn said.

"No, I went mad for a bit but I was lucky one of my teachers helped me realize what was going on and made me talk to him. Wonderful man, drop-dead gorgeous, openly gay and an amazing teacher. He awakened my passion for history and I think I was a bit in love with him as well. Perhaps I have a thing for teachers?" he added, locking gazes with Iestyn.

Blushing, Iestyn replied, "Well, it sounds like they had a positive impact on your life. I've bought ice cream for afters or we can just have coffee. I have a machine that does all sorts of clever things."

"Yeah, I have one of those too. It came with the kitchen. I've no idea how it works. Perhaps you can come round and show me sometime soon."

Iestyn got up, taking the plates into the kitchen.

Dan's words hung in the air for a moment until he broke the silence again. "Do you fancy a day out somewhere after New Year's? We could go down to the Gower and find a pub for lunch. I know a few good ones and I love the beach in winter when there's hardly anyone about but dog walkers."

Less chance of being spotted as well. The fear of his private life being exposed was an ever-present concern and now he might subject Iestyn to the possibility of being scrutinized by the papers. *Why can't things be simple?*

"I seem to remember there's a nice pub at Ogmore. And if the machine does cappuccino, I'll have one of those."

He watched Iestyn move back and forth across the kitchen making the coffee. As he padded about in his bare feet, Iestyn seemed much more at home in there than Dan did in his designer version. He leaned back on the sofa enjoying this vision of cozy domesticity.

"I'll just make myself comfortable then, shall I?"

Iestyn set out the things he needed, making a cappuccino for Dan and an espresso for himself. He'd had a few beers and wanted to revive his wits. Nervousness had claimed him at the thought of what might happen. He was actually going to sit next to Dan on the sofa. His stomach churned, every nerve going to high alert. *I wonder if Dan is this nervous? Has there been anyone since Aron? Oh God, please let me be more than just a rebound shag.* He leaned against the counter and took a few deep breaths. He knew Dan was very careful about any sort of relationship because of his public profile but he was there, in his living room, waiting for him. *Get in there, you idiot.*

He put the mugs on the coffee table and sat next to Dan.

"I was just looking at your book collection," Dan said, waving his hand toward the large bookcase that occupied most of the wall to his left. "There's a few in there I'd love to read. I have an e-reader but I do like to read print books. I've not had time to read the *Shardlakes*. Are they any good?"

"Yes, I enjoyed reading them. I haven't read the most recent one yet. I'm reading the latest Ken Follett and that's taking me a bit of time."

"Mmm, this is good coffee," Dan said. "Restaurants, even good ones, don't seem to be able to stop it from being bitter, but this is lovely and smooth." He leaned over and kissed Iestyn gently on the lips.

"That was pretty smooth as well," Iestyn observed.

He leaned back, parting his lips to allow Dan to kiss him harder. Taking the opportunity, Dan slipped his tongue into Iestyn's mouth. Iestyn groaned as a thrill wound through him to his cock, which quickly filled and hardened. The taste of the coffee Dan had drunk mixed with his personal flavor, further tantalizing his senses.

Dan cupped the back of Iestyn's head with one hand, digging his fingers deep into Iestyn's hair. With his senses reeling and a maddening yet delightful pulsing in his cock, Iestyn desperately wanted to give himself over to the sensations his new would-be lover inspired. By now, Dan had pulled Iestyn's shirt out with his other hand and Iestyn jumped as fingers touched his bare flesh for the first time. He knew Dan had felt the lurch when he pulled away and smiled indulgently at him.

"You are going to have to breathe out, you know," Dan said as he leaned in, pushed up the cotton shirt and kissed Iestyn's stomach.

"I know," Iestyn replied. "It's just… Oh, God."

Dan placed a series of small kisses across his skin, higher and higher up his chest until he reached a nipple. Iestyn couldn't help himself. He whimpered as the warmth of Dan's tongue flicked over it then circled the areola. It was as if his nipple had a direct line to his cock and it hardened even more. Dan's growing erection pressed into his thigh. Iestyn pushed his hands under the back of Dan's T-shirt as their lips met once again. He pulled the material up. He badly wanted to see Dan's chest, to know if the adverts had really been telling the truth.

As if reading his mind, Dan explained, "They make me wax for the photo shoots, but I'm a bit stubbly again. I didn't want to presume anything about tonight. Um, it's been a while for me and— Shit, look, this is a bit of an admission but there's only been one person since Aron and for seven years there was only him."

Iestyn could tell Dan was embarrassed, but he had to admit that despite his worries about being a rebound shag, he found it rather sweet. At least it meant Dan wasn't the sort of man to sleep around.

"I have to be so careful," Dan continued. "The only other bloke I've had sex with was a footballer who's so deep in the closet he's way past Narnia. I have no worries about him spilling any beans."

Iestyn didn't know whether to feel flattered or worried. "You must know I fancy you and I hope you fancy me too, even though I'm a little out of shape so..."

Dan took off his T-shirt then pulled him down so that he was almost on top of him. They were now chest to chest and skin to skin. Iestyn ground himself into Dan's groin. The friction in his jeans invigorated him and he knew if he kept crushing himself against Dan, he'd come in his pants. He reached for his belt but Dan was there before him, pulling down the zip and plunging into Iestyn's boxers. When Dan made contact with Iestyn's cock, Iestyn gasped and thrust upwards, lifting his hips high enough to allow Dan to push down Iestyn's jeans and clutch his arse. The man really did have strong hands. Iestyn loved the feel of all the rough callouses from Dan handling thousands of rugby balls, or maybe they were from all those sessions on the rowing machine he imagined Dan did weekly. Iestyn delved between their bodies, desperate now to undo Dan's jeans and feel his cock. He stroked over the fabric and knew instantly from the size of the bulge beneath his fingertips that Dan had no reason to be worried about his equipment. With Dan's belt undone, Iestyn pushed his fingers between the buttons and on into Dan's briefs. Touching skin, he grinned at the long, low moan Dan uttered into Iestyn's neck.

He wrapped his hand around Dan's shaft and began stroking it none too gently. Dan's hand joined his and took both their cocks in his massive grip, pressing them together. His thumb swept over the head of Iestyn's cock, collecting pre-cum and using it to aid his strokes up and down, up and down. Iestyn lost himself in the sensations. It was like the other man's hand had been created just for this task. Sod the rugby balls—those hands were made for *his* balls! Iestyn knew he wanted to feel that hand everywhere. He let Dan continue. Iestyn relished the deliciousness of another cock pressed against his own, conscious of just how heavily both of them were breathing.

"So good," Iestyn managed to growl.

Dan pulled down Iestyn's foreskin, exposing the more sensitive tip.

"Oh, God. Yeah, just like that. Please, I'm so close... Don't stop." His balls tightened and he knew he was going to come. He hoped he wasn't too far ahead of Dan, but seconds later, Dan pushed up and threw his head back. Iestyn followed him over the edge. A sticky warmth erupted between them. Iestyn lay back and attempted to get his breathing back under control, pleased to hear that Dan was similarly affected and breathing just as heavily against Iestyn's chest.

"Need to move," Iestyn said first. "Or we're going to be in a mess."

"Nghh," was all Dan could manage in reply.

Iestyn literally peeled himself off Dan. A little embarrassed, he pushed himself back into his pants, padded into the kitchen and grabbed a tea towel. He wiped down his stomach then ran the towel under his nose. He could shove it into the washer later or keep it. Was that just a little kinky? He felt like—what was her name?—Monica Lewinsky, who'd put that dress in her mother's freezer. Gee, perhaps he was kinky, but the smell of them both had been incredible. Any more of that and he'd be getting hard again. Of course, he'd managed to stain his jeans but he didn't care about that as he wasn't going anywhere. It was probably a good job Dan had worn black. Had he planned this, then?

When he got back into the other room, Dan had tidied himself up a little. Iestyn sat next to him and wiped his stomach, breathing in the aroma of him. Dan simply watched him. Only if Iestyn looked close enough could he see that Dan's jeans were slightly damp.

"You okay?" Dan asked.

"Yeah, I'm fine," Iestyn replied, not sure if he should add any more to his comment. Should he say the sex had been amazing, because it would be the truth?

"Still want to see me again?" Dan questioned.

Iestyn smiled, leaned over and kissed him. "I thought we had a lunch date next week and a trip out — unless you've changed your mind?"

"Now you're fishing, Iestyn Jones. Nothing that's happened here would make me change my mind. I'd love another coffee, please, then I'll phone a taxi and go home. I know you won't change your mind about the New Year's party but I'll phone you afterwards. Are you doing anything?"

Dan followed Iestyn into the kitchen and took a seat at the table while Iestyn made another coffee for them both. "Yeah, I'm out with the usual crowd, but I suspect it could be a bit of a different night as they all seem to be... Perhaps I'll leave that for another occasion. And you can tell me all about your friends and your teammates."

Thirty minutes and several kisses later, Dan got up to go to the taxi waiting at the door.

"Thanks, it's been a lovely evening." Dan kissed him again before opening the door. "Happy New Year, sir," he said.

"Happy New Year to you too." Iestyn laughed. "Have a lovely party. I'll be thinking of you at midnight."

"I'll text your kiss to you," Dan said.

"Go on, before the taxi driver leans on his horn and wakes the neighborhood," Iestyn said.

Dan rushed down the path and into the car.

He waved as the taxi moved off and Iestyn closed the door. "Oh God, Iestyn Jones," he said. "There's no hope for you now."

Chapter Twelve

This is going to be a fun evening. Iestyn got ready to go to the pub with the others. Yesterday, the day after the night before with Dan, he'd spoken to Julie, who'd been out for her date with Matt. He'd also spoken to Kate, who'd had a long talk with Sian. One of those occasions had gone better than the other, but Kate and Sian didn't want to talk about it and certainly didn't want Matt to know, fearing his usual comments about women together, which would invariably get him a slap from Julie and a Paddington Bear stare from Iestyn.

He hoped Julie and Matt's decision was that they'd made a mistake but were okay about it. And lastly, there was the fact that he would be there missing the person he really wanted to see at midnight. If he closed his eyes, he could see Dan's large hands and imagine them touching him. Somehow, the tea towel had found its way to his bedroom and was currently under his pillow.

Well, they can't arrest me for it, can they?

Instead of wallowing in self-pity, he decided to get a bit drunk, which was probably the wrong decision, but he didn't particularly want to be sober if there was going to be an atmosphere.

He closed his computer. Dan had sent him a photo of himself in his kitchen with the food set out by the catering company and a 'wish you were here' message. Dressed in black trousers, blue shirt and a black waistcoat, Dan looked positively edible, and Iestyn worried that he'd made the wrong choice. If this relationship was going anywhere, they'd have to meet each other's friends at some point, and Iestyn had already decided that he wanted their romance to go somewhere. He'd also had an email wishing him Happy New Year from Gareth in Barbados. He was by the swimming pool looking tanned. Iestyn wondered who'd taken the photo, as there were hints of a new woman in the email. Perhaps Gee really had found a bored millionairess after all.

It was time to go—time to face the music. It couldn't be that bad, could it?

* * * *

Across town, in his fifteenth floor apartment, Dan looked around him. His guests were due at eight thirty. He hadn't lived in this place for long. He'd bought it for the roof garden that gave him a view across to Cardiff Bay. Having the twenty-four-hour concierge was good as well. The feeling of security it gave was a real plus. He'd given the concierge on duty a list for the evening and all the guests had a password. Some might consider it overkill but he wanted his private life to stay as private as possible. He'd invited about twenty people—some of his teammates from the Giants and Wales teams and some of his old school friends. When he'd split with Aron, it had shocked many of them and they'd found it difficult to adapt to him as an individual and not part of 'Az and Dan', as they'd been at school. Evan, Beth and Hayley formed his close circle of friends and all were coming tonight.

He wondered what Hayley would wear. She liked to dress outrageously and was beginning to make a name for herself in the fashion world after completing her degree in Leeds.

Evan had finally worn Beth down and they'd been together for two years.

Mac, his best friend on the Giants team, would also be there. He was Welsh through and through, but his great grandfather had brought the name McDonald down from Scotland when he'd come to work at Cardiff docks. There were a few others from the Giants coming with their partners and that was all. He wished Iestyn had agreed to come but he understood it was early in their relationship. He hadn't even told Hayley about him yet. He was going to talk to her tonight. He knew there was something between him and Iestyn that he hoped would go somewhere but he wasn't sure Iestyn really understood what he was getting into yet. Dan looked at the text he'd received from him and wished he could receive those kisses in person.

Hayley was the first to arrive, as instructed, so they could talk without interruption. She'd been upset when he'd split with Aron but had supported him. Dan knew she was still in touch with his ex but also that she would keep his new relationship to herself if he asked her to.

"You look stunning," he said when he opened the door. She was dressed head to toe in tartan fabric that hugged every curve until it reached her knees then flared out, not quite hitting the floor thus showing off the tartan shoes too. Wearing them, she easily reached six foot. She wore a sporran on her belt and her long hair was plaited through with tartan ribbons.

"Well, it is Hogmanay," she replied. "I thought I'd dress appropriately, although these shoes may come off. Proper taxi shoes, these are. So, my mysterious friend, what did you want to talk to me about?"

Dan couldn't help smiling.

"You've found a new man, haven't you?" she said excitedly. "Oh! Interesting! Give me a drink and tell me all about him. I want to know everything down to his inside leg measurement, assuming you've already discovered his inside leg measurement, that is."

Dan blushed. She was one of the few people who could do that to him. He shrugged.

"Okay then, where did you meet him? What does he look like? What does he do? Do you think he's a keeper? Is he cute? Come on, Danny. Spill the beans."

He flinched. "You know I hate it when you call me that, and it's early days yet. I met him before Christmas when I was out skating with Mac. He fell at my feet and didn't know who I was, which I have to say doesn't happen to me very often these days, so I was a bit intrigued. I gave him my number, just in case."

Hayley raised her eyebrows.

"Yeah, I know, but something told me he'd phone. Then I overheard the kids ribbing him and I found out he was gay. So my gaydar was working after all. He rang and we went out to dinner."

"He has kids? You said there were kids?" Hayley looked confused.

"No, stupid, he's a teacher. He teaches history at St Illtyd's. He's tall, although not as tall as me, and he's got dark hair and these amazing blue-gray eyes." Dan drifted for a moment.

"You're really into him, aren't you? Please tell me he's out, unlike your little footie friend. Does he realize what he's taking on with you? The papers will jump on this if they find out. You were lucky no one noticed you at St David's. You know what it was like when Aron left. They wanted all the details and were desperate to find out if either of you had been playing away. I always wondered if they hacked your phone."

"Me too. As to if he'll cope, I don't know. He's out at work and with his family, so that isn't a problem, but I'm not sure he understands what it'll be like when the media finds out he's going out with me."

"Well, you are the most eligible gay man in the country and one of the few in any sport. You're a gay ambassador, whether you want to be or not. Just by being there, you make it possible for more gay kids to come into sport. And you could be named Welsh captain for the home internationals. He must realize you have a public profile."

The buzzer warned Dan that others were coming up. Soon everyone was there and the party began to warm up. He was drinking the non-alcoholic wine tonight to keep his head as host and because they had training—not that this stopped Mac and the others.

"Please eat something, Mac," he warned. "You know if you've got a thick head, you don't run as fast. I promised the boss I'd keep an eye on all of you tonight. Can't let the fastest winger in the country get out of shape!"

"All right, Dad, I'll be good. I'll just have a few then go on the water. Oh, by the way, did that bloke who fell on you phone?"

Dan found himself smiling again.

"Ah, I think that's my answer. So did you get laid then?"

"Fucking hell, Mac! Not all of us are like you, and you're going to have to do a lot better than that if you think Hayley's going to have anything to do with you."

"You've got to admit she does look bloody edible in that dress. Those curves are to die for. I always was a sucker for curves and red hair."

Dan fixed him with a stare.

Mac held up his hands. "Okay, I'll be good. I promise. So why isn't your new man here tonight then?"

"He's out with his friends, and it really is a bit soon for him to be exposed to everyone, especially you, but I like him."

* * * *

In the pub, Iestyn was on his third pint and heading toward being tipsy. Matt had gone off hunting some woman who'd given him the eye at the bar. Kate and Sian had heads down, whispering to each other. He couldn't help noticing their hands accidentally brushing. He was simply trying not to be miserable.

"Well, this is fun, isn't it?" Julie said. "So are we both going to get pissed?"

"Seems like a plan," Iestyn said. "Are you really all right about Matt? You've liked him for such a long time."

"Yeah, actually I'm fine about it. I think I just fancied the image of him, not the reality. When we went out, he watched every woman who came into the room. I could almost see the calculations in his head as he gave them scores out of ten. I should have known, really. He's not going to change until he finds some woman he can't live without and I'm definitely not that woman. At least I realized that quickly. Perhaps this rugby player of yours, when we finally get to meet him, will have some fit friends on the team and I can find a handsome sportsman." She paused. "Hmm, I think I need to study the Welsh team to see if there are any likely candidates."

"I'll see what I can do. We're going for a run down the coast sometime soon, so I'll ask him then. I can do a dinner party to introduce you to him. My family wants to meet him as well. The poor man doesn't know what he's letting himself in for, getting mixed up with me."

* * * *

Half an hour before the witching hour, Dan stood in the kitchen getting more drinks for everyone. Mac followed him in.

"I've set the fireworks out on the balcony. There's only a few."

Dan put the beers down and looked at Mac. "If I disappear, will you keep an eye on things?" he asked.

"Disappear where?"

"I know this is mad but the pub Iestyn's in is about fifteen minutes from here. If I go now, I can find him before midnight." He looked at Mac's face, which was a mixture of surprise and... What? Indulgence?

"You soppy sod! Be careful you aren't seen. Can you imagine the papers picking up on this?"

"Everyone'll be too pissed to notice," Dan said hopefully.

"Go on. I'll tell people you've gone to see your nan if you want."

Dan hugged his friend and grabbed his coat. The lift seemed to take forever. The drive went without a hitch, as the streets were fairly clear, and he pulled into the car park at eleven fifty-two. He texted Iestyn.

Come out to the car park. I'm in the black SUV near the gate. Want to see you.

Would Iestyn think he was mad?

* * * *

When his phone buzzed, Iestyn took it out expecting to find a kiss or two from Dan for midnight. "What?" he exclaimed.

"What is it?" Julie asked.

He showed her the phone.

"Bloody hell! Why are you still here? Get out and find him. I'll be fine."

Iestyn kissed her. "That's your New Year's kiss," he said. His heart was pounding nineteen to the dozen. He couldn't believe that Dan had left his party to find him.

He slipped out of the back door. It didn't appear as if anyone was paying him attention as he stood at the door looking around the car park. Headlights flashed once from across the gravel, and he ran over and opened the SUV's passenger door.

"Get in," Dan said. He'd parked so that the front of the car faced away from the pub.

"I can't believe you're here," Iestyn said, trying to catch his breath. "I didn't expect this. What about your party?"

"I left Mac in charge. I suddenly realized I wanted to give you a New Year's kiss in person, if that's all right with you."

Iestyn still couldn't believe it. Is *this man really that perfect?* "Go on then," he said. "I think it's seconds from midnight."

Iestyn leaned across until their lips met. Dan cupped either side of his face as he sank into the kiss. Nothing else mattered to either of them at that moment and they continued kissing. Dan bit Iestyn's lower lip and sucked it as he reached out with his tongue looking for more contact. Finally, they broke apart.

"*Blwyddyn Newydd Dda,*" Dan said, grinning broadly.

"Happy New Year to you too," Iestyn replied, taking hold of Dan's hand. "Nice car," he added. "You'd better get back to your party."

"Wish you'd come with me," Dan said.

"Can't. I shouldn't leave Julie. I'll see you Tuesday. We'll go in my car, yeah." He started to open the door but Dan pulled him in for another brief kiss.

Iestyn sat back and grinned. "If you keep doing that, I'll never get out of here." He caught Dan's glance toward the back seat. "Don't even think about it. I'm way too old to contort myself enough to have sex with you in the back of your car."

"Spoilsport," Dan replied, laughing.

Reluctantly, Iestyn opened the door and stepped out then watched the SUV pull out. If it was cold, he couldn't feel it. There was no ground under his feet as he made his way back to the pub.

Shit, can I fall in love so quickly? The only answer he could find in his head was a resounding *Yes*!

Chapter Thirteen

Dan didn't get to take Iestyn out to the pub or on a romantic walk along the beach.

"I've cleared it with the management," Graeme Starr of the Starr Agency said. "Both the Giants and the Wales think it will be good publicity for the game, and it won't do you any harm, either, so it's a photo shoot and an interview. They want you to come to London and bring your Wales kit with you. I've booked you into the Londinium for Monday night. It's a boutique place that's central. Well, they're paying and the shoot is Tuesday. You even get to keep your clothes on for this one. Well, mostly. There'll be three others there as well, all-out sportsmen, so you can guess who. They wanted to get all four of you for an issue, as you've been in before."

Dan had little choice but to accept the offer. He'd always been determined not to hide his sexuality for or from anyone, however difficult it got. He'd had his fair share of banter from the crowd about 'taking it up the arse', to which Mac had usually commented that 'they should be so lucky!' When it came to formal occasions with partners, he'd always taken his boyfriend with him. It wasn't that he wanted to be a role model or a pin-up for *Gay Times*, but someone had to show that a person could be gay and play sports. It saddened him that they had to go to Scandinavia to find a gay footballer for the shoot. He knew there were many such players in the league. Hell, he'd been chatted up by several. A few high-profile ex footballers were now moving into management. However, with the exception of that one time, he'd turned down anyone in the closet. Now, however, he had to make a decision. Graeme had said he could take someone with him if he wanted to. Dan had hinted that there was someone in his life.

"Bring him along," Graeme had said. "If he's going to be important to you, I'll need to meet him anyway, as things will have to be managed."

Dan hated this but he was realistic enough to know that Graeme was right. He hoped Iestyn would be able to cope.

Graeme would be there, of course, looking after his client's interests. Even though he had mentioned the possibility to his agent, Dan wasn't sure whether he should ask Iestyn if he fancied a trip to the capital. Would Iestyn want to stay the night with him in the hotel? Was it too soon? Would he think Dan was pushing him to take things further too quickly? Well, there was only one way of finding out, so he picked up the phone.

"I'm sorry about the trip to the beach," Dan said. "But I know you're not back at work until Wednesday and I could get you back for Tuesday night, so I wanted to ask if you'd like to come to London with me. I have a hotel booked on Monday night then the shoot is Tuesday. I could sneak you in as Graeme's assistant—he's my agent. After that we might have a bit of time before we get back, though probably not much. It might be a bit boring for you but I just wondered. There's no pressure if you don't want to go." Dan stopped abruptly.

He'd barely given Iestyn time to collect his thoughts. "Sorry, I know I've sprung this on you at short notice."

He could almost hear Iestyn trying to work out in his mind how to answer.

"Umm. Sorry. This is a bit of a surprise. I don't know if I can go to London just before I go back to work. Would we be late? Wouldn't I be in the way?"

Dan guessed there were questions Iestyn hadn't asked.

Quiet followed for about ten seconds before Iestyn said, "Oh fuck it! Why not?"

"I'll pick you up tomorrow morning at ten. We'll see if we can get tickets for a show at the last minute and have dinner. I doubt if anyone will recognize me there. I'm only a rugby player after all, not some celebrity."

* * * *

As soon as he had put the phone down, Iestyn gulped, realizing what he'd done. He had just agreed to go to London, to stay in a hotel room with the most famous rugby player in Wales. England might be safer for them both, but he doubted Wales would be the same. Perhaps it was better this way, easier to be together. Then there was the issue of 'sleeping together' or just actually sleeping together. Iestyn wasn't sure what he was ready for. He knew some people could fuck each other stupid within minutes of meeting, but he wasn't that sort of bloke. He wasn't even sure what he wanted to do.

He phoned Julie.

"No, I haven't got anything special to do," she said. "Yes, I'm sure I can put down these theory exams I'm supposed to be marking for a couple of hours for you to make me dinner and listen to your angst. I'll be over at seven. Make sure the wine is cooled. After marking this lot, I'll need something decent to drink."

* * * *

"So," she continued a little while later, having consumed two glasses of wine whilst trying desperately not to spill spaghetti down her front, "you're worried he's going to expect you to take one for the team, so to speak."

"Jesus, Julie, you're as bad as Matt. This matters to me. I thought you'd understand, being female. This is like letting him into a place that belongs to me, and he's already far more into my head than I thought possible after so little time. I haven't slept with that many people. You know it's different with men."

"Ah, the sixty-four thousand dollar question of who tops and who bottoms," she said, trying to suppress a giggle. "Doesn't that just sort of work itself out? You don't care that much, do you? Bloody hell, the things I end up talking about with you!"

"No, I don't care, but he might. Look at the size of him, Julie. He's got muscles where I didn't know they existed and he's a natural leader."

"That is rather a stereotype, isn't it? Come on. Tell the truth. This isn't about who fucks who, is it? Or if you even fuck at all," Julie said. "You're worried about not having a six-pack or him seeing you naked.

He does have a tight butt, I'll admit." She poured herself another glass. "But it's not like you need a paper bag over your head, and he obviously likes you, even if your six-pack isn't exactly...prominent. You could always turn the lights out if you're that worried."

"Thanks, you're being really helpful, and it wouldn't be the first time."

"What? I thought you were worried about having sex with him and you've already played hunt the sausage!"

"Oh, he found the sausage all right! Oh, yeah." Iestyn drifted off for a moment. He was feeling a little tipsy himself now. "But this is different. This is sharing a bed. It's almost like being a couple."

"Look, Iestyn, so you go away with him. You go to dinner and see a show. You go back to the hotel and see what happens. Try talking to him. Unlike most men, you can string a few words together to make whole sentences. Hasn't he proved to be more than just some unfeeling sportsman, unlike our dickhead friend?"

"Yeah, he has, and I know you're right."

They talked about Kate and Sian for a while.

"They seemed happy on New Year's Eve but Sian hasn't said anything to me," Julie said "Has Kate talked to you since?"

"No, not a word, but as long as they're happy, who cares? We need to find you a decent man now, Julie. Perhaps I'll ask Dan if he's got any desperate teammates."

She punched him hard on the arm. "You've already mentioned that—and I'll give you bloody desperate. I can survive without a man, you know."

Iestyn made a noise that defied description and started humming *Good Vibrations*.

"Bastard. I've no idea why I put up with you. Anyway, you can talk. I've seen what's in that bottom drawer of yours. Now, I like a good solid cock as much as the next person but—"

"Well, seeing as I *am* the next person that's true," Iestyn said. "And that thing is nothing to do with me. It was Matt's idea of a joke."

"I might have guessed. He is such a prick himself." She picked up the bottle and drained its contents. "Bloody hell! That was the second bottle. I think I need to use the bathroom."

"I'll come up too. You'd better stay tonight. No taxi will want to have you. Come and help me decide what to wear."

In his bedroom, Iestyn opened his cupboard doors and looked inside. Julie was lying on the bed propped up on one elbow, trying desperately to stay awake.

"Now, what clothes do I take with me?"

"Where are you staying?" she asked.

"I don't know but I imagine it'll be somewhere reasonable. Don't the magazines usually pay for these things? I'm just wondering if I need a suit for the theater and dinner. These days, people seem to go in jeans and T-shirts."

"Take a suit and jeans, the red and the dark gray shirts and a jumper. It's a pity you don't have a Wales strip. You two could have a private ruck and maul session."

"Really?" She giggled and fell back on the bed, laughing at her own joke while he gathered the clothes and put them in his small suitcase.

"Okay, I think I'm sorted now. I'll put the suit in tomorrow. Boxers or briefs?"

"Oh, briefs, definitely, but no patterns, and not those ones Gareth got you with chess pieces on them. Will you be taking your little buzzing friend from the drawer or does Dan have ample equipment?"

"Sure you don't want it? Far more reliable than a man."

"Yes, I know," Julie replied pointedly.

Iestyn closed the suitcase and hung the suit over the wardrobe door. "Thanks, Jules. I really do appreciate your help." He fell down on the bed beside her. They lay comfortably as Iestyn put his arm around her and she pulled into his side.

"I know, but there is a price for this service," she said, looking up at him with eyes full of mischief.

Iestyn raised an eyebrow.

"I expect full details of everything that happens and marks out of ten. Or perhaps you could give him a grade if I provide the criteria."

"You are a bad woman."

"But you love me anyway."

"Yep, I do." He hugged her tightly.

"D'you want one of my shirts to sleep in? The spare bed is made up," he said. "Come on. Let's get you up. You're not going to be sick, are you?"

"You know me, Iestyn. I can take my drink. Anyway, you need your beauty sleep—big day tomorrow. And I get to meet the incredibly handsome Dan Morgan."

Iestyn looked at her.

"What, you thought I'd just disappear before he came? Not a chance. I want introductions and everything. Now, I'm going to bed. I'll see you in the morning and I'd like tea and toast, please."

A little while later, Iestyn turned the light off and stared at the ceiling, wondering about what the next day would bring.

Chapter Fourteen

Iestyn crawled out of bed then stepped into the shower. *Why did I drink so much last night?* He washed, shaved and put on black jeans and a jumper with a red T-shirt underneath. The click of the bathroom door told him that Julie was up and about.

Downstairs, he made the tea and toast she'd requested. In the mornings, it had to be tea for him as well. He didn't feel ready for the day unless he'd had a mug and it had to be extra strong. He knew what Julie was like, so he made a pot to cater for her needs. His suitcase was in the hall, and it was forty minutes before Dan was due to arrive. He hoped the tea and toast would quiet the flock of seagulls currently swirling around in his stomach.

"You look like death," he said as Julie entered the kitchen.

She clutched at the mug of tea he'd just poured for her. "I'll need more than this," she murmured.

"I'm prepared. I made a pot, since I know what you're like in the morning."

The toast popped up. Iestyn collected it and spread on butter and jam. Julie fell on it hungrily and sat at the kitchen table.

"No paper?" she questioned.

"No, I canceled it as part of my fitness regime," he replied. "If I want one, I have to go out to the newsagents."

"Which is what, all of ten doors down?" She laughed. "You should get a dog and train it to collect one. Or you could take it for a walk as well."

"Too much bother," he said. "Will you lock up for me? Give yourself a bit of time for the alcohol to clear. We wouldn't want you getting stopped by the police, now, would we?"

At nine fifty a knock sounded at the door.

"He's early," Iestyn said. "Do I look all right?"

"Oh, for God's sake, you look fine! Now answer the door so I can meet him."

When he opened up, the body in front of him almost filled the entire doorframe. Dan looked good dressed from head to toe in black, his blond hair spiked up at the top and gelled at the side, and his blue eyes sparkling, making it plain that he hadn't been drinking the night before. Iestyn was surprised that Dan wasn't covered up, as it was light now and someone might spot him.

"Come in," he said. "I'll just get my jacket. I love yours by the way. That leather looks really soft."

Dan smirked and, before Iestyn had a chance to move, the rugby player had closed the door and pulled him into a kiss. Surprised, Iestyn kissed back, open-mouthed, losing himself in the scent and taste of Dan—until he heard a cough behind them. Dan sprang back, hitting his head on the coat stand to the side of the door.

"Sorry. This is Julie," Iestyn explained whilst Dan rubbed his scalp.

"I guessed that from your description, but I must say her skin seems to have cleared up wonderfully, and that's a great wig if she really is bald."

Julie frowned and looked at her best friend.

He held up his hands. "Honestly, I said nothing of the sort."

Dan laughed his deep chuckle that always made Iestyn want to kiss him again.

"She stayed overnight. For some unknown reason, she wanted to meet you this morning and..." He leaned in and whispered rather loudly, "She was as pissed as a newt last night."

"And he was, of course, stone-cold sober. He talks when he's drunk, you know. Tells me everything," she added, winking at Dan.

Looking embarrassed, Dan put out his hand. "It's nice to meet you, Julie."

"You too," she said. She turned to Iestyn and pulled a face. "Oh, my God, he's gorgeous, and you were right about those hands," she mouthed.

Dan chuckled again. "Are you ready to go?" As he spoke, the phone rang in the other room.

"I'll get it," Julie said. "You get off. It's probably only someone trying to sell you something."

He opened the door and followed Dan down the short path. He was just stowing the suitcase in the boot when Julie appeared at the door.

"Iestyn!"

He looked up at her face and knew that it was serious.

"What is it?" he asked.

"Iessie, it's your mam on the phone." He ran back to the door. "Julie, what is it?"

"Oh, Iessie, it's your dad. Your mam said he got up early this morning and told her he'd manage by himself. When she came downstairs, she found him in his chair. He's dead, Iessie."

Dan appeared behind him and Iestyn turned back to look at him. "I'll get your case."

"I need to talk to her." Iestyn couldn't quite take in the news. Inside, he picked up the phone.

Dan and Julie waited nearby while he talked.

"I'll be over as soon as I can, Mam. I'll call Huw and Rhian. Okay, Mam, you talk to the paramedics."

Dan hovered while he talked. Julie sat next to him on the sofa.

Iestyn looked up. "I can't go."

It didn't really need saying, but Dan nodded.

"I know," Dan stated, "and I wish I didn't have to, but I'll be back tomorrow night. I'll phone you tonight, so leave your mobile on."

Iestyn got up, but Dan pulled him into a hug and kissed his forehead. He really didn't want to let go as Dan surrounded him. He just wanted to cry in Dan's arms and have him say that it wasn't real, that his father wasn't really dead.

"I'm so sorry about your dad. Go look after your mum."

Iestyn guessed that Dan was thinking about his own mother. "Drive carefully, Dan," he said. "You'll be out among the English."

"I'll be fine."

He sat on the arm of the sofa while Julie showed Dan to the door. "Don't worry. We'll take good care of him," she said. "It's been nice to meet you. I hope your trip goes all right."

He knew Dan had to go—it was his job—but Iestyn wished with all his heart that he was staying to help him get through the next few days.

Chapter Fifteen

The drive to London gave Dan time to think about Iestyn. He wished he could have stayed with him but he knew he didn't really have enough of a place in the man's life to support him through this. They weren't really a couple—not yet—but Dan hoped they might be soon. He also hoped Iestyn would feel that he could depend on him, talk to him. He knew what it was like to have a parent die. He thought about his own mother. She was the only parent he'd ever known. He'd wondered, when he became well known, if his father would come crawling out of the woodwork to claim his son, but whoever the bastard was who had abandoned his mother had never shown his face. Dan hadn't really missed him.

Growing up, he'd had his granddad, who'd taken him to his first rugby match at the Arms Park virtually as soon as he could walk. He'd seemed so big, his granddad, Bobby Morgan. Dan knew that he looked like him, as his nan reminded him all the time when she was reminiscing about the husband she had lost far too early. The old man had told him all about the

Welsh greats—Barry John, Gareth Edwards, Phil Bennett, JPR, JJ—the team that had beaten all challengers and had been immortalized in song by Max Boyce. His granddad had also provided his first experience of death. Dan could recall the morning of the funeral. He'd been eleven years old. It had been a cold day and he was trying to be the man of the family, now that there was only him, his mum and Nan. Nan had been stoic and hadn't cried. They'd sung *Men of Harlech*—not really a funeral hymn, but it had been his granddad's favorite song, from his favorite film, *Zulu*. The church had been packed.

After his granddad's death, his nan had taken him to watch Cardiff play. He hadn't been told much when his mam was ill for the first time, not until she was better, but the cancer had come back and she'd ignored it for too long. He'd always said that if ever he captained Wales, he would dedicate it to the memory of his granddad.

* * * *

Back in Cardiff, Iestyn arrived home. Another car sat in the drive, which he guessed was the doctor's. His father would still be there. He hesitated at the door.

As if she guessed his thoughts, Julie spoke to reassure him. "Come on, Iessie. Your mum's going to need you now. It won't be fun but you've got to cope." Julie took his arm.

"I've never seen a dead body before," he said.

"It'll just be like he's asleep," she explained. "And you've seen that before. It won't be easy but it helped me to think that they were asleep—my parents, I mean."

They went inside. The doctor was talking to Iestyn's mother. He glanced over at his dad in the chair. Julie had been right. His father did simply appear to be asleep. He wasn't quite sure what to do. Did he touch him? Kiss him? His mother peered up at Iestyn. Her eyes were red but she'd stopped crying. She looked years older than she had the last time he'd seen her.

"Mam," he said quietly.

She got up and they held each other for a while.

"He didn't suffer, Iessie. They're going to have to do a post-mortem but the doctor thinks it was a heart attack. We're just waiting for Williams Funeral Home to arrive to take him. They'll sort everything out."

The bell rang and Julie hurried to the door. The couple from the funeral home carefully explained everything that would happen and that someone would come round the next day to discuss arrangements for the funeral. Iestyn watched as they carefully took his father away.

"I'll put the kettle on," Julie said.

Iestyn sat with his mam on the sofa. Suddenly the room seemed empty without his dad in his usual spot. He found he had no tears yet and wondered if that was normal. Before he could think anymore, Huw arrived.

"They've just taken Dad," Iestyn explained.

Rhian got there fifteen minutes later. Julie made tea for everyone and sat quietly to one side for a while as the siblings talked to their mother about what had happened. She then phoned a taxi and tried to catch Iestyn's eye.

"I'll be off," Julie said. "I'll pick up my car from yours and I'll ring you later. I'm so sorry, Iessie." She gave him a big hug, said brief goodbyes to the rest of the family and left.

The family stayed together for a while and made arrangements, knowing that Williams would be there the next day to discuss the funeral service in more detail.

"Your dad knew what he wanted. He had it all planned," his mother explained.

Iestyn stayed with her that night. Looking after him gave her something to do, she said, and he didn't want her there alone.

"I'll have to get used to it sometime," she'd said to him, "but not yet."

She'd gone to bed early and he'd heard her crying for the first time. He realized that his parents had barely spent a night apart since they'd married, aside from a brief stay his dad had had in hospital a few years back.

His phone rang. He smiled when Dan's name flashed up.

"Hi," Iestyn said. "How's London?"

"London is fine. How's things with you? How's your mum doing?"

"She's trying to be brave," Iestyn replied. "But I heard her crying just now. I still can't believe he's gone. It's like he's in the hospital or something and he's going to be coming home. He was still here when I arrived and he just looked like he was asleep. I guess it'll hit me more when I go downstairs tomorrow and his chair is empty." All at once, tears began to fall for the first time. He shook uncontrollably and wished that the rugby player's strong arms were holding him. "Oh, Dan, my dad's dead. I'm never going to see him again."

"I know," Dan whispered. "I wish I could hug you, make it all better for you, but I can't."

"At least he didn't suffer," Iestyn continued, wiping his face. "He would have wanted it like this, at home, with his own things around him. Mam says he left instructions for his funeral. We're going to talk about it tomorrow." He wiped his eyes again and blew his nose. "Sorry about that. Tell me what's happening with you."

"The shoot and interview are tomorrow morning," Dan said. "I'll be home tomorrow night. I could come round if you want, but I don't want to interfere."

"I don't know, Dan. I'm going to stay with my mam for a while. I have to ring work. I'm not sure how long I'll be off. It depends when the funeral is but we'll find that out tomorrow. Ring me when you get back, yeah? Is the hotel nice? Tell me what the room looks like." The realization that they'd have been there together now, if things had gone to plan, hit him.

"It's not exactly luxury but it's comfortable. Even the bed, which I'm lying on now, thinking of you and what we did on the sofa, is long enough not to have my feet hanging over the end." Dan changed the subject. "I had dinner with Graeme, my agent, and discussed what I'd say tomorrow. They always try to dig for information about my private life, especially since I split with Aron. I wish you were here with me and not having to deal with…"

"I wish I was there as well," Iestyn whispered. Suddenly very tired, he said, "I'm going to go to bed now. I hope the shoot goes well. I can't wait to read it and see the pictures. Ring me."

"Yeah, okay. I'll ring you tomorrow. Iestyn, I really am sorry. Try to get some sleep."

Iestyn made his way up to bed. He decided not to look in on his mam and went to his own room.

Hugging his pillow, wishing it was Dan, he went to sleep.

* * * *

The next day, the family was together again. Huw took the lead, being the eldest. Ben had decided that he wanted to stay at home, as he had school the next day.

"I don't think he's ready to come here yet," Huw explained. "He's been quiet since we told him about Dad. His friend Adam came over so we've left them to it. Sue will be back this afternoon anyway."

He'd brought Megs, who immediately had gone to her granddad's chair and looked around, confused. She'd scrambled up into the seat and looked at everyone.

"Grannad?" she'd questioned.

Iestyn had forced back the tears as his mother had simply picked Megs up and said, "Granddad isn't here anymore, darling. You'll have to dance for us instead."

"Dance," Megs had echoed.

There hadn't been a dry eye in the room as she'd begun to sway to the music in her own head, whilst caught up in her grandmother's arms. Rhian had taken the twins to their playgroup as usual. They hadn't really understood when she'd tried to explain to them what had happened.

The funeral director arrived at ten thirty on the dot. He was younger than they'd expected. Somehow Iestyn always expected them to be old.

The director introduced himself. "Hello, everyone, I'm Tom Williams. First, let me say how sorry I am for your loss. My job is to find out what you want for the funeral. The results of the post-mortem will be available later today. You can ring this number after three this afternoon. So, let's get started."

Someone made tea for everyone. In their dad's file, there was a copy of his will, all his insurance documents, his account details and his funeral plan. Tom made notes about everything. Iestyn helped him take down all their names and together they drafted the entry for the local papers, announcing the funeral.

"This is a busy time of year," Tom declared. "Once the post-mortem has been completed, we'll return the body to our premises. You'll be able to visit, if you like. We can have the funeral a fortnight from today. We can do it at the crematorium—or perhaps you attend a particular church?"

"What d'you think, Mam?" Iestyn asked. Throughout the discussion, she'd sat ramrod straight, staring into the distance, and he wasn't sure how much she'd heard.

"The crematorium will be fine," she answered, turning to face the funeral director. "My husband was not a religious man. Geraint planned a humanist funeral. He knew someone who can lead the service. I have the name here. It seems he had already spoken to him about his ideas for the service. I'm going to ring him later. There are various songs he requested and if anyone wants to speak, that's fine. Now for the tricky bit. I know it's usual for the cremation to take place after the service, but Geraint was very definite about not being there in a box. He instructed he was to be cremated beforehand then just his ashes should be at the funeral, before we took them to be scattered at sea. Can we do that?"

"I will check for you, Mrs Jones, and let you know. It depends on the crematorium but I can't see that it will be a problem. The music is easily sorted if you put it on a tape or CD. We have a large collection and I think we have *Old and Wise* already, as well as the Glen Miller, but we don't have a copy of *Chess*." Tom delved into his file again. "We can also produce a program for the day. Is there any image you'd like on the front, something Mr Jones was interested in, perhaps a hobby or sport?"

Iestyn smiled, knowing there was an obvious choice. He saw that his mother and siblings were thinking exactly the same. Their father had only ever had one vice—horse racing. It had been his passion and he'd still had a bet regularly, but never too much, of course.

"There's that picture of him at the races a few years back," Rhian said. "You know, after he'd had that big win. We could put that on the front. That was his best win ever at Chepstow. I remember the bookie wasn't at all impressed at losing three thousand pounds."

Eventually, Iestyn sighed once everything was decided. Megs had danced for everyone and this time it brought a much-needed smile to their faces. They had lunch and said their goodbyes again, leaving Iestyn with his mam.

"You don't need to stay, darling," she said. "I'm sure you'd rather be off with your new friend. Do I call him your boyfriend yet?"

"I don't know, Mam. Anyway, he's in London until later doing an interview and photo shoot for a magazine. He did ask if he could come round when I said I was staying here with you."

"Give him a ring and tell him to come to dinner. I'd like to meet the man who's put a smile on my baby's face again."

"I'll text him. He's probably in the middle of things now."

About thirty minutes later, his phone beeped.

Be there at six. Send postcode for satnav. Dan. XX

Iestyn swallowed. His new boyfriend was about to meet his mam!

Chapter Sixteen

Dan's journey home was disrupted by an accident just after the tollbooths on the bridge into Wales. He tapped the steering wheel in frustration and looked at the clock every other minute. He desperately didn't want to be late, not when he was meeting Iestyn's mother for the first time. The shoot had gone well, except for the curve ball question asking if he was seeing anyone at the moment. He'd hesitated just a little too long before saying no.

"Do I sense a reluctance to admit anything?" the interviewer, Suzie, had asked.

Dan hoped they wouldn't go digging. Afterward he'd asked, off the record, if they could leave out that question. "You know what it's like. If there's any hint that I'm seeing someone, the papers will be after a story and—"

"You don't want to scare him off yet," she'd said perceptively.

She'd smiled and he'd hoped that it was sincere.

Once past the accident, he put his foot down a bit. It had grown dark by the time he hit the rush hour around Newport and Cardiff. He had to admit that he'd been surprised at the dinner invitation. It wasn't the best of circumstances to be meeting one's boyfriend's mother when his father — her husband — had just died.

"Look, it'll take her mind off things — and mine too," Iestyn had explained. "And you had to meet her sometime. At least this way you don't have to face the whole family at once, which, believe me, is a good thing."

He pressed his hands free and heard Iestyn say, "Hello?"

"I'll be there around six thirty. Sorry, there was an accident on the motorway and I'm running a bit late," he said.

"Don't worry. Just get yourself here in one piece. I hope you're hungry. Mam has made cottage pie and apple and rhubarb crumble. I know you said you had to eat a lot to keep up the calorie intake. She's been busy all afternoon. We saw the funeral director this morning and I'm going with Mam tomorrow to register Dad's death now that we have a cause. It seems he had a coronary thrombosis. Nothing anyone could have done about it. I'll see you in a bit."

* * * *

Iestyn ended the call and called out to his mam, "He'll be here at six thirty."

"That's fine," she replied, coming into the room. She sat beside him on the sofa. "You like him, don't you?"

"Yes, Mam, I do, but I'm not stupid. He's gorgeous, and somewhat famous, as well as being on the rebound. He was with one bloke since he was sixteen and he's never really been with anyone else."

"Some men are stayers, Iessie. Look at me and your dad. Your grandparents thought I'd lost my mind. I was just out of university after getting my PhD when I announced I was getting married to your dad, a builder. The first time he met them properly, you could have cut the atmosphere with a knife. He had his best suit on and fidgeted with his tie. He never was that keen on wearing one. In those days, he still got his hands dirty and was working for your Uncle Stan on the building sites. Relations thawed a bit when he started his own company and he got involved in the school's building program. He traveled all over the country then." She hooked her arm into his. "You can't control who you fall in love with, and I fell in love with your dad the moment I laid eyes on him, half naked and covered in brick dust with sweat dripping between his shoulder blades. It was quite an image, I can tell you, and first impressions matter. Anyway, Dan must like you or he wouldn't be coming here."

At six-thirty, the doorbell rang. "I'll get it," he shouted to his mam, who was busy in the kitchen. He opened the door and his knees turned weak. Dan appeared a little ruffled but incredibly sexy. Iestyn was absolutely certain no human being should be able to look that adorable in a black cardigan. His blue eyes sparkled and his hair looked like it hadn't seen a comb for months. It had probably taken an age to style it like that. Black jeans hugged his hips and his chest stretched the fabric of the pale blue shirt. He carried a large bunch of flowers.

"For your mum," he explained. "If she isn't out of the house with them already."

"Sorry, come in," Iestyn said.

After he closed the door, Dan stood for a moment. Iestyn reached up to kiss him, knocking Iestyn's glasses slightly.

Dan obviously hadn't expected it. Adjusting them, appearing a little self-conscious, Dan kissed him back then whispered, "Glasses are cool. I've always had a thing for them."

Pulling himself together, Iestyn said, "Come on. Mam's really looking forward to meeting you. She was reminiscing about the first time she met Dad earlier. She really loved him so much."

Dan squeezed his hand then followed him down the hallway.

Chuckling as they all reached the living room at the same time, Iestyn motioned for Dan to hand over the flowers.

"It's good to meet you, Mrs Jones," Dan said. "And I'm really sorry about Mr Jones. It would have been good to talk rugby with him, if he liked rugby, that is. I still have to persuade Iestyn away from his chessboard."

"It was his dad who taught him how to play, but Geraint loved his rugby as well—and call me Mary. Mrs Jones is so very formal. These flowers are lovely and colorful. I'll just go and find a vase. Iessie, will you come out and get the plates and some beers?"

"Beer okay?" he asked his smiling rugby player.

"Iessie?" Dan questioned.

"Yeah, it's a family thing." Heat flooded his cheeks.

"I like it," Dan replied, twinkling more than the polestar on a clear night. "It's cute and it suits you."

Iestyn had been called many things in his life but cute wasn't one of them. He wasn't quite sure whether to be pleased or offended.

In the kitchen, his mother was taking out the cottage pie.

"I'll take that in, Mam. It looks like it weighs a ton. You bring the plates and beers."

"He is magnificent," his mother whispered. "He's like some huge lion with a great blond mane. I bet that hair is a nightmare to control. He must be what? Six foot five at least, and he's built like the proverbial outhouse." She winked at him. "And the size of those hands and feet!"

Mortified, he stared at his feet and bit his lip as heat surged into his cheeks once more. His mother lifted his chin.

"Aww. You're so cute when you blush."

He wanted the ground to open up and swallow him. "Mam, for God's sake, he's just next door, and for the record, he's six foot six. As for his feet, I'm not saying anything."

Back under control, he followed his mother into the living room. They sat at the table and began to eat.

"This is lovely, Mary. I can see Iestyn inherited his culinary skills from you. He makes a mean curry himself."

When he saw his mother smile, he wondered if Dan could get any more perfect.

"Oh, I can do basics like this, Dan, but I have to admit I'm not the best housewife in the world. We've always had a cleaner because, if it had been left to me, we'd have been covered in dust. Housework really isn't my thing."

Dan swallowed another large mouthful. "I believe your specialism is poetry," he said. "We did Welsh poets in school. My favorite was always RS Thomas. I loved what he said about being Welsh."

Iestyn listened to Dan cite one of the poet's most famous verses in his beautiful baritone voice and sighed inwardly. The quote would undoubtedly get his mother started.

"Sorry, I'm showing off a bit." Dan appeared slightly sheepish. "I looked up your stuff about Welsh poets and I know RS Thomas is your favorite. But I do think he really understood what it is to be Welsh. I know when we line up and they play the national anthems, we all sing. It touches some part of me that's so deep and makes me so proud that I can represent my country."

"Spoken like a true Welshman," she said. "When do they tell you who's in the squad for the Six Nations?"

"Sometime later this month."

"And do you think you'll be named captain?"

"I hope so," Dan admitted. "Ever since I started playing rugby, it's been my sole ambition. I'd love to captain Wales."

Iestyn listened and watched as Dan and his mam talked rugby, poetry and what it meant to be Welsh. Dan shoveled the food down in between discussions. "It's so wonderful to have a home-cooked meal. I'm afraid I don't always eat as well as I should."

Iestyn almost expected him to lick the plate clean.

His mother beamed. "I'll get the crumble. Custard or cream?" she asked.

"Oh, custard, please," Dan replied. "I have to keep up the calories or I'll fade away. Training uses a great deal of energy so I get to eat a lot, although it is supposed to be good food and not chocolate and pizza. Apple and rhubarb will help my five a day."

"It must be great to be able to eat anything," Iestyn said, feeling self-conscious again.

"Nah, it's only because I have to train so much. When I stop playing, I'm going to have to be careful. Anyway," he said, leaning forward so his lips were a fraction away from Iestyn's ear, "I like the way you look, so stop worrying."

Iestyn smiled, not quite believing him.

"What do you weigh?" Mary asked, when she put the crumble on the table. Her son looked up, amazed that she should ask, but Dan didn't bat an eyelid.

"Just over seventeen stone, but I'm not the heaviest in the squad, and my height stretches it out. I need the height in the lineouts." Dan dug his spoon into the crumble and ate with an enthusiasm Iestyn couldn't help but envy.

"This crumble is wonderful as well, Mary." He polished off the whole bowl in another few huge mouthfuls.

"Well, you've certainly got an appetite," Mary said when he put down the spoon having practically scraped the dish clean.

"I hope I get to come back again soon."

Mary picked up his bowl and put her hand on his shoulder. She smiled at Iestyn and then looked back at Dan. "You can come here any time you want, Dan."

Iestyn couldn't help himself. "I think she likes you," he said.

"And I like her, very much." He stretched his arms above his head and yawned.

"D'you want another beer?" Iestyn asked. "I'm not back in work tomorrow, which is going to be a bit strange, so I can afford to have a bit of a drink."

"Better not. I'm a bit tired already and I have to drive home," Dan said.

"You could stay here," Mary replied, coming in from the kitchen.

Turning simultaneously, Iestyn and Dan looked at each other.

"It's fine by me. For goodness sake, Iessie, we're all grown-ups. And I can always put my headphones in." She laughed.

It's good to hear her laugh. Iestyn grinned.

"If that's all right with you, I'd like that," Dan said to them both.

"Hmm, yeah," Iestyn said, not quite believing that they were going to spend their first night together in his bed, with his mother across the landing. Life was indeed strange.

Mary went up to bed after the ten o'clock news. Iestyn talked for a bit about his school and why he'd become a teacher. Dan's idolization of several of his teachers was clear. Iestyn wondered if any of the kids he'd inspired to go on to study history felt the same about him. He knew he was a role model in school, being 'out and proud', and it pleased him to be able to show teenagers that they could be that way too.

"Let's go to bed," Dan said suddenly. "It's been a long day and I'm really tired. I need my sleep, as well as my food."

Dan seemed to fill Iestyn's bedroom, even though it was a reasonable size. It would be a bit of a squash for both of them and Dan's feet would probably be over the end of the bed.

"I'm used to it," he said. "Am I okay to use the bathroom first?"

"Yeah, sure, and there's a new toothbrush in the cupboard by the sink. Mam's always doing buy one, get one free."

Iestyn waited but Dan wasn't very long.

"All right if I get in?" he asked. "Are you okay with me sleeping on the left?"

"Yes, that's fine," Iestyn replied, leaving the room. When he returned from the bathroom, Dan was lying on his side, his feet just tucked under the duvet. He was flicking through a book. "Is this good? I've read *The Saga of Exiles* but not those that followed."

"I'm re-reading it while I'm here and, yes, it's good." He stood for a while, unsure what to do next.

"Iestyn, get undressed and get in here, will you?"

He removed most of his clothes as instructed but then sat on the edge of the bed.

"It's all right," Dan said. "I promise I'll behave myself."

"It's not that." He turned slightly. "It's just that this is the first time you'll see me without my glasses."

"And?" Dan said curiously.

"People who don't wear glasses don't understand. Not having them on makes me feel a bit exposed, as if you're seeing the real me. The best I can explain it is how some women feel appearing in public without makeup on."

Dan sat up and leaned toward him. He reached over and took off Iestyn's glasses. "My, but, Mr Jones, you're beautiful." He gave Iestyn the glasses and took his hand. Turning it over, he kissed Iestyn's palm gently.

Iestyn's stomach turned over at such an intimate gesture. He put his glasses safely on the bedside table and, leaving his briefs on, he dragged the duvet back and got into bed. Dan put out an arm and Iestyn found himself snuggling in with his head on his rugby player's broad, firm chest. He noticed that the blond stubble was gone, obviously waxed for the photos. He pulled the light switch and plunged them into darkness.

"Your mum seems to be coping pretty well," Dan said. "How about you?"

"It's odd without him. I can't quite believe it, even though his body was still here when I got home. Did you see your mam...? You know, after? I don't know if I want to go to the funeral home. Most of me doesn't, but I think Huw and Rhian may go. I'm going to miss him such a lot." With that, he realized he was crying.

Dan hugged him tighter and let him cry. He stroked Iestyn's hair. The sensation was incredibly soothing and just like his mam used to do when he'd been ill as a child.

"I'm sorry. I'm getting you all wet," he eventually said.

"It's okay, Iessie. I'm glad I'm here for you."

Dan leaned in and kissed him gently but not for long. It was nice, but he knew that it was all about comfort and nothing to do with sex. Dan kissed him again on the top of his head and wrapped both arms around him. Iestyn closed his eyes and drifted off to sleep.

Chapter Seventeen

To Iestyn it seemed strange to be back at work on Monday morning. His mother had insisted that she would be fine on her own and that she needed to get used to the idea of being alone, so he'd gone back to his own house. Dan had been busy since he'd stayed over, training with the Welsh squad as well as for the Giants. The squad had been named for the Six Nations that weekend. As yet, there'd been no announcement about who was going to be captain for the first game against Ireland at the beginning of February. They'd also set the date for the funeral, which was going to take place on Friday. The funeral directors had organized everything, as his father had wanted.

"I won't come to the funeral," Dan explained over the phone the night before.

"It's all right. I didn't expect you to. You didn't know him after all."

"I'd have come to support you, but if I was there…"

"It's okay, Dan. I get it. People would want to know why you were there and the funeral would end up being about that rather than about my dad. This is one of the problems, isn't it?"

"Yeah, it is. Still want to be involved with me?"

"Stop fishing," Iestyn said. "You know I do and I know that sometime we're going to have to go public. Perhaps I should kiss you at the Millennium Stadium, or join the wives and girlfriends for the photo call. Do rugby players have WAGs like footballers do?"

"Sort of, but the wives and girlfriends don't get called WAGs in the same way, and they don't usually come on tour. You'll be coming to the home games, though, won't you?" he asked.

"It'll be the first time I've been to a rugby match," Iestyn admitted. "But I won't have to sit with the others if you get me tickets, will I?"

"Not if you don't want to. I can get a couple of tickets in the main stand," Dan explained.

"I think I'll bring Julie, if that's all right. It'll stop Matt or Huw complaining."

"No problem. The first home game is against Scotland."

He hesitated for a minute and Iestyn wondered what was coming next.

"D'you fancy coming to Paris with me for the game? Friday we're at the team hotel, but I can book us in somewhere on Saturday night and meet you after the game. We can fly back on Sunday so you'll be back in time for work."

Iestyn thought for about ten seconds before saying, "A night in Paris with you? I think I could cope with that."

* * * *

Iestyn finished tidying up his desk and sorting out the work for the rest of the day. He was just getting up to go when he heard a voice.

"Sorry about your dad," Matt said. "How's your mum coping?"

"She's fine. Has her moments, of course, but she's made of strong stuff. Did I miss anything while I was off last week?"

"Nah, but you could have told me about Kate and Sian. I put my foot right in it there."

"Putting your foot in it is your specialty, Matt. What did you do this time?" He walked with Matt to the staffroom for the daily briefing. Once again, Iestyn wondered why he put up with his friend after he related his latest faux pas.

"I can't believe you actually asked Kate if she was into pussy now."

"I meant it as a joke. They were looking at these paintings of naked women. I didn't bloody know, did I?"

"I'm not surprised she slapped your face. I think I'll look for a diversity course you can go on."

"Might be worth it if I get a day off. Oh, and I got a call from the Giants outreach department. They're going to send some players over after the Six Nations. So is Lover Boy getting you tickets for the home matches then?"

Iestyn knew he had to be firm in his decision. "I'm going to the Scotland game with Julie."

"What! Bloody hell, Iestyn, she knows nothing about rugby, except that some of the players are good-looking! Can't you get another ticket?" Matt's frustration was obvious.

"I'm not asking him. I knew you and Huw would be the same, so that's why I'm taking Julie. Don't pout. It doesn't suit you."

"I don't bloody pout," Matt said.

"Yes, you do," Julie said, as she met them at the staffroom door. "Told him you're taking me then?" she queried.

"Yep," he said, opening the door. "I think he's going to sulk."

* * * *

After briefing, a few people said how sorry they were to hear about his loss. Other members of staff popped into his classroom throughout the day. Everyone offered their condolences. He decided to tell the kids about his dad. The information would soon get around and this way he'd avoid more difficult conversations. Kids always wanted to know what was going on. It was weird how much things had changed since his school days. If Iestyn's teachers had been absent, he and his classmates would never have questioned why. However, he had no chance to explain as the questions began as soon as his form came through the door.

"You all right, sir?" Sophie asked. "It's not like you to be off."

"That must have been some hangover, sir," Josh added.

"Nice to see you here on time, Josh. New Year's resolution, was it? Good choice. The truth is that my father died suddenly last week, and that's why I was off."

Josh looked suitably embarrassed, which was an achievement in itself.

"Sorry, sir. I was just…"

"Joshing, yeah, I know. It's okay. Come on. Let's get on with the usual. So what did everyone get for Christmas?"

As they reeled off lists that included BlackBerrys and iPods, Iestyn thought things had definitely changed since he was at school.

* * * *

The days passed by in a blur of activity. He spoke to Dan on the phone but that was all, and he missed him. Friday was the funeral. He just wanted to get through the day and come out at the other end.

For a winter's day, the weather was kind. The sun shined brightly over the city of Cardiff, attempting to warm the cool January air. The whole family was together and it was strange looking at so many people with variations of the same face. The Jones gene was very dominant and his father's strong features were everywhere. Megs and the twins had been left with a childminder for the day, so Ben was the only grandchild present. When the cars pulled up, Iestyn and his family took their places.

His father's friend, Sam Smith, who was acting as celebrant, was waiting for them at the crematorium. The ashes had already been placed at the front of the room next to the family photograph and Geraint's chessboard. Somehow it was easier not to have his body there. Iestyn was grateful for his father's organizational skills and that he'd been far-sighted enough to write things down. He'd been the same with his will, which Rhian's husband Gareth had sorted. It was useful to have a tame solicitor in the family. He looked around and saw that nearly everyone had worn something red or green, as his father had requested — Welsh colors for a man proud of his roots. Ben had his rugby shirt on, as did many others under their suits.

If Dan had been there, it would have overshadowed the whole occasion. He'd spoken to him that morning and they'd arranged to have dinner at Dan's flat on Saturday night. There was the unspoken invitation to stay over, but Dan had also invited Julie and his friend Mac, so they could begin the process of introducing their circles of friends to each other.

The music began and *Anthem* from *Chess* filled the air. Iestyn heard his mother take a deep breath and knew that the music would make her more emotional. His parents had seen the musical many times, and his father had loved the song, particularly Josh Groban's version of it. He took his mother's arm and they led everyone else into the room.

It didn't take long, really. Sam Smith spoke well about a man with whom he'd shared many pints at their local pub. When the haunting notes of *Moonlight Serenade* began, his mother struggled to keep from crying. It was the music they'd danced to for the first time. On his other side, Rhian took his hand, tears falling down her cheeks.

Finally, Huw got up and spoke about their father and the service finished with *Old and Wise*. As he listened to the words, Iestyn realized he was crying as well. When the service was complete, people milled around for a while, talking in small huddles before making their way to the function room at the back of his father's regular haunt. The alcohol flowed and the mourners ate heartily. Iestyn drank more than a few beers to toast his father and celebrate the life of a man he'd admired so much. By the time Julie and the others arrived straight from school, he was a little tipsy. Julie looked worried and hugged him.

"Are you all right?" she asked.

"I'm fine. It was a lovely service, exactly how Dad would have wanted it." The way his friends gathered around him made him feel warm inside—or maybe it was the alcohol. It didn't really matter. He was just glad to know they were there.

"I'm going now, Iessie," his mother said at around five. She'd been there for four hours. "I'm very tired."

She was staying with Rhian that night so Iestyn didn't worry. He knew she'd be well looked after.

"Phone me when you get home," she told him. "I know what you lot are like on a Friday night."

"I'll look after him," Julie said.

"Us too," Gareth added. "We'll get him home, Mrs Jones."

They did get him home as promised, slightly worse for drink. Gareth's snores from the spare room reached Iestyn as he texted Dan to wish him luck for the next day. He was sure that his dad would have been happy with how the day had gone. He looked at the ceiling out of habit more than any beliefs.

"I hope it was what you wanted, Dad. I'll miss you. We all will. You did a great job with all of us, and it's not every father who could claim that. Goodnight, Dad. Rest in peace."

Chapter Eighteen

The concierge had been warned to expect them. Iestyn emerged from the taxi and looked up. Dan lived on the top floor of a fifteen-story apartment block — mostly, he'd explained, because of the view. The advertising contracts he had allowed him such luxurious living. Iestyn gulped at the thought of being so high and wished that he'd never watched *Towering Inferno* as a child.

"Would it be impolite to ask about evacuation procedures in case of fire?" he said to Julie, who had a similar look on her face.

"Take the lift over there," the small, balding man behind the desk told them.

It was fast, which pleased Iestyn to no end. He wasn't keen on small spaces, really, but this lift even had a seat. They emerged into a small hallway with three doors. Dan lived behind door B and he answered immediately.

"Come in," Dan said.

He kissed Iestyn as if it was something he did all the time and led them into the main room.

Iestyn stood there doing fish impersonations as he and Julie took in their surroundings. They stood in a large space. To one side there was a kitchen area, fitted with every mod con known to man, including the coffee machine. A large oak table with black leather chairs sat in front of the floor-to-ceiling windows. On the other side of the room there was a massive corner sofa in white leather covered with red scatter cushions. Bookcases containing books, DVDs and assorted collectables took up one entire wall and provided the only real color in the room other than the red accessories.

Another wall sported a forty-two-inch plasma screen. Iestyn thought about his own house where every room was packed with things, in a totally organized way, of course, and wondered how much this reflected Dan's personality or that of some interior designer. Music drifted from the system in the corner. Iestyn was surprised to hear that Dan had chosen Adele to listen to as he cooked.

"It's gorgeous," Julie said. "The views must be amazing when it's light enough to see, although just seeing all the lights out there is quite spectacular."

"The view is one of the reasons I bought it and it's central for the city. Come and sit. What can I get you to drink?" Dan asked. "I've red or white, or beer if you prefer," he said to Iestyn. "The roof garden is the other reason I moved here, but it's a bit cold out there now. I should buy one of those patio heaters. It'll be great for barbecues when it's warmer. Mac should be here soon. He got a bit of a kicking this afternoon so had to be checked over, but he's all right."

Iestyn hadn't wanted to mention the match since the Giants had lost by one point.

"He was a bit worried about getting injured before the Six Nations," Dan continued, whilst stirring a large pan.

"You're cooking!" Iestyn said in surprise, coming up behind him. He'd warned Julie earlier that Dan didn't cook.

"No, I'm warming," he replied. "My nan came over this afternoon and made the Bolognese sauce. I'm just cooking the pasta. I've cheesy garlic bread and salad to go with it, so nothing complicated. I hope that's all right. Come taste."

Iestyn opened his mouth after Dan blew on the spoon.

"Don't say it," he warned Julie, who smiled at them both.

"What? You just look so…domestic."

They both looked at her, then at each other. The buzzer sounded, destroying the moment.

Dan put down the spoon. "That'll be Mac."

The door opened a few minutes later. The man who entered the room sported a black eye and a wicked smile. Dan made the introductions.

"Mac, this is Iestyn and his friend Julie. This is Mac, the best winger in the world," Dan said, proudly putting his hand on the other man's shoulder. The first thing that struck Iestyn was how much smaller Mac was compared to Dan, but then everyone was. He was dark, not blond, with almost black eyes. His physique was similar to Matt's but on a smaller scale, and he gave the impression of speed and stealth rather than simple strength as Dan did. In fact, Mac was as physically opposite to Dan as a man could get.

"I know," Mac said, catching the look. "Little and large, but then again, everyone's little compared to him. I'm built for speed."

"Hey, I can run," Dan said indignantly.

"Yeah, *into* things," Mac replied, punching his friend playfully. "But that's what you're supposed to do." He sniffed the air. "Have you cooked?"

"Sort of," Dan admitted, "and it'll be ready in a few minutes. You and Julie sit at the table, will you? Iessie, would you give me a hand?"

Heat burned Iestyn's cheeks at Dan's use of his family's pet name. It seemed so intimate. Even Julie rarely used that name. She grinned at him then allowed Mac to escort her to the table.

As he stood at Dan's side, tossing the salad in a bowl and adding dressing, for the first time in a while, Iestyn allowed a moment of happiness to wash over him. From the way Dan glanced his way, he guessed he might be experiencing the same feeling. Iestyn allowed himself the small indulgence of imagining the two of them hosting dinner parties for their mutual friends.

Dan served out four portions of Bolognese pasta and took them to the table, as Iestyn placed the garlic bread on a tray and added Parmesan to the mix. Finally, when they sat down to eat, Iestyn couldn't help noticing that conversation flowed easily between Mac and his best friend. He looked at Dan then nodded toward them.

Dan smiled, leaned over and whispered, "Shall we play matchmakers?"

"I know what you told me about him, and Julie hasn't had the best of luck with men recently."

"Depends what she wants. Mac is fun. He just needs a good woman to keep him in order, like I need a good man."

With that, Dan slipped a hand under the table and ran his fingers up Iestyn's thigh, causing him to wriggle nervously on his chair and give the other man a look.

"Oh, I'm really scared!" Dan said and continued moving his hand ever higher.

The room in Iestyn's trousers kept diminishing so he placed his free hand over Dan's and moved it away. Bringing it above the table, he kissed Dan's palm and put it down.

He noticed that the room had gone silent. Mac coughed.

"Other people in the room, you two," Mac said, laughing.

Iestyn noticed that Julie was wearing her 'Aw, that's so cute' face, which she kept for him and pictures of kittens and puppies.

"Well, you two were so busy talking to each other that we got distracted," he replied pointedly.

Julie tossed her red hair and fought off a blush. "Mac was telling me about when they went to New Zealand to play the All Blacks. You know, I've always fancied going. This food is wonderful, Dan. Please tell your nan she makes a lovely sauce."

Iestyn swallowed a chuckle when Julie made the obvious change of subject.

"You must have been all over the world," he said to Dan and Mac.

"Yeah, I suppose we have," Dan replied. "Although we don't usually get to see much of the country, unless we're staying somewhere for a while, and I hate flying, so I'm usually as out of it as possible. The World Cup in South Africa was amazing. I was only twenty and it was the first time I'd spent so long away from home. We saw quite a few of the towns and cities but the best bit was the safari. I'd only seen animals in the zoo before then. I'd never even been to Longleat, and we saw elephants, rhinos, lions, giraffes, loads of antelopes and zebras. We also went to a place where they helped abandoned or injured animals and kept them. They had these cheetah cubs and we got to feed them. They took quite a shine to Mac and kept rubbing themselves against him, just like a cat would."

"What can I say? It must be my animal magnetism," Mac boasted.

"I've the photos somewhere," Dan continued. "I'll have to get them out. We did quite well in that tournament and got to the quarters, but were beaten by the Aussies. We're hoping to go at least one better this time round when we go to Australia."

"So when's the World Cup, then?" Iestyn asked.

"September. I'll be away for six weeks hopefully. There are lots of things going on this year," Dan explained.

"And they'd better make you captain," Mac said.

"I have to say you look like a man who *should* be captain," Julie purred, batting her eyelids.

Dan looked at Iestyn, confusion all over his face, until Iestyn and Julie collapsed in fits of laughter.

"Stop it, you know what happened last time you did that. He thought you were serious and I could have missed the love of my life. I'm not doing that again, so stop scaring him off," Iestyn warned.

"Oh, I don't scare so easily," Dan said, looking straight at Iestyn. "Especially when I have something I want in my sights."

Iestyn gulped and shivered under Dan's gaze.

Mac nudged Julie. "Now you know why he scares the opposition. He fixes them with that stare."

"I don't think it's scaring Iestyn," she whispered back. "I think we may have to make ourselves scarce."

"Not until I've had pudding," Mac said. "So, Big Man, what's for afters?" Mac asked, deliberately racking up the innuendo. "Assuming, that is, there *is* food involved and not just the two of you disappearing into the bedroom?"

"Ha bloody ha," Dan said. "You know there's pudding 'cause you're here. He has the sweetest tooth on the team. It's marbled chocolate cheesecake and cream, and yes, my nan did make it. Then Iestyn is going to show me how to work that coffee machine. He's a bit of a connoisseur, you know."

Dan got up, Iestyn following him with the rest of the plates.

"Sorry about Mac and his comments," Dan said. "I don't expect you to stay tonight but you can if you want to. I'm not pushing you into anything. I want to take this slowly as well." He placed a hand on Iestyn's. "I'm not really sure how this dating thing goes. You've more experience of that than me."

"I'm no expert. And, believe me, I've made some mistakes, so I can live with taking things slowly." Changing the subject before the conversation turned into a confessional of past romantic disasters, Iestyn said, "I'm looking forward to seeing your first game against Ireland. I used to watch sometimes with my dad and Huw, but it'll be different now I know some of the team." He turned to look at Mac and Julie, who were once again absorbed in conversation. "They're getting on well. I'm assuming that Mac is single at the moment. Julie's just had a bit of a brief fling with a mutual friend of ours that turned out to be a big mistake. I wouldn't want Mac messing her around."

"Mac has a bit of a thing for redheads and, to be honest, Julie is *very* much his type. Wait until he finds out she's a music teacher. He thinks he's a rock god on the side. He plays a mean guitar and he's got a half-decent voice, not that I'd ever tell him that."

"So, d'you sing?" Iestyn asked. "We have a Friday karaoke and takeaway night."

"I can sing a bit," Dan said sheepishly.

"Well, you've certainly got the equipment for it," Iestyn said, placing a hand on Dan's chest. "Let's get this machine working, then."

The room soon filled with the aroma of coffee as they ate their desserts.

"Bloody hell, this is good," Mac said when he took his first sip. "You'd better give Dan lessons on how to use it properly."

Half an hour later, Julie yawned and Iestyn said that they'd better be getting home. Mac had decided to crash in the spare room once he had realized that he wasn't going to be playing gooseberry. Dan spoke to the concierge, and within a few minutes, their taxi had arrived. Outside the lift, Dan gently pressed his lips to Iestyn's.

"Night, Iessie. I'll call you tomorrow and let you know what I'm up to this week. I've got to talk to Graeme to sort out some interviews and other stuff. The captain for the first game should be named in the next few days, so who knows? I've really enjoyed tonight." He kissed Julie's cheek. "It's been good to see you again too, Julie. I hope you'll come again."

"Thanks for having me." She winked. "And thank your nan for a lovely meal!"

Dan laughed that deep throaty laugh that did strange things to Iestyn's stomach.

Back home, having dropped Julie off at her house, Iestyn turned on his laptop when he got into bed. He'd been playing chess against one of his regular competitors. He logged on to the game and noted that

Aztec had made his next move. Iestyn moved his bishop to try to block. Aztec challenged his skill and often won their encounters. He made a few more moves before he signed off for the night and snuggled into his duvet, contented with the way the evening had gone.

Chapter Nineteen

The next two weeks passed by in a blur of exam preparation with lunchtime and extra after school sessions for the pupils involved. When Iestyn wasn't working, he tried to spend time with his mother. She appeared to be coping well but had buried herself in research for her book. Iestyn worried that she might break at some point, but Rhian reckoned that was unlikely. Huw took Megs around often and she provided an entertaining distraction, although she still asked for Grannad. When she did, Mary would scoop the toddler up into her arms and dance around the room.

"You'll have to make do with Nanna, I'm afraid, my angel, but I'll dance with you." She'd whirl Megs round to the music and Megs would smile and giggle. Watching them brought a tear to Iestyn's eye then, when she'd had enough, Megs would insist on sitting in Grannad's seat to eat. Neither Iestyn nor anyone else could help getting emotional watching the little girl as she sat in that large armchair talking away to herself.

* * * *

"We'll have to get Skype," Dan suggested late one night, as he lay in his bed breathing heavily into his phone as Iestyn did the same. "Then we could see each other while we do that!" He realized this sort of 'discussion' had begun to be a bit of a habit for them.

"Oh, I don't know," Iestyn said. "I think imagination is a wonderful thing and so does another part of me. It must be your voice because…"

"What?" Dan said, guessing that Iestyn was a little embarrassed by their recent activity. He deliberately lowered his voice again. "Does this make you all hard and needy, Mr Jones? Does it make you want to touch yourself and imagine that it's my hands wrapped around your cock?"

"Stop it," Iestyn replied, squirming. "I've got to get up early in the morning to be there in time for last-minute revision with Year Eleven, and aren't you supposed to lay off sex when you're playing?"

"Old wives' tale," Dan said. "That's never been a rule for rugby players. But I suppose I'd better let you get some much needed beauty sleep."

"Bastard," Iestyn replied. "You were the one saying you wanted to watch me on Skype. Maybe next time we're in the same room, I'll let you watch for real."

Dan's cock responded to the suggestion. "Oh yes, please, sir, and maybe we can take things a bit further."

"I think that would be acceptable," Iestyn said. "Now, I'm going to bed to dream of rugby players grabbing me in my own private ruck and maul. Did I ever say how sexy I think your fullback is?"

Dan heard him put the phone down. He smiled, hung up his receiver and pulled the duvet over his head.

* * * *

"Did you see the news?" Julie asked at lunchtime. "Dan has been named as captain for the first match against Ireland."

"What!" Iestyn took out his phone and realized he'd switched it off. There was a text from Dan. He tried ringing but it went straight to voicemail. "I heard the news. It's fantastic. We need to celebrate. Can you get to mine Saturday night after the game? We could do takeaway and what we talked about last night, if you want—"

Julie coughed. "Just before you get any more detailed," she said, smiling.

Each class seemed to last a lifetime as he watched the clock all day, waiting for the final bell to ring to let him leave work. At lunchtime, he checked the news feeds on his computer. Dan's appointment as captain was the headline in all the local media. Seeing the name of the man he now thought of as his boyfriend trending on Twitter was somewhat disconcerting but he pushed those thoughts aside. Today was a day for celebration.

Dan called later that night. "Sorry I couldn't call earlier. Graeme had me doing interviews all over the place."

"Yeah, I saw you on *Wales Today*. You looked good and I'm so proud to be going out with you."

"Is that what we're doing here?" Dan questioned. "I want it to be what we're doing, if you do."

"Dan, you know I do. I want to be your boyfriend—if that's the right word—but we both know it's not that simple. You're a celebrity and I'm a schoolteacher. I need to understand what I'm getting into but I like you, Dan. I *more* than like you."

"I like you too," Dan replied, cautiously. "And I know if you go out with me there's baggage, but I'd love it if we could go legit. Perhaps if you talk to Graeme, we could sort out how to handle the press and things. We can talk about it tomorrow. We're in Gloucester so I'll be back by eight. I could come round to yours and we could get to know each other better."

"Hmm, sounds good to me."

"Oh, I nearly forgot—how was the exam this afternoon?"

"It was the Suffragettes and it seemed fair. The kids had a good go at it anyway. Look, I'll see you tomorrow. Hope you win and congratulations. I know you're going to be amazing."

Iestyn was like a cat on a hot tin roof most of the day and reading the papers hadn't made him feel any better. Dan was everywhere—an interview in *The Independent* and a story in *The Mirror*. They'd obviously had the same picture released to every paper, and Dan looked stunning wearing his kit. Iestyn found it hard to drag his eyes away from the man's thighs and his imagination worked overtime envisaging where he could put them. The interview concentrated on the rugby player and how he felt about captaining his country. However, the other story also talked about Dan's sexuality and his previous relationship with Aron Roberts. The press noted that he hadn't been seen with anyone since and that it was a shame that was the case, unless anyone knew differently. The challenge was there for the public to tell if they knew anything, complete with the usual contact telephone number.

Iestyn wondered about his neighbors and if anyone had noticed Dan visiting and reported it to the papers. He began to worry and he almost wished he'd said he'd cook, as it would have given him something to do. He popped out and did his weekly shopping to keep busy, buying a bigger variety of breakfast things just in case then he returned and cleaned the house, especially his bedroom. He'd bought necessary supplies, not knowing exactly what Dan had planned, put on fresh bedding and made sure that the bathroom sparkled.

After that, he awarded himself with a large cup of coffee, lay back, put some music on and let his mind wander. When he woke, the room was dark and his coffee cold. He turned on the TV and checked the results. "Yes, the Giants won forty to fifteen," he said, aloud to himself. He checked the try scorers, amazed to find that Dan had scored. He would be in a brilliant mood when he arrived having been named as captain and scoring a rare try.

Iestyn rushed upstairs to change. He put on blue jeans and a shirt and ran some gel through his hair. He looked in the mirror.

"Stop it! He knows I haven't got a six-pack and pecs to die for and he still wants more of me."

Iestyn told himself that there were no plans for tonight. They would do whatever felt right. He hoped Dan would stay the night. It had been a while since he'd slept with his arms around a warm body in his own bed, and part of him looked forward to that possibility even more than the sex. He hummed to himself. *Well, maybe the same as.*

Downstairs, he ordered pizza, knowing what Dan wanted then he waited. Dan had texted that he would arrive on time. Mac was going to drop him off on his way to Julie's. Iestyn smiled to himself. *She'd kept that quiet.*

He jumped when the doorbell rang, unsure if it was Dan or the pizza. It turned out to be the deliveryman. Iestyn paid him and saw Mac pull up at the curb at the same time.

Dan must have seen the other person on the doorstep, so he waited in the car. Iestyn watched him pull a hat over his distinctive hair but there was nothing he could do to disguise his body. When the deliveryman had gone, Dan moved swiftly into the house.

"Sorry! I didn't want to be seen. We really do need you to speak with Graeme," Dan said. "I want to be able to take you out with me."

A sudden sense of fear made Iestyn's stomach churn. For now, it was just him and Dan, but Dan wasn't only his—he was public property and the public always wanted to know more. He was going to have to make preparations to become part of that world to be the man photographed next to Dan, at least until it was no longer news.

Dan hung his coat on one of the hooks in the hall then turned and smiled. Iestyn could almost feel the excitement pulsating around him. He gulped, attempting to swallow his fear.

Iestyn led Dan into the kitchen. Dan waited while he put the pizza down on the counter before putting his arms around Iestyn and kissing the back of his neck.

Iestyn turned in his arms. "It means a lot to me that you want to be seen with me," he said. It felt wonderful to be back in Dan's arms again.

Dan bent down and kissed him. As the kiss intensified, Iestyn opened his mouth and Dan tentatively pushed his tongue in, running it over Iestyn's teeth. Iestyn responded by pushing his own tongue into Dan's welcoming mouth until he could taste the coffee that Dan had obviously drunk recently. Dan's sheer physical presence could have been intimidating but Iestyn took the lead and reached up with his hands to cup the back of Dan's head and pull him closer. Iestyn used his tongue to explore every area of the warm, wet surface until Dan finally changed his angle and began pushing back. Iestyn opened his lips wider as Dan's tongue penetrated farther and he started pulling at Iestyn's shirt. He knew he needed to bring this to an end before they got too carried away. Reluctantly, he broke their kiss, breathing heavily to see Dan grinning at him with mischief in his eyes

"Sorry, I missed you," Iestyn said. "We'd better eat this pizza before it gets cold, or I may just drag you to bed now."

Dan raised an eyebrow and placed a hand over the bulge in Iestyn's jeans, making him groan.

"That's really not fair," Iestyn said. "Eat first, then bed." He reached into the fridge and pulled out two beers.

Dan came up behind him again. "I missed you too. I've been thinking about you all day and your arse looks so very tempting in those jeans. You'd better not bend over or I won't be held responsible for my actions."

Heat flared across his face and he fought to stop himself shaking. He really wasn't used to this level of flirting but he wanted to give as good as he got. "Maybe you'll be the one bending over," he said.

Dan met his gaze, took a bite of the pizza slice he'd taken from the box, chewed slowly then said, "That works for me."

Every nerve ending in Iestyn's body reacted as if someone had connected him to the electricity grid. His cock wanted desperately to get out of his pants and into something else. Iestyn pictured Dan bent over the desk in the corner of the room, his arse framed by his jockstrap, waiting for him. Was he even wearing a jockstrap, and since when did Iestyn fantasize about men wearing them? Shit, he needed to calm down and think of something to say.

"Any chance of one of your coffees?" Dan asked, his tone hopeful. "My mouth seems to have gone a bit dry."

"Yeah, of course," Iestyn said. Why did this feel awkward all of a sudden? Was it easier if it was spontaneous like before? He went to the kitchen and turned on the machine. A few minutes later, he returned, mugs in hand, to find that both the man and the pizza had disappeared.

"Coffee's ready," he shouted.

"Bring it up here," Dan shouted back.

Iestyn took the stairs as quickly as possible. He found Dan sitting on the side of the bed, still fully clothed.

"I thought we'd move things on before I got too tired. It was a pretty full-on game today."

"You scored a try. You don't score very often, do you?" Dan fixed him with a stare then he realized what he'd said. "Sorry, I didn't mean that quite how it sounded."

"Iessie, put the coffee down and come over here."

Iestyn did as he was told. Dan wrapped his arms around him and pulled him to his body. He began to open Iestyn's shirt and nuzzled his middle. "Mmm, you feel good, so warm and soft. There's not a blemish on you. I have scars all over. Kiss me."

Iestyn reached down, feeling more confident about being naked with the gorgeous man next to him. They kissed, allowing each other to explore with tongue and teeth. Iestyn pushed Dan back and fell on top of him, kissing his neck and sucking on his earlobe. When Dan groaned, Iestyn's cock responded.

"Ever thought about playing rugby?" Dan asked. "You should—that was some tackle. Now, teach, I think we're wearing too many clothes."

"What about the pizza?" Iestyn said.

"Sod the pizza. I'm hungry for other things."

Smiling in agreement, Iestyn shrugged off his shirt then started undoing the buttons on Dan's. Dan impatiently tugged it over his head. Iestyn got up and attempted to undo the zip on his jeans.

"Let me," Dan said, rising to help. He removed Iestyn's shaking hand and, in one swift action, stripped off the offending item of clothing leaving only Iestyn's cotton briefs between his flesh and Dan's grinning mouth. He shivered as Dan ran his tongue over his lips, looked down at Iestyn's crotch then looked up at him again. Iestyn's cock was more than interested in what that tongue could do.

Dan placed a hand on each hip and slowly dragged the last remaining piece of clothing down. Iestyn held his breath. It was like waiting to see what people thought of the gifts you'd bought them at Christmas. He fell back to earth as Dan engulfed him in his hot, wet mouth. He groaned then looked down, meeting Dan's gaze, his eyes full of mischief and desire. He watched as Dan moved his mouth up and down and allowed himself to feel as Dan expertly worked tongue and teeth, lips and even throat.

Shit, how the hell is he doing that? Does the man have no gag reflex at all? Iestyn was surely going to ask him about that when his brain managed to get back out of his cock and into his head. *God he is good!* Iestyn buried his hands in that blond mop of hair. He wanted to thrust into him, to fuck that gorgeous mouth.

Dan splayed his hands across Iestyn's arse, pulling him closer then gently probed a finger between his cheeks to caress and tease at Iestyn's opening. Iestyn wanted to say something, to tell Dan how good it felt, but words didn't seem to be enough. He didn't want to come so soon. He pushed back on Dan's head.

"Too good. I'm gonna come if you continue, and I'm not sure if my knees will hold me up," he explained.

Dan pulled away, trailing saliva and pre-cum with his tongue as he did. "I thought that was the idea?"

"It is but I want to see you. I want to be naked with you. I want to touch you too. Tell me what you like, what makes you feel good. I want to learn it all. Take off your clothes and show me."

Dan removed the rest of his clothes and scooted back on the bed. On his knees, Iestyn followed him until he straddled Dan's hips. Their cocks touched as Iestyn leaned down to kiss Dan. As Iestyn kissed his neck, Dan reached to do the same. Capturing an earlobe and sucking gently, Iestyn heard Dan groan again and he began to work his way down Dan's chest. He discovered a few scars and a livid purple bruise just along his soon-to-be lover's hip.

"Got a kick in a ruck," Dan explained. "I scored from the penalty. As we were so near, we decided to run it. Oh yeah, I like that."

Iestyn had a nipple between his teeth, tugging gently. Then he swirled his tongue over the now-engorged nub. By the time he got to Dan's cock, it was standing at attention, waiting for him and looking impressive. For a moment, he sat back on his heels and just stared, his mouth watering with anticipation.

"Would you like measurements?" Dan said, grinning. "I think yours is longer but mine's thicker, if we're comparing." Iestyn pressed a finger to the slit. He spread the pre-cum around the head.

"Please, stop teasing," Dan said, reaching out.

Iestyn took one of his hands and swallowed two fingers, sucking gently.

"You're killing me," Dan continued. "Need…"

Iestyn released Dan's fingers and finally took hold of Dan's cock. He tasted the salty liquid on his tongue and relished the feel of the soft downy hair against his face. He allowed one hand to stray to touch his own cock, whilst with his other, he held Dan's balls, rolling them gently. He took the other man as deeply into his mouth as he could manage. He knew that this was something he was good at and, judging by the sounds issuing from Dan, he knew his confidence was well placed.

"Bloody hell, Iessie, that tongue of yours is amazing. I need to come." The raw need in his gravelly voice revealed how much he wanted this.

Iestyn looked up and winked. Dan tensed and gathered himself, then shouted his name as he poured himself into Iestyn's mouth. Iestyn relished the taste of every salty drop as it spurted onto his tongue. He continued until Dan was spent. Iestyn used his hand to squeeze out every last drop. Close to climaxing himself, he sat back on his heels again and continued to pump his own cock.

"Well, you said you wanted to watch for real," he said to Dan.

"Yeah, go on. I want to see you come all over me."

Dan's broad chest was still heaving and his eyes remained wide with excitement. The mere sound of that low growling voice made Iestyn's cock harden even further.

The thought of covering that abdomen and chest in white, sticky liquid was too much for Iestyn. He sensed he was going to explode. His whole body focused solely on the sensation of his hand stroking his cock. Tingles danced down his spine, his balls began to tighten until finally he shuddered, sending cum all over Dan's perfect six-pack until it pooled in the grooves between the muscles. Flecks reached Dan's chest and chin and he snaked his tongue out to taste it. Dan ran one finger through the liquid on his abdomen and sucked on it, moaning as he did.

Iestyn fell down next to him, tucking himself under Dan's arm and placing his head on that chiseled chest he admired so much. Stickiness tugged on his cheek but he didn't care. It somehow connected them and made them one.

Dan kissed his forehead. "You are amazing, Mr Jones. We must never get Skype. Otherwise, I'll want that show every night." He yawned. "Sorry, bit tired now. You've worn me out."

Seconds later, Iestyn heard snoring. He levered himself out from under Dan's arm and drew the duvet, which had ended up on the floor, over them. Dan shifted as Iestyn moved toward him then turned on his side. Iestyn spooned against his big lover and wrapped an arm around him. It was nice to do this once more. His last thought before he too drifted off to sleep was that they could have fun cleaning the mess off as they showered in the morning.

Chapter Twenty

A week later, Iestyn and the others were sitting in the pub eating lunch, waiting for the game to start. They'd arrived early to get good seats. Usually, Iestyn just went for the chat and paid little attention to the game, but this time he had a more important reason to be there. For a change, Huw had decided to join them and he proved to be worse than Matt, constantly ribbing him about Dan.

The build-up to the game was mostly about the man he now called his boyfriend. It told the tale of Dan's youth and how he'd been spotted in school by a local scout who knew one of Dan's teachers. The scout had recommended Dan to Glamorgan Giants and from there he'd progressed through the squad going full-time after successfully completing his A levels. Of course, there was also some conversation about Dan being gay. The panel included the only other rugby player who'd come out after he'd finished playing for Wales. There had been magazine and newspaper articles all over the place about Dan being the first openly gay captain of a national squad. Even in the program for the game, it was mentioned that any homophobic chanting would result in banning the perpetrator from all matches.

* * * *

In the dressing room, Dan paced, nervous and excited all at the same time. This was his big moment, his first match as captain of his country. He thought his heart would jump out of his chest. Mac and the others watched him pace.

"You're going to wear a groove in the floor if you keep that up, Big Man," Mac said.

"Yeah, Morgan, come on. We know what we're doing. The boss has planned every move and we're all behind you, you know that." Luke Hathaway was the tall fullback Iestyn had mentioned.

"Well, not that close behind you," Mac said, laughing. "We wouldn't want to get you too excited!"

"Piss off, McDonald! You just do your job down that wing and score us a few tries. Playing the Irish here is never that easy and I want us to win this Grand Slam, but to do that we've got to win here, defeat the English at Twickenham and get our revenge on the French. After the World Cup, we're on a roll. Right everyone? Got your kit on? Let's go out and throw a few balls about!" He looked at the smiling faces around him. "Oh, for fuck's sake, can't I say anything without it being innuendo?"

Mac got up and put an arm around his shoulder. "Nope, I don't think so."

* * * *

In the pub, Huw talked rugby with Gareth and Matt while Iestyn talked rugby players with Julie. This was the first time he'd been able to talk to her in depth, as she'd been off sick in the previous week.

"So, how was your dinner with Mac, then?" he asked.

"It was very nice," she replied, somewhat cryptically.

"Is that all I'm getting, then? It was very nice? *Are* you going out again?" Iestyn asked.

"Probably. Look, the food was wonderful and he was interesting and attentive. He didn't push his luck after taking me home. He just kissed me goodnight."

"But that's good, isn't it?" Dan said.

Julie shrugged. "I suppose so. I guess I'm just not used to it."

At that moment, the squads emerged from the tunnel to huge noise and applause from the crowd. Everyone in the pub turned to look at the enormous plasma screen and waited for the national anthems to begin. Iestyn watched as Dan led Prince William down the line, introducing his players. Part of him couldn't believe that was his boyfriend captaining their national team and mixing with royalty. Julie nudged him as he introduced Mac to the Prince.

"They look good, don't they?" she said.

Iestyn couldn't take his attention from the screen. He nodded. Dan looked bloody amazing. His hair was all over the place, as usual, and his chest looked as if it was trying to get out of his shirt. The black armband that denoted his role as captain stretched around his biceps.

The introduction to the anthems began. The whole Welsh team and everyone in the pub sang their lungs out—the Welsh certainly could make a loud noise when singing. The whistle blew and the game began.

Throughout it was tight. The points went to Ireland to begin with and Wales played catch up. There were penalties on either side, and it was scrappy. Ireland went into half-time with the lead. Iestyn couldn't say that he watched the whole game. He only had eyes for Dan and got annoyed when the cameras didn't show him. At every lineout, he saw his boyfriend's huge frame reach skywards as he leaped high in the air. Iestyn noted Dan's huge hands as he palmed the ball and Iestyn remembered how they'd surrounded both of their cocks that first time.

At every scrum, he saw Dan bent over ready to push his head forward, and Iestyn imagined him naked, on his knees, bent over in front of him, waiting for the other man to push into him. He hoped Dan would let him do that very thing sometime. He ached to be inside his boyfriend and his cock hardened at his thought. He needed to get himself under control. As he shivered with anticipation, he realized Julie was speaking to him.

"Sorry," he replied. "Did you say something?"

"I was just asking if you were all right. You've been so quiet and you just shivered."

"I'm fine, just thinking about something."

She grinned. "Hmm, that something wouldn't be anything to do with a certain Welshman bending over, then?"

His retort was lost in the noise that erupted in the room.

Mac had dodged his way past two Irish players and was running down the wing to the line. He flung himself forward, putting Wales a point back in the lead. The cheers nearly deafened Iestyn. Dan lifted

Mac up in celebration. Iestyn checked his watch. There were ten tense minutes to go. He watched, living every move as both sides made mistakes. Then with sixty seconds remaining on the clock, Ireland scored an easy penalty. Wales was going to lose by two points. Dreams of the Triple Crown and the Grand Slam were fading by the second.

"Come on, lads. One last push," Matt shouted.

As if they'd heard him, the Welsh team kept pressing forward. Just one mistake would give Wales a penalty. The tension in the room was almost palpable. Iestyn took hold of Julie's arm. Then one of the Irish put a hand in the wrong place. With eighty minutes gone, the last kick of the game would be a penalty for Wales. Iestyn watched Dan talk to the handsome Welsh fullback. Iestyn couldn't help feeling scared for the player whose boot would determine if Wales won or lost. A hush descended on the crowd in the stadium. Everyone watched the Welsh fullback carry the ball and place it carefully on the ground.

Iestyn scanned the room. Every person in the bar was staring at the screen. Every set of hands, including his own, were joined together in prayer, hoping the ball would go between the posts. Time seemed to stand still as he watched the ball lift over the bar.

The whistle blew and Wales had won by a point. Iestyn sat back while those around him cheered. He watched Dan and the others dance around in victory. He thought he was going to burst with pride. Dan had captained his team to victory. He wished he could be there. He was jealous of every man who hugged him. He hadn't realized how much he missed him until that moment of victory when they were so far apart.

The camera panned to the stand where the families and girlfriends of the players stood cheering. Sudden understanding hit Iestyn between the eyes. Would he be expected to sit there with the other WAGs? He was relieved to see that there were some male family members but he would be alone if he was ever there. He would be the only boyfriend. Whilst other people cheered, he wasn't sure what to feel.

"Iessie, it'll be all right," Julie said, somehow understanding his mood. "You love him, don't you?"

"Yeah, I think so, but look at him, Julie. He's going to be all over the press again tomorrow."

The teams were going back into the stand.

"Only you can decide if you can cope with that. Most of the time he's just a rugby player who happens to be gay. Now he's in the news, but after the Six Nations, he'll just be playing for Glamorgan Giants. It'll be a nine-day wonder, if you time it properly. Didn't you say his agent had a few ideas?"

"Yes, he has some plans. I hope it's not *Hello!* or something similar. It could be one of the gay ones, I suppose."

"Well, little bro, I'm off," Huw said. "He did well. You must be chuffed. Mam said you must bring him around again."

"I'll see. He's pretty busy at the moment. Say hello to everyone for me," Iestyn said. His phoned buzzed.

We won! Time on Weds. Fancy meeting my nan for dinner? Call later.

He smiled then he said, "Shit, Dan's nan!"

* * * *

They managed a few phone calls. The team was together in training before the Scotland game, which would be at the Millennium Stadium the following Saturday. It would be Iestyn's first live game.

As he was leaving on Wednesday, Matt shouted to him in the car park.

"Wait up, Iestyn!"

He turned to see the PE teacher rushing across the tarmac.

"You're seeing Dan tonight, aren't you?"

Iestyn wondered how he knew and raised an eyebrow as he got in his car. He rolled down the window. "D'you think you could shout that any louder? I think they missed the announcement in New York!"

Matt looked around at the empty space. "Piss off, there's no one here," he said, smiling.

"You were saying?" Iestyn said, somewhat testily.

"I was wondering if you could ask if there was any chance your boyfriend could get any more tickets for Saturday's game, as I assume you're still insisting on taking Julie."

"For fuck's sake, Matt. Dan has given me two tickets and that's it!" He did wonder if Mac would have spare tickets but perhaps he gave them to family members. He didn't say anything, as he was still annoyed with his friend for asking.

"Just thought I'd ask," he said. "Don't ask, don't get. Have a good evening, but don't wear him out!"

Iestyn smirked before he wound up the window. "Anyone would think you were jealous, the way you go on." He put the car into gear and drove off.

Once home, he got ready. He'd decided to wear a suit and tie to see Dan's nan. He had no idea what to expect. The woman had helped hold Dan together when his mam had been ill and he thought she was bound to be protective of her grandson. He imagined he was only the second man Dan had brought home. He swallowed hard. How would he measure up to Aron?

The suit was his best one and it fitted well. He'd indulged himself last year, using the money he'd earned from exam marking and had one made to measure. It certainly hugged his arse. He chose his tie carefully. The blue silk one his mother had given him for his birthday last year went well. A tie really finished an outfit. As he tied his Windsor knot, he thought about his dad, who'd taught him how to tie a tie properly. If he'd still been alive, he'd have taken him to the game on Saturday.

His phone buzzed. Dan was waiting for him outside.

He pulled on his overcoat, grabbed the flower bouquet and moved quickly to the car. Its darkened side windows protected the identity of the driver but, even so, Dan had on his knitted hat that covered his unmistakable unruly hair. Iestyn slid into the passenger seat, wanting to kiss him so badly.

"Oh, my God!" Dan said when he saw him. "Why didn't you warn me you were dressing up like that? I'm going to have a hard-on at my nan's sitting opposite you dressed in that suit." He looked at his watch. "I wish we had long enough to find somewhere to ease the sudden tension in my trousers."

Taken aback by the outburst, Iestyn didn't say anything. He was so nervous about meeting Dan's nan that all thoughts of sex had disappeared, but here was this stunning man talking about arousal just from seeing him in a suit.

"But you've seen me in a suit before," he said.

"I know, but I was so nervous about meeting you for the first time, my libido must have decided to go into hiding."

Iestyn looked at him, totally surprised by his confession. "You were nervous?"

Dan glanced across at him. "Of course I was nervous. I hadn't been out on a first date with a stranger forever. I'm still not sure what made me give you my card when you fell at my feet."

"I'm really glad you did. Just to be sure, is there any other type of clothing I should avoid wearing, so you can keep your cock under control whilst visiting family members?" he asked, teasing by stroking Dan's thigh.

He was tempted to check whether Dan was telling the truth, but as they were driving through the streets of Cardiff, it probably wasn't a good idea. 'I was just stroking the captain of Wales' crotch when we crashed into the storefront, Constable' would not be an explanation he'd like to give to the local police.

Dan hadn't answered his question and appeared to be concentrating on the road.

"Just suits, then?" Iestyn continued.

"Well, there is something else, but tonight's not the night to discuss my proclivities. By the way, Nan takes a bit of getting used to. Don't worry if she's rude. She *always* is."

Iestyn thought about his own nan.

"I bet she'll be an angel compared to mine. What do I call her?" he asked.

"Mrs Morgan. She'll tell you if you can call her Betty. She'll like the flowers. Nice touch remembering some."

Dan parked his car on the quiet street. It looked like any other terraced house in Cardiff with three rooms downstairs and two bedrooms. He'd wanted to buy his nan a bungalow but she'd told him that she would stay there as long as she could. "Your granddad lived and died here with me and I won't leave unless I have to," she'd told him firmly.

Dan had nodded and accepted her decision. The time might come when she'd have to change her mind but at least he had the means to make sure she would be well looked after. He squeezed Iestyn's hand, then got out and looked around before they entered the house straight from the pavement, without knocking.

"Nan, we're here. Are you in the kitchen?"

A voice replied, "Yes, *cariad*. I'm just checking on dinner. Sit and I'll be out now."

Dan gestured to the second door off the hall, told Iestyn to sit and went into the kitchen.

Voices sounded from the kitchen. Iestyn strained to hear exactly what they were saying until Dan and his nan emerged side by side.

Iestyn got up immediately. Dan and his nan made an interesting pair. Dan was well over six feet and, if his nan was much above five feet, it would surprise Iestyn. She looked remarkably like Tweety Pie's mother. She'd swept her gray hair back into a rather elaborate bun. She wore an apron over her green skirt and jumper and furry green slippers shod her feet.

Iestyn stepped forward to hand over the flowers. "I bought you these, Mrs Morgan, to say thank you for inviting me."

"Thank you, young man. It's nice to see you've brought someone with manners," she said, looking at Dan. "I believe you're a schoolteacher." She turned her attention back to Iestyn. "That must be hard work but then you do get the holidays, don't you?"

Iestyn tried to smile. At least she hadn't mentioned that he was carrying a bit of extra weight like his nan would have done.

"You did well on Saturday, *cariad*. You need to have a word with the prop, though—you know, the one that does the throw-ins. He sometimes makes the wrong decision about who to throw the ball to."

Dan smiled. "Yes, Nan. I'll have a word."

"So, Iestyn, isn't it? That's a good Welsh name. Has your family been in Wales for long? Dan told me about your father. That must have been very difficult for you, coming so suddenly, but easier for him." She didn't wait for him to answer. "Now sit yourself at the table. Dan, come and give me a hand with the dish. I know what you're like over my cottage pie, so I've made a lot. You need to keep your strength up and it looks as if your friend has a healthy appetite."

She turned and went into the kitchen.

Dan shrugged and mouthed, "So far, so good!"

Iestyn watched as Dan shoveled the food into his mouth at breakneck speed. The man could certainly eat.

"This is amazing, Nan." It only took a few minutes until he'd cleared his plate and asked for seconds.

Iestyn savored each mouthful. It was almost as good as his own mother's cottage pie with the same mix of beef and vegetables in a thick gravy, topped with mashed potato and cheese. The only discernible difference was that his mum used sweet potato as well.

"This is really delicious," Iestyn agreed. He looked on as Dan cleared his second plate in record time.

"You not having any more?" Mrs Morgan asked Iestyn in an accusatory tone. "Probably just as well, as there's apple pie for afters. Dan loves my apple pie, don't you?"

Dan nodded as he ate the last mouthful of meat and potato mash.

"It's on the side and there's cream in the fridge. Go get them for me, *cariad*." Dan cleared the plates and took them through. Mrs Morgan leaned toward him and whispered, "You seem like a sensible young man. He needs someone level-headed and I'm glad you're a bit older than he is. He hasn't had an easy life, what with being gay and his mam's illness. Don't mess him around. If you're not prepared to deal with the situation he's in now, back away before he gets too involved with you. He may be big and strong on the outside but he just wants to be loved. D'you think you can love him?"

Iestyn spluttered. He hadn't expected to be questioned so directly. "I've only known him a couple of months, Mrs Morgan."

"No excuses. I knew as soon as I met my husband."

The woman certainly took no prisoners.

"I think I could love him, Mrs Morgan. I'm just amazed he's given me the time of day. I'm nothing special and he could have anyone looking as he does and being who he is."

"Good, that's all I needed to know, and you can call me Betty." She turned to the kitchen. "What's taking you so long, Daniel?"

"Just putting the dishes in the dishwasher, Nan," Dan replied.

"I don't know why he bothers. He bought that for me but I don't trust it. I'll just take the plates out later and wash them properly."

"I don't have a dishwasher either," he said. "Dan has loads of gadgets in his flat but I had to teach him how to use the coffee machine. Oh, and that Bolognese you made was lovely."

Iestyn was rewarded with a smile and a pat on his hand.

"You'll do," she said.

* * * *

They left at eleven.

"I wish I didn't have to drive you home," Dan said.

"You could stay," Iestyn replied. "You did before."

"I'd love to but I can't risk anything getting out and hitting the headlines at the moment. When the Six Nations is over, we'll let the press have the story and it'll be a nine-day wonder. Graeme says we just need to be in control of the information. But you are definitely coming to my flat sometime in that suit."

He pulled up outside Iestyn's house. "I want to kiss you goodnight but I'd better not. Look, we have a free weekend when you're on half term. I know we talked about you coming out to Paris but we could go away for a few days somewhere no one knows about rugby. We could go somewhere else in Europe."

"I can't," Iestyn said. "I've got mountains of coursework to mark over half term. It would take up the whole baggage allowance. If I go anywhere, it would have to be in Britain. We could find a cottage somewhere remote, with a log fire and just stay in the warm together," he said. "We could go to Cornwall. It won't be busy in February. I'll have a look online. If we book it in my name, we shouldn't have any problems." The thought of a naked Dan laid out on a fur rug in front of a log fire sent messages south.

"You haven't told me about your other clothes fetish," Iestyn added.

Dan leaned in and whispered into his ear. "Are you shocked?" he said, a tremor in his voice.

"No," Iestyn replied emphatically, "but I'll admit I'm a bit curious and more than a little excited!"

Chapter Twenty-One

Iestyn got lucky. After a few hours online, he found exactly what he was looking for. It was the perfect place for him and Dan, and it was free for the week. That weekend, Wales would be playing France in Paris so they'd be able to travel down early on Sunday morning and be there in just a few hours. He checked that this was all right with the owner and booked it. The cottage was basically a glorified wooden hut with one main room and a bathroom but it was on its own and overlooked a beautiful beach. It would be cold in winter but there was a log fire and a king-size bed. There was a luxury hamper provided and they could pick up other food on the way. Iestyn could combine the holiday with marking essays. Hopefully, they would be able to stroll along the beach, even if the weather was cold. And all of this was just three weeks away.

On Saturday, he was going to watch Wales play Scotland. This would be his first live game and he was looking forward to it. Even if he couldn't quite sit in the executive seats, at least he would have Julie with him, so he could talk about Dan. The following week Wales was going to be in Rome playing Italy. He wouldn't be able to see Dan then since the team were going out there a couple of days earlier to settle in and train. At least they had Skype and, as Mac knew about them, even sharing a room posed no problems. Dan would still be able to talk. Mac was pretty good about giving them space. He rang Dan.

"Hi, it's me," he said.

"Hello, it's me. Recovered from the trauma of meeting my nan, then?"

Iestyn could almost feel the warmth of Dan's smile in his voice. He allowed himself to think about how good that baritone voice would sound talking dirty to him. His body reacted instantaneously, pulling him back to his senses. He really didn't want to be marking essays about the Welsh industrial revolution feeling that excited.

"She's lovely," he replied. "I think she liked me."

"Oh, yeah, she approved of you, especially that you were in education. Nan considers learning to be very important. She's a big fan of the teaching profession."

Much like her grandson.

"I guess me and Nan have a lot in common," Dan confirmed.

"As long as you just confine it to this member of the teaching profession," he growled.

"Oh, baby, talk dirty to me," Dan growled back. "Go on, tell me what you're wearing."

"What would you like me to be wearing?" And suddenly his cock was paying attention again. "Oh, yeah, I think we established that last night. The question is — do I wear it under the suit or over it? Now a corset might make a neat waistcoat. I've been looking online. I don't suppose there are any pictures of you dressed as Frank-n-Furter?"

"Oh God, Iessie, stop it. You're killing me here and, well, there might be. So did you find somewhere for us to go on holiday? And yes, that was a totally unsubtle change of subject."

"That's why I'm ringing. I found us the perfect beach house in Cornwall. It's pretty isolated and overlooks a beautiful bay. There's a log stove and a king-size bed. I checked and we can go down on Sunday after the game. I think we'd better take your SUV, as it's a single track to the house. Will we get a chance to see each other after the Ireland game? Mam suggested Sunday lunch with the family, if you can face it."

"I should be able to manage that. I have to say it'll be good to get some time alone without worrying about who might be watching us," Dan said, "although I'd better remember to pack my hat. Let your mam know I'd be pleased to come to lunch."

"I'm not sure who else will be there but, knowing my family, they'll all want to meet you. It'll be safer if there are a lot of us and it's pretty private on the drive with the trees and shrubs obscuring the view. Anyway, I'll let you know so you can be prepared. You know Mam. She likes to have people around. Right, I need to get on with some work now. These essays won't mark themselves and I've just got five left to do."

"Remember, you need to get some sleep as well," Dan said. "I don't want you all exhausted on our week away. I have plans for that body of yours—big plans."

"Hey, I won't be playing France the day before," Iestyn replied. "I think you might want a rest. Perhaps I'll give you one of my all-over massages. Ever had an

Australian? I read about it on the net and I'm dying to go down under." He didn't give Dan a chance to reply but knew his boyfriend would be looking that up on some website. "Night, Dan. Sleep well."

* * * *

Iestyn and Julie got to the Millennium Stadium around two, having had lunch in the city. Their tickets were for the East Stand above the entrance tunnel.

"I didn't realize this place was so big," Julie said.

Iestyn looked at her. "Yeah, I know. It's big from the outside but it's massive in here. How much can we actually see from here, I wonder?"

The stadium began to fill up. All around them people were singing hymns and Max Boyce classics. Supporters were dressed as dragons, leeks, daffodils and painted in Welsh colors. Iestyn felt a little underdressed in jeans and a Wales shirt. It was a cold February day and they'd both dressed to be warm. Julie snuggled into him.

"D'you wish we were over there?" she asked, looking over to where the friends and relatives of the players were sitting.

"Well, you wouldn't be out of place, would you? You could sit there as Mac's girlfriend without sticking out in the crowd, but me? I'm not old enough to be someone's dad."

"You could be the brother of a player," she protested. "I don't really understand what your problem is. He's gay and everyone knows he's gay. It's not like he's going to be outed if you're seen together, and you're out too. Work knows about you — and your family. What's the big deal?"

"I don't exactly know, Julie, and keep your voice down a bit. Dan is public property. People want to know what he's doing. He appears in adverts. He's a poster boy for gay rights. He's appeared on the front page of *The Sun*, for Christ's sake. When we go public, there will be people looking into my life. I'm a teacher. How long before someone asks whether a gay man should be educating children? D'you know how many teachers actually come out? I was reading in the *Times Ed* that there is only one head teacher *out* in the country. I don't see Kate and Sian rushing to declare that they're together now. I'm going to have to talk to Neil before we talk to the press to let him know there may be interest in the school. It's a lot to contemplate."

Suddenly cheering erupted all around and the teams ran onto the pitch. Dan stood out immediately, his shock of blond hair all over the place, as usual. He looked like some sort of Norse god — like Thor without the winged helmet or hammer.

The teams finally took their positions for the anthems. Princess Anne, who came to every Scotland match, was taken down the Welsh line with Dan introducing his team. With an electric atmosphere and the roof closed, the sound reverberated around the stands as the crowd sang the national anthems at the tops of their voices.

Strangely emotional, Iestyn realized his team, his country and his boyfriend were on that pitch, leading his nation, hopefully, to victory. His heart swelled with pride. When the teams parted and went to their respective ends, Dan stopped and peered up at Iestyn's stand. Iestyn knew the rugby player was looking for him. He wanted to stand and wave, but knew he couldn't. Then they found each other and, for a moment, their gazes locked. For Iestyn, it was magical. The smile lighting up the Welsh captain's face on a cold Saturday afternoon in February was aimed just at Iestyn.

Then battle commenced.

It was a tough first half, neither side ready to give anything away. It wasn't very pretty, either, so at half-time the score was three–three. Iestyn and Julie stayed in their seats rather than attempt to get to the bar. Julie had fetched them both coffees just before the whistle to avoid the crowds.

"It looks so much more aggressive when you see it for real," Julie said. "The way the scrum just locks together and the power… I'm not surprised they end up bruised all over. It's pretty close at the moment."

Iestyn was much happier watching the second half as Wales took control of the action. Dan launched himself at a throw-in and tipped it to Mac, who took it down the line for the first Welsh try. Two more followed. Scotland managed to get one back and the score ended twenty-seven to thirteen. Wales' second win, on their way, hopefully, to both the Triple Crown and the Grand Slam.

Dan glanced up as they went into the tunnel. It saddened Iestyn that he wasn't going to be at that night's winning party. Julie was going with Mac. It would be her first official outing as his girlfriend, although she claimed she wasn't giving herself that title. This was a test for her and Mac to see if she could hack it.

"Who'd have thought I'd ever be a WAG" she said when they got to Iestyn's car.

"Who'd have thought you'd ever be a rugby player's girlfriend?" Iestyn replied.

"I'm not his girlfriend yet," she protested.

"What? You're telling me you're just friends with benefits?"

"Actually, he hasn't had any benefits."

Iestyn stared at her. "Really?"

"Don't look so shocked," she said, getting into the passenger seat. "You know I said I wasn't going to make the same mistake as before. I might let him have a little fun tonight. I'll see."

"So going for the 'treat 'em mean keep 'em keen' routine, then," he said, laughing. "Good luck with that."

"I'm guessing you haven't fucked Dan either. Am I right?"

Iestyn nearly hit a bollard and had to drag the wheel over to avoid it. "Shit, Julie, not when I'm driving. And what sort of a question is that?"

"Well, you seem to think you can ask if I've shagged Mac, so I'm just guessing this holiday is to allow you two to get down and dirty together in private. Think he'll let you top?"

Once again, Iestyn had to jerk the wheel. "Will you stop doing that while I'm driving, or neither of us will get our wish." *He did hint but there's no way I'm telling her about that.* "And no, I've no idea if he'll let me top, as you so delicately put it. He's a big bloke but I don't want to stereotype him, and anyway, I'm flexible, if I have to be."

"So a week tomorrow you'll be off to Cornwall for a romantic tryst in a beach house with a log fire and a big bed with a view of the sea. He'll be a bit knackered flying back from Paris overnight. Still, I expect the sea air will be invigorating."

"I hope so," Iestyn said, smiling. "But first we've got to get through Sunday lunch with my family."

* * * *

The next day, Iestyn drove his hatchback into the underground car park below Dan's apartment block. He spotted his boyfriend's SUV and pulled up behind it. Dan appeared from nowhere, carrying a large bouquet of flowers and a couple of bags. He got in.

"I feel like I'm having some secret affair with a married man," Iestyn said. "It's quite sexy, really. You might want to stow those on the back seat."

Dan grinned at him under his usual hat pulled low over his face. "Hmm, I bet most secret affairs don't involve going to dinner with the family."

"No, you may well have a point there," Iestyn conceded.

"I'm looking forward to a roast beef dinner, even if I do have to deal with your rugby mad brother and nephew. So what did you think of your first live match, then?" Dan asked.

Iestyn headed out of the car park and began the drive through town. It would take about forty minutes to get to Sully.

"It wasn't exactly the prettiest game I've ever seen," Iestyn began. "But the atmosphere was amazing. My boyfriend being the captain made it much more interesting, especially as he looks so good in shorts. You must be pleased—two games and two wins."

"Yeah, so far so good, but the French are going to be tough and it's a bit of a grudge match after the World Cup. If you think yesterday's match wasn't pretty, I expect there's going to be a hell of a lot of scrapping at the Stade de France. I already have a few bruises from yesterday. Tomorrow I get my whole body massage from Sven."

"Sven," Iestyn spluttered. "You have a masseur called Sven? I don't believe it."

Dan smiled. "I wish. No, actually he's just a physio called Fred who's nearly sixty, but he does have lovely hands. Now tell me all about this luxury hut you've booked us into.

Iestyn described the small cottage, emphasizing the king-size bed, the wood-burning fire and the secluded nature of the beach it overlooked. Occasionally, he glanced across as if to reaffirm that he was in a relationship with this glorious specimen of manhood who was hunched in the limited space the small car provided.

"It sounds wonderful," Dan said, putting his hand on Iestyn's thigh. "I can't wait to have you all to myself."

"Stop it. I know you're only trying to get your own back for what happened on the journey to your nan's house."

"Is it working?"

Iestyn didn't even need to look at him to know that his eyes would be shining with mischief. He picked up Dan's hand, allowing it to lightly brush over his own groin before putting it back on the wheel.

"You tell me."

Laughter erupted from Dan and Iestyn grinned as he turned into the wide street where his parents had lived for the whole of their marriage. Finally, he pulled into the drive of his family home.

Unlike most people, his mother parked in her garage, giving room for three more cars on the driveway his father's company had laid. No one could see through the trees so they entered without being observed.

"Bloody hell! That smells good," Dan said as he entered the living room.

"I bought more, especially since you were coming," Mary Jones shouted through from the kitchen. "I hope you don't mind it medium. I know what you men are like when it comes to red meat."

Iestyn punched Dan as he sniggered. "Shut up! That's my mother and you're making meat jokes!"

Dan walked to the kitchen and gave Mary the bunch of flowers. "I got these for you," he said. "Do you have a vase handy?"

"Oh, they're lovely, Dan. There are some vases in the cupboard. You'll need the large one for those. Just put them in and I'll sort them later."

Catching their conversation as he came through, Iestyn kissed his mother before turning around when he heard the front door open. A small body trundled toward them.

"Iessie, Iessie, up, up," Megs said.

Iestyn picked her up and swung her around. She giggled madly as her parents looked on.

Dan smiled and wondered. He'd often thought about children, and Iestyn looked so natural holding his niece, making her pull faces and blow raspberries.

"Oh, for God's sake, Iessie," his mother said. "Now she'll be blowing raspberries at everyone. I have enough trouble with Ben teaching her rude words."

Iestyn's brother, Huw, came in behind his wife and daughter. Ben brought up the rear.

"Dan, this is Huw and Susan, and this lovely lady is my niece, Megs, who knows exactly how to get her Uncle Iestyn to do whatever she wants."

"I must ask her for tips, then," Dan replied, smirking. "It's good to meet you both. I brought you something from yesterday's game." Dan picked up the bag and handed it to Huw.

"Bloody hell! Is this a ball from the match?" he asked excitedly, as he spun it around between his fingers.

"Yes, and I've signed it for you," Dan explained.

"Oh, my God, this is amazing!"

Iestyn winked at Dan then said, "I think your daddy is quite pleased with that, Megs."

Huw was still examining the ball. "I know exactly where this is going to be on display."

"I got some signed photos for Ben as well," Dan said.

Huw turned round to find his eldest child staring at the rugby player, his mouth hanging open. "So nice to see you without your phone attached to your ear," his father said. He looked at Dan. "We didn't tell him you'd be here, so I think he's a little shell-shocked. Ben, are you going to say something?"

"Umm, yeah, thanks," Ben mumbled.

He reached for his mobile, but Huw stopped him.

"Ben, you have to keep this to yourself for a while — until Uncle Iestyn and Mr Morgan speak to the papers — or it might cause problems. We're trusting you with this."

Ben gave them one of those looks that said 'I'm not stupid'. "I didn't say anything after Christmas. I can keep a secret and it'll be great to be able to tell the others that my uncle is going out with the Welsh captain when it's finally out."

"Thanks, Ben. And lastly, here's something for the most important person in the room." Dan handed over a cuddly dragon wearing a Wales shirt.

"Teddy," Megs said, holding it up to Iestyn.

Iestyn smiled in agreement

"So, what did you think of the match?" Dan asked.

The conversation then centered on the game for the next twenty minutes, helping Dan feel comfortable. Iestyn's sister, Rhian, and her twins arrived soon after. She announced that Gareth was away on a case.

Dan had brought miniature Welsh rugby kits for the boys, who he thought would consider themselves too old for cuddly toys.

Dinner began promptly at one thirty. Dan stood, not knowing where to sit. He had assumed that Huw would take the chair at the head of the table until Mary suggested that he sit there, startling him.

"You may as well," she said. "Then Iessie can sit to your side."

Everyone took a seat.

"This all looks amazing," Dan said. "I rarely get to eat a good roast these days. In training, it's all stuff that's good for us and lots of carbohydrates."

"Help yourself, everyone," Iestyn's mam said. "I bought a large slab of beef and made extra Yorkies and roasties."

Dan enjoyed continued talk about the chances of Wales beating the French, then Iestyn mentioned that they were going away on the Sunday.

Dan wasn't sure what reaction Iestyn's announcement would get. After all, they'd only been together for a few weeks and it did sort of confirm that they were sleeping together. From everyone's faces, it was clear that no one was bothered by this development.

"Oh, that sounds gorgeous," Rhian said. "Gareth and I could do with a little holiday if only we could get someone to look after these two."

"I think they might be a bit much for me, love," Mary said. "You know I would if I could."

"We could," Sue said. "We've already got this little monster, so two more wouldn't make a difference and Ben would help, wouldn't you?"

"Huh, I guess I could teach them to kick a ball or something," the boy conceded.

Dan listened to the family talking. He'd never had anything like this. All his life there had only been him, his mum, then his nan and granddad. He had no brothers, sisters or cousins that he knew of. His mother had been an only child, as his nan had nearly died giving birth to her. It felt good to be part of this family. He watched as Megs ate her mashed-up vegetables without complaint, although some of it ended up on the highchair tray—and was that a sprout in her hair? Ben pushed his food around until his father looked at him.

Dan really did enjoy the food. He also adored feeling Iestyn squeeze his thigh affectionately under the table.

He looked up from his plate as each sibling then decided to tell stories about the other.

"D'you remember when you ate all those green tomatoes because you thought they were apples?" Rhian said to Iestyn. "God, you were so sick."

"Well, you made mud pies on the kitchen floor," Huw said. "Trouble was you used some of the compost heap and the kitchen stank after that. Mam used to go mad because you always got so dirty. She gave up putting you in nice dresses."

"You weren't so innocent," Mary said to Huw. "You once stood on the compost heap playing king of the castle. You also took out a box of washing powder when it was windy and spun around to see how far it would go. When it rained, the garden was covered with suds."

"At least I didn't get caught with gay porn mags under my pillow," Huw said, looking at Iestyn. "You know Mam read them, don't you?"

Iestyn looked at his mam, eyebrows raised in horror.

Dan suppressed a chuckle.

"Well, love, they were very interesting and I wanted to make sure that when you finally came out, I would know as much as I could. There was a number for a parents' group in one of the adverts and they were very helpful."

"You rang them?" Iestyn said, his face now bright scarlet.

Ben was paying much more attention to the conversation.

"You were fifteen and I didn't know what experiences you'd already had, if any. Anyway, perhaps this isn't proper conversation for the dinner table."

"Aw, just when it was getting interesting," Ben said grumpily. "I do know what being gay means, you know. I'm eleven, not five."

"We know you do, dear, but now really isn't the time. Right, let's clear the table. It's apple and rhubarb crumble for afters. My family has their favorites. Iestyn, would you go and get it, please."

After the meal, they drank lots of tea. Dan once again sat and listened, far too comfortable in the armchair that had been Iestyn's father's usual seat. Megs had insisted on sitting on his knee where she promptly fell asleep.

Sue leaned over. "You can come again if you can get her to sleep for an hour. How are you at reading stories at bedtime? We could do with a decent babysitter and you could bring your boyfriend if you want."

Dan smiled and looked at Iestyn. He liked the way it felt to have Megs asleep in his arms. "As soon as the Six Nations is over, we're all yours, aren't we, Iestyn?" Dan genuinely meant it.

"As long as we can use the hot tub," Iestyn said, smirking.

"They have a hot tub?" Dan asked. "Oh, we'll definitely babysit, then."

"I think we'd better leave that until we're away. You're welcome to use it then," Huw said.

* * * *

Sometime later, a hand stroked Dan's thigh and he moaned.

"Dan, wake up. You're snoring," Iestyn said.

Dan opened his eyes and sat up, waking Megs as well. "Sorry. I nodded off, didn't I?"

"Yup, time to get you home, and I've still got marking I need to do. Coursework is bloody endless."

Dan passed Megs to her father. "It's been a lovely afternoon. I don't get to do this very often. Thanks for having me, Mary."

"It's been a pleasure, love. I enjoy watching a man with a good appetite. Geraint used to be just the same in the early days when he was working. He was always ravenous."

"We'll get off now, Mam," Iestyn told her, "if that's all right. See you lot again soon. I'll send some photos of the beach."

The family all hugged one another, including him in the hugging session.

A warm feeling of contentment took over his body on the journey home. He was full of fabulous food and he'd been welcomed into this wonderful family like a long lost relative. The whole afternoon could not have gone any better.

"That was really lovely," he said to Iestyn. "Your family is so amazing. I've no close family like that and I like yours a lot."

"And they like you. Megs seems to be a big fan and you're a natural with her. You don't have to babysit, you know."

"I want to. It'll be fun. You're okay about that, aren't you?" he asked.

"I guess so," Iestyn replied. He turned into the car park a little while later.

There was no one around so Dan leaned across and they allowed themselves the luxury of a brief snogging session until Dan yawned again.

"You better get some sleep," Iestyn said. "Are you back in training tomorrow?"

"I've got a couple of meetings that Graeme has organized. Then I'm back with the lads on Tuesday and we're off to Paris on Thursday. I'll phone you later to say goodnight." Dan kissed Iestyn again. He was so looking forward to the following week, when they would have time together with no interruptions. He walked swiftly to the lift then turned to wave as Iestyn reversed then finally drove out through the gate.

* * * *

The week passed quickly for Iestyn. He'd been busy at work. And intensive training with the Welsh team had left Dan with little time to call. Iestyn got most of his information from the news reports in the build-up to the next game.

Dan had pulled a shoulder in training and it was uncertain that he'd even begin the match. Intense physio got him to the start line. It was a tough and scrappy first half with Wales just edging a lead. Dan had picked up the ball from a ruck and charged straight into the huge French number eight. As he watched on the TV, Iestyn could see that Dan was in pain when he got up. For the rest of the half Dan didn't leap as high at the throw-ins and whenever he landed, he winced after tipping over the ball to the scrum half. When the teams came back after half-time, it was announced that the captain wouldn't return. Iestyn hoped it wouldn't mean the end of their holiday too. He was more than looking forward to it. As if he'd been reading Iestyn's mind, Dan texted.

Am ok – just a precaution. Needs strapping and rest. Have two weeks. Pick me up as agreed. Love you.

Iestyn stared at the phone. Love you? Did Dan realize he'd said that to him for the first time in a text? He started pressing buttons.

Good news. See you eight a.m. Take care. Love you too.

Suddenly it was so easy for him to say. The next day couldn't come quickly enough.

Chapter Twenty-Two

"You mean I get to drive your precious SUV?" Iestyn said.

He was back in the car park underneath Dan's building, loading up for their trip to Cornwall. It was still dark. Dan had managed about five hours in bed after flying back from the Welsh victory in Paris.

"Well, I can't drive with this bloody shoulder, can I? So I guess that leaves you." He passed over the key.

Iestyn smiled and turned it. The engine purred and he shifted it into gear.

"Be careful. Watch the barrier. You know the way to the motorway, don't you?"

"Oh for fuck's sake, Dan, I know how to drive! Now shut up and close your eyes. It's a few minutes to the M4 then it's motorway all the way down to the A391. I have driven to Cornwall before, which is more than you have. We can stop and get lunch nearby and pick up some food in Bude, although there's a hamper in the house. The road down to the beach hut is a bit narrow but I doubt it's used much, as there are only a few houses at the end and it's hardly beach weather.

Hopefully, it won't be too cold. The forecast is a bit mixed but we might get some nice walks on the beach."

"And hopefully some nice days in bed," Dan added.

"Oh, no. No sex for you. You've got to rest that shoulder."

Iestyn looked straight ahead, but he sensed Dan staring at him, open-mouthed.

"Got yer," Iestyn replied.

"Hmm, I can see you're going to be trouble." Dan yawned.

"Why don't you get some sleep?" Iestyn suggested.

"All right but you'd better take care of my baby." Dan laid his head back and was soon snoring quietly.

The miles rolled by and soon they were leaving Wales. The sun was finally beginning to come up and show its face rather weakly when they reached the first service station on the M5. Dan stirred as Iestyn drove into the car park.

"I'll get us a couple of egg and bacon rolls for breakfast," he said. "You stay here. I'll grab a couple of coffees as well and the papers. There should be a report of the match. How much d'you wanna bet they'll say you're doubtful for the rest of the Six Nations?"

He was right, of course. There were various assessments of Dan's injuries and reports of how the French had targeted him.

"Not available for interview. Believed to be resting. I know where he is," Iestyn said, smirking. "Oh, yeah, he's with his boyfriend, going to hide for a few days in Cornwall where, if he's lucky, he'll get one of his boyfriend's special massages."

Dan snickered and raised an eyebrow.

"Well, possibly one of them, if you behave yourself," Iestyn said.

They stopped and got some food at a supermarket in Bude and finally arrived at the house just after lunch.

"Bloody hell!" Iestyn said. "That road down is a bit steep and narrow, isn't it? I don't think I'll be doing it in the dark, so we'll have to stay in and amuse ourselves somehow." He smirked at Dan. "Mind you, look at the view of the beach and there's not a soul on it."

"I'm not surprised, really. It is a bit cold and inaccessible."

Iestyn shot him a worried look. "But it is lovely and all the better for us if no one is here. Come on, you. Let's get the stuff into the house. The key is supposed to be under the red plant pot on the window sill, isn't it?"

"Yeah, that looks like the one over there."

"I'll get it and leave you with the bags." Dan grinned and held his shoulder. "I won't be able to carry anything with this arm — sorry."

"It's all right, my wounded soldier. I'm a big boy and I can manage a few bags. You go and get in. The first fire is supposed to be set up but it will need lighting. There's central heating as well and, if we're too cold, we can snuggle under the duvet, eating bad food and watching the box."

Iestyn got all the bags in and collapsed onto the king-size bed. "Well, it's certainly compact and bijou," he said, looking around. "It's really a well-appointed beach hut and this bed is comfortable so I think it'll be long enough for you," he added.

Dan sat in one of the armchairs. "It's basically a kitchen at one end and a bedsit at the other." He got up and joined Iestyn on the bed. "Mmm, you're right about this bed. Let's get unpacked and lounge around for a bit before you make us a sumptuous repast."

* * * *

It got dark quickly in February, even in Cornwall, so they didn't go out. Iestyn noticed Dan was dead on his feet anyway, the result of yesterday's game. He said his shoulder wasn't too bad or they wouldn't have let him come away, but he'd been warned to be careful with it all the same. Iestyn made pizzas. They sat watching the box set of *West Wing*, which Dan hadn't seen, eating the pizza then ice cream for afters. It was relaxed and homey to be able to spend so much time together. This holiday would be the longest that they'd managed since meeting. Iestyn thought it would show both of them if they really had a future together and if he was going to be able to cope with being the boyfriend of a semi-famous sportsman.

After three episodes, Dan was snoring next to Iestyn. It was still before ten, so he turned off the machine and took out his book. Settling next to Dan, he read for a bit until he too slept.

* * * *

When he woke up in the morning, he was still spooned next to Dan and sporting an impressive erection that was currently pressing into Dan's arse. Iestyn allowed himself to fantasize for a moment or two about an early morning fuck.

It was still dark out. The sun wouldn't be up for a few hours. The room wasn't cold but it wasn't red-hot, either. He wondered absent-mindedly when the heating would come on. Saying nothing, he snuggled into Dan's back until sleep overtook Iestyn once more.

When Iestyn woke up again a few hours later, Dan was still snoring. He slipped out of bed and, after popping into the bathroom, made a cup of tea and settled down with some marking at the kitchen table. It felt good that Dan was there with him, even if he was asleep. He could hear Dan breathing as Iestyn tried to get his mind into essays on the causes of World War I. Every so often, he'd steal a look over to Dan as he lay there. Iestyn indulged himself in fantasies about them living together, about this being how they might be. He found that he wanted it more than he'd expected He tutted aloud as he read through the piece in front of him.

"You should have woken me," he heard Dan say.

"You were fast asleep and I had work to do. How's the shoulder feeling?"

Dan moved his arm around. "It's still a bit stiff. I don't think it's anything serious but that French prop was targeting me and we didn't want to risk it being worse, so they took me off again. I've two weeks before the Italian game then it's the final match against England, probably for the Grand Slam. The physio just said to rest it and get some gentle exercise this week and then I can try some more serious training next week." He winked at him. "You'll just have to be gentle with me." He pulled back the sheet.

Iestyn gasped. Dan was magnificent but there were bruises all over his chest. Obviously, the prop had connected a few times. A pair of tightie-whities clung to his every contour. It didn't help Iestyn's equilibrium when Dan got up and sashayed to the bathroom, shaking his arse as he went.

"Those are some bruises you've got there," Iestyn said when he returned. "Is that one a boot?"

Dan shrugged. "It's par for the course in a game, really." He pulled on jeans and a T-shirt and strolled to where Iestyn was sitting at the other end of the hut. He slung his arms around Iestyn and gawked over his shoulder to see what he was doing.

"Bloody teachers! Only work a few hours a day and have so many holidays, so why are you here at eight in the morning marking stuff while it's still dark? I'll do you some toast. We can have some of the jam in that hamper." He examined the contents. "Oh, and there's some shortbread as well. D'you want more tea?"

"Yes, please. I'll just do my batch of five then we'll have a trip out, shall we? I can only do five before I want to rant too much and it is boring reading the same thing over and over again."

By nine, the sun had risen and was making an effort to smile down on the sand and sea outside the cottage. Dean shielded his eyes from the glare and contemplated the empty beach. Occasional gusts of wind whipped up surf and spray, creating white tops on the incoming waves. It was beautiful.

"We should have brought wetsuits then we could have tried surfing," Dan said.

Iestyn pulled a face at the idea. "It's February, in case you haven't noticed and, although the sun is shining, I bet that wind is making it cold. Shall we go and find out in a bit?"

"Yep, let's go for a walk and see how far we can get then find somewhere for lunch," Dan agreed.

"You sure you want to be seen? We can always eat in. I don't mind," Iestyn said.

Dan leaned in and kissed him quickly.

"We should be all right. I doubt if anyone down here will really know who I am. It's not really a big rugby area. Perhaps I should get some hair dye for a disguise or a mustache. I could buy some glasses or borrow your spare pair."

Iestyn looked at him. "You wouldn't be able to see a thing. You know I'm short-sighted as hell. Come on, let's get our coats on and brave the wind."

It wasn't a big beach. A path meandered down to the sand. They had no idea whether the tide was in but it seemed so. The sand at the top appeared dry and there were large rocks that had obviously fallen from the cliff at the other side. Only seagulls kept them company. Even so, it surprised Iestyn when Dan took his hand as they walked. That simple move sent warmth pulsating through him. After about fifteen minutes of walking, they had reached the other side.

"We might be able to clamber over the rock," Iestyn said. "We could do with looking at Google to see what's on the other side at each end or we might be able to find a path over the top. Otherwise, we'll have to do a reccy in the car."

Iestyn lay back on a rock and Dan leaned into him. It seemed natural to put his arms around Dan as he moved in for a kiss. They didn't get carried away but Iestyn placed his head on Dan's chest for a while before shivering. It was cold in the breeze. Finally, they sat on the rocks looking out to sea. To the left, two people appeared dressed in wetsuits and carrying boards. They ran toward the waves and threw themselves in.

"They must be mad," Iestyn said.

"Surfers are," Dan agreed, "but it is fun. I bet you've never even tried. What about kite flying? We could probably buy one somewhere round here and have a go. The wind is certainly right for it. It'll be fun. Let's walk back to the other end and take some photos to send back to Julie and Mac. D'you think they'll get together properly? I must admit that Mac is quite smitten. I thought he'd gotten stuck on my friend Hayley, but she wasn't interested. Julie's having a positive effect on him, I think."

"Well, she's always been there for me. I've known her nearly all my life. She got hurt by her first husband but I think she likes Mac. She's a bit wary after that brief fling with our friend Matt, who's a bit of a plonker. Well, he is a PE teacher. I hope Mac won't mess her around."

"Sometime my friends need to meet your friends. I'll have to have a party or something after the Six Nations finishes where we can get them all together."

The offer really pleased Iestyn. Dan was obviously seeing this as a long-term thing. At some point, they needed to address that 'love' word they'd both used in their texts.

They found a pub in a nearby village and settled into a corner with Dan facing away from the room. The food was good and Dan piled his plate high with beef and vegetables. Iestyn envied the way Dan just put away the sticky toffee pudding he'd declined.

"Do you really worry about being fat?" Dan asked.

"I'm a gay man. Aren't we all supposed to be buff or bears? And I'm neither. I'm just ordinary, I guess. Matt says I should exercise more."

Dan quirked an eyebrow. "I'm sure I could devise a routine for you. We could start tonight if you want." He moved his arm and winced.

"Would you like me to give you one of my famous massages later? I'll be gentle, I promise," Iestyn said.

"Do I have to wait until tonight? We've nothing else to do this afternoon and I have been told to rest," Dan replied.

"Sounds like a plan to me. I'll pay. You wait for me in the car."

Forty minutes later, they arrived back at the hut. A few people stood skimming stones on the beach so Dan decided to have a rest while Iestyn did a bit more marking. It grew dark soon and Dan made an offer Iestyn couldn't refuse.

"That bath looks like it would take both of us."

The bath was a luxury one with a double end and Jacuzzi jets.

Iestyn lay with his back against the end of the tub. Somehow, Dan had managed to sit between his legs and had his head back on Iestyn as he was gently soaping Dan's chest. Unable to resist tweaking Dan's nipples, he gave each a gentle squeeze and was gratified to see a response as the tip of the other man's cock emerged just through the bubbles. He smiled as Dan turned his head and looked up at him.

"Now see what you've done, and there's something hard sticking into my back too. I didn't notice a toy submarine in here earlier."

"Hmph," Iestyn replied. "I'll give you toy submarine."

"Really," Dan said. "I'll look forward to that."

Iestyn wondered for a moment. They'd never really talked about what sort of sex they both liked. Fucking was the automatic last stage in Iestyn's mind but he'd assumed that Dan would want to top. Perhaps now was the ideal time to talk about it. Iestyn was certain that they were heading to bed from here.

"Water's getting a bit cold," Dan said. "Let's get out and you can give me that massage. I've some stuff in my bag the physio recommended."

Moments later, Dan was lying on his stomach on the bed. The sight threatened to take Iestyn's breath away. From his size fifteen feet, through his strong calves and huge thighs, past his amazingly tight bubble butt, onto the wide shoulders and blond mop of hair, the rugby player's body was perfect. In fact, he was marred only by the livid bruising across his back and down his left hip. For a while, Iestyn just stood and stared, unable to move.

"Are you just going to stand there and look or give me that massage you promised?" Dan asked.

A chuckle lurked in his voice. Iestyn guessed that Dan knew the effect he was having on him. Iestyn's cock was certainly taking notice. Would he get to bury it in that glorious arse? *Down boy! We don't know whether you get that, so control yourself!*

Iestyn positioned himself so he straddled Dan's muscular thighs. The action wasn't easy to do, even for a man of his not inconsiderable size. He poured some of the massage oil onto his hands and warmed it up before rubbing it into Dan's shoulder muscles. He worked gently around the injured shoulder and just rubbed harder into the rest of Dan's back and sides. He deliberately avoided putting the lotion on Dan's neck and into the hollow at the bottom of his spine. He was dying to lick both so he bent over, moved Dan's hair aside and kissed the back of his neck. Dan groaned. Iestyn shuffled down so that he could kiss that hollow. He let his tongue swirl around then began moving across each cheek, taking little nips as he did so.

He wondered if he dared go further. It had been a while since he'd used his tongue to delve into another man. Steve would never do it to him so he hadn't done it back. Gently he spread Dan's arse cheeks apart and trailed his tongue down his crack between them. Dan tasted of vanilla and toffee bubble bath. Tentatively, he licked at his hole.

"Oh, God," Dan gasped. "That feels so good."

Encouraged, Iestyn poked his tongue in further but only enough to prod at the ring of muscles and try to push past them. He grabbed a pillow, urging Dan to lift, then continued licking and pressing at Dan's entrance. He wanted to ease a finger inside him too. He longed to sink his cock inside his boyfriend, but he just kept licking and sucking at that hole.

"Iessie, will you please fuck me before I die of frustration?"

Iestyn looked up in surprise. "Really? I don't have to if you don't want me to."

"I want you to. I like being fucked. You do fuck, don't you?" he said.

"Yeah, but I thought you might want to fuck me instead. I didn't expect you to…well, you know."

Dan looked over his shoulder. "I might want to fuck you sometime, but right now I want to feel you inside me when I come, because if my cock gets any harder, I'll be drilling a hole in the mattress. The lube is in the bag, along with the condoms. Just remember that it's been a while for me and that I'll need a decent amount of preparation, though that's a talented tongue you have there."

Iestyn quickly recovered from his surprise and smiled to himself. He retrieved the lube and started to open Dan up. Tight muscles surrounded his finger. When Dan raised his arse taking him in farther, he added a second and searched for that little bundle of nerves. When Dan jerked, he knew he'd found it. A bolt of desire surged south in Iestyn every time he delved his fingers inwards. Although he could feel Dan's passage pulling him deeper with every thrust, he pinched himself to make sure he wasn't dreaming. Dan's groans grew louder.

"You all right?" Iestyn asked, checking before he put in a third finger.

"Yeah. Burns a little but it's so good." He trembled under Iestyn's touch. "Fuck me, Iessie, please. I want to feel you inside me. Give me a minute to turn over. I want to see you."

"Okay," Iestyn replied. "I'd like that too." He got off him and withdrew a condom from the bag. He hoped that sometime soon they would be able to make love without this barrier between them. He longed to fill Dan up with his cum. He knelt between Dan's legs.

"Let me," Dan said, taking the condom and rolling it slowly onto Iestyn's fully erect cock.

He quivered with anticipation as Dan lay back on the bed and lifted his legs so they hung over Iestyn's shoulders displaying himself, all wet and gleaming.

"Oh, God," Iestyn said as he tried to control his emotions. He wasn't sure about the exact proportions of fear and excitement he was feeling.

"You're thinking too much, teach. If you don't get a move on, I'm going to start without you." Dan placed a hand on his cock and moved up and down slowly. Just for emphasis, he raised his hips toward Iestyn.

"Greedy bugger," he replied. "I can see you're going to need some training."

"Stop talking, Iessie, and start fucking!" Dan ordered.

"Oh, I just love a bossy bottom." He grinned and lined himself up. Finally, he began edging in slowly, making sure he wasn't hurting his lover.

"Wow, that's good," Dan said. "Now fuck me like there's no tomorrow. I'm a big boy, Iessie, not some fragile creature, and I want to know that I've been had."

"I love a challenge. You may live to regret that." He pulled himself fully out then slammed back in. Then he set a pace he hoped he could maintain.

The smell of sex filled the hut. Skin slapped against skin as Dan continued to say "More", "Harder", "Faster" and other words Iestyn couldn't make out. Iestyn couldn't believe he had such a powerful body writhing beneath him, begging him for more, craving every thrust of his cock. He'd never expected this scenario. Oh, he'd imagined it in his wildest dreams that he'd get to have this gorgeous man writhing and begging for more under him, but he'd really thought that it would remain just that—a dream.

He leaned over, almost bending Dan in half so he could capture his bottom lip and suck on it. Dan's cock rubbed against his abdomen. Gradually, he kissed down from Dan's lip to his chest. He desperately wanted to leave marks on that muscled chest but he knew he couldn't. There would be no way Dan could pass those off as bruises from a rugby match. His need to mark Dan as his own startled Iestyn.

Pulling up again, he balanced himself enough to wrap one hand around Dan's cock. Establishing a rhythm that matched his thrusts, he moved his fist up and down the engorged shaft from balls to tip. He couldn't wait to see cum splash all over the other man's broad chest, filling the grooves of his perfect six-pack.

"Let me," Dan said, replacing Iestyn's hand with his own. "I want you to hold my balls."

As soon as he began gently rolling them between his fingers, Iestyn knew Dan's climax wasn't far away. He picked up his pace, thrusting again and again at that spot within.

"Oh, God, that's so good. I'm gonna come," Dan groaned.

Their eyes met as Dan's arse contracted around Iestyn's cock, pushing him over into his own orgasm. White sticky liquid pooled over Dan's stomach and chest as Iestyn poured himself into the condom, wishing he was filling Dan's passage instead. It seemed like his whole body had waited all his life for this moment—totally in control and totally out of control at the same time. For a while, he lay on top of Dan, still deep inside him. He didn't want to lose that connection, that heat all around him. He wanted to rub up and down Dan's chest, coating his own seed in Dan's cum so they were joined together.

Finally, he pulled out and lay next to Dan. He trailed his fingers through the mess on his chest and sucked on his fingers. He could have sworn that Dan's cock twitched as he did. Dan leaned over and kissed him, filling Iestyn's mouth with tongue as he examined everything within. Iestyn ground his cock against Dan's. Was it possible that they were both ready to go again? He shoved Dan off and came up for air.

Dan gazed at him, his fringe falling into his eyes. "I love you, Iestyn Jones, and that was incredible."

"I love you too, *cariad*," Iestyn replied. He knew that it was true. He'd thought he'd been in love before but not like this, never like this. He lifted Dan's good arm and laid his head on his chest.

"So does that mean you're ready for us to go public?" Dan asked. He knew it was asking a lot of the reticent teacher but he figured Graeme would know what to do and, after a while, some other story, like phone hacking or the spending cuts, would hit the news. Iestyn looked up at him and Dan's heart skipped more than a few beats. The last person who'd looked at him like that had been Az.

As if reading his mind, Iestyn said, "If you're sure I'm who you want. You've only just come out of a long relationship. I don't want to go through everything if you're not sure. This is going to mean interest in both of us. Are you positive this agent of yours knows what he's doing? I'll have to warn the head before it hits the press but...I think we're worth it." Dan leaned down and kissed him. "Let's have our week and after the England game, we'll go public."

Dan loved every moment of their week. He couldn't get enough of Iestyn below him, or above him—he didn't care, as so long as they were together. At the start and end of each day they made love like they were teenagers again. Dan said more than once that it was a good job he'd bought a big tube of lube, as they got through a lot. The weather stayed fine—cold but sunny. Occasionally, Dan walked by himself while Iestyn marked, but usually Iestyn accompanied him as they strolled side by side along various beaches, or scrambled over rocks near the hut. Iestyn found some board games in a cupboard and began to teach Dan how to play chess. He showed him how to move each piece and slowly Dan improved under Iestyn's patient tutelage. Iestyn had also allowed Dan to persuade him to eat Cornish pasties and the odd scone with clotted cream. Dan figured they'd work some of it off somehow.

* * * *

On Friday afternoon, Iestyn took Dan on one last stroll down the beach. He sat on a large rock and pulled Dan toward him, kissing him gently, luxuriating in the proximity of their bodies in the February sunshine.

Was that a noise?

Fear gripped him. He pushed Dan off and looked around but couldn't see anyone.

"What?" Dan asked as he scanned the beach too.

"Nothing," Iestyn replied, taking his hand once more. "I'm just being paranoid. I wish we never had to leave here and go back to the real world."

"I know. It's been good, hasn't it? We just need to get past the Six Nations then no more hiding in the shadows. If we let the information out carefully, I'm sure it will be all right."

Iestyn heard a car pull away up the lane but thought nothing of it as they strolled back along the beach, hand in hand.

Chapter Twenty-Three

Back at work, Iestyn had trouble stopping himself from daydreaming about the previous week. It had been perfect. Even the weather had been dry, if a little cold. However, there was a big gray cloud on the horizon and he kept trying to work out exactly what he was going to say to Neil Griffiths, the head of the school. He knew he had to tell him something.

Last night he had met Graeme, Dan's agent. They had gone through the press release to be issued after the England game. There would be a photo session as well. It was going to be a simple declaration that they were together, with enough information about him, hopefully, to stop the papers digging any further into his background. After all, it was only a rugby player he was going out with, not an A-list celebrity who was being dragged out of the closet by a set of kiss-and-tell pictures. He was worried about it all the same. He wasn't looking forward to the comments some people might make. He looked up as Maisie, the newest recruit to the Humanities Department, came through the door. Sometimes she made him feel like an old fogey but her enthusiasm was infectious.

"Hi, Maisie, I've had a look at the Year Nine exercise books and they're really doing well. How have things been going over the last couple of weeks? I feel like we haven't caught up as often as we should have. I hope that's because you think things are progressing nicely. We have someone coming in to look at a few lessons. Do you mind if he comes in to see you?"

"Wow, I've only been teaching six months and I get someone coming in to see how I do it. That's cool. To be honest, I'm used to being observed, so it's no problem. Is he one of these ex stockbroker types who's decided to do his bit for society?"

"I've no idea but he is in his mid-thirties. I'll introduce you on Friday when he's coming in to get his timetable," Iestyn explained.

"Ah, well, perhaps he'll be tall, dark and handsome as well as rich, and sweep one of us off our feet," she replied, laughing.

Iestyn frowned.

"Sorry, was that inappropriate?" She looked worried.

"No, it's fine but I don't think that's likely."

"Why? If you were straight, I'd fancy you myself." She laughed then stopped. "Sorry again. Sometimes I can't seem to help myself. I'll take my foot out of my mouth, leave these lesson plans with you and get off, shall I?"

"I think that's best," Iestyn agreed. God, she was so young. He wasn't sure he could remember ever being that young. The bell sounded and he beckoned his Year Twelves into the room.

* * * *

"How's the shoulder doing?" Mac asked at Dan's flat.

"Got the all clear, so should be all right to face the Italians on Saturday. Resting it last week really did it some good and Iestyn has such healing hands."

"Wow, who knew getting a hand job or two could help fix your shoulder! I'll use that excuse next time I get an injury. You had a good time, then. That smile hasn't left your face and you keep going off into la-la land."

"Yeah, we had a good time, a *really* good time. Mac, I think I love him. I think I'm *in* love with him. We're going to go public after the England game. Graeme has everything worked out. Last week was so good, and Iestyn is amazing in bed."

"Whoa, too much information," Mac protested. "But I am pleased for you. Are you sure you're over Aron now? It's just…if you let this bloke down, I think Julie will kill you, then she'll kill me, and I like her. I *really* like her. She even has me listening to classical music. I could listen to her playing all night. Man, the way she runs her fingers over the keys. Your bloke isn't the only one who's good with his hands."

For a moment, he stared off into space, and Dan smiled, knowing that someone else had it bad too. "So back to full training tomorrow then," Mac continued, back in the room. "Fancy some company here tonight and then we can go together tomorrow?"

"Sounds like a plan. We can get some takeaway and slob out tonight," Dan said.

* * * *

The game against Italy came and went and, although the Italians had improved considerably, the result was never in doubt. Iestyn attended with Julie and they shouted themselves hoarse, but then so did everyone else. He knew he wouldn't see the Welsh captain in the following week, because next it was the big one. Even if Wales wasn't in line to win the Grand Slam, beating England was the ultimate aim of every Six Nations Tournament. They would be playing at Twickenham and tickets were going for ridiculous prices. Iestyn was a mixture of nerves and excitement. After the game, whatever the result, they were going to go public in a series of photos and an interview. Graeme hadn't yet decided who would get the exclusive but he knew that even the broadsheets would be interested. After captaining the Welsh team to victory — if Dan did — the only out rugby player, who also happened to be the Welsh captain, would be news.

* * * *

Tuesday morning he went to pick up his paper from the corner shop. Usually Des, who did the early morning shift, was chatty, but this morning he handed over the paper and just stared at him. For a moment, Iestyn wondered if he'd developed some strange spot on his face that hadn't been there when he'd shaved that morning. He walked back to his car and threw the paper into the passenger seat. He whistled as he went up the corridor to his classroom and settled down to sort out all that he needed for the day. He had a meeting with Sam that morning after lesson one. He'd worked out everything he was going to say.

"Bloody hell, there you are!" Matt said as he barged into the room.

"Where's the fire?" Iestyn asked.

"There," Matt replied, placing the tabloid newspaper on his desk.

Iestyn looked at the headline—*Welsh Captain's Mystery Lover*—screamed from the page. There was a photograph underneath. It had obviously been taken on that last day in Cornwall, when they'd kissed on the beach. Under the photo was a brief paragraph about Dan. With trembling fingers, Iestyn turned the page to where the story continued. On page three, there was a picture from Dan's last photo shoot for a charity calendar. He was wearing very little but a rugby ball and an enormous smile. The paper asked for people to contact them if they knew who the mystery man was.

"Shit!" Iestyn said, his heart pounding as if it was going to jump out of his chest. A wave of nausea swept over him. "Shit! Shit! Shit!" He pulled his phone from his pocket. Dan was away with the team, so he probably wouldn't have seen the story. It went to voicemail, so Iestyn left a message asking him to call.

"What are you going to do?" Matt asked.

The door opened again and Julie came in. "Have you seen it?" she asked.

"He has now," Matt said. "I repeat, what are you going to do? It won't take long for them to get your name. Half the kids in Year Ten were there when he gave you his number. Weren't you seeing Neil today?"

"Yes, lesson two. I bet they've done this deliberately before the England game. They must have had that photo for a while and now there'll be maximum publicity. The rest of the press are going to be all over this like a rash."

Matt rolled his eyes. "Of course they are. He's the only out gay rugby player in the country. He's an icon for sports all over the world, as well as for gay rights. They'll want to know everything about you. I hope you haven't got too many skeletons in your closet."

Iestyn tried to think what any of his previous lovers could say about him. He hadn't had many but there had been a few one-night stands along the way. His phone rang. He looked at the name. Mam.

"Oh, hell!" he said, pressing a button. "Hello, Mam."

"Have you seen the paper today, Iessie? There's a story about you and Dan. Have you spoken to him yet?" She sounded worried.

"Yes, I have seen it and no, I haven't spoken to Dan. He's holed up with the Welsh team and probably incommunicado."

"Oh, Iessie, I know you wanted to keep this quiet until after the England game and now… I thought you were being careful."

"We were. It was just a kiss on the beach and now they'll find out who I am. Come to think of it, my newsagent looked at me funny this morning and, bloody hell, he has my address. I know we were stupid. It was just one of those spur of the moment things."

"If they find out who you are, I guess I'll get some news reporter asking questions."

"Shit! Sorry, Mam, I'd not thought about that. If they do, say nothing."

"You know me, love. I'll cope. I'm just worried about you."

"Thanks, Mam, and I love you too. I'll call you later."

He looked at Matt and Julie. "Mam's worried the press might call her. You know, what does she think about her son going out with the most eligible gay bachelor in Britain?" He almost laughed. His phone beeped again and again. There were messages from his brother and sister. He texted back.

Yes, I know and no, I've no idea.

"It's probably going to be the talk of the school today," Julie said. "What are you going to say?"

"I could try 'Shut up and get on with your work'," Iestyn replied. "With any luck, they won't recognize me. It's not the clearest of images."

"Ha bloody ha! You'd better hope none of this lot read the papers. Trouble is it'll be in them all tomorrow and all over the TV. You've got to face it, Iestyn. It's news and your private life is about to be taken apart and examined."

Iestyn put his head in his hands and tried to control the feelings of panic threatening to overwhelm him.

"Are you sure he's worth it?" Matt asked.

"You can't ask him that," Julie said. She turned to Iestyn. "At least you're out and not stuck in the closet. Imagine that! And you were going public next week anyway."

"I know, but on Saturday Wales will play a huge game against England. Dan will be captaining them and all the talk will be about this. If I'm there, the press will want some words from me. There's nothing controlled about this. It's not like we had it planned. If Wales lose the Triple Crown and the Grand Slam, it'll somehow be my fault. I bet there'll be stories of how we were at it like rabbits in Cornwall and I wore him out, or that he's too distracted. He can't afford to make one mistake and now I can't be at the match either, because by then they'll know who I am."

The bell sounded. Matt and Julie rushed off to their own classes. Luckily, his form seemed absorbed in discussing some party and none of them mentioned the paper.

Josh strolled in late as usual at the end of registration. "Can you mark me in, sir?"

Iestyn nodded, still distracted.

"It must be a bit of a disappointment, the paper, sir. You must be gutted."

Iestyn snapped his head up, afraid of what was coming next. His whole body tensed in anticipation.

"I guess you and Dan Morgan didn't hook up after all, as he's got himself a new boyfriend."

Iestyn said nothing but he did allow himself a slight smile. Perhaps he was going to get away with it after all. However, he knew his talk with the head, scheduled for after break, wasn't going to be quite as simple.

* * * *

Waiting outside the head's room always made Iestyn feel like a naughty schoolboy who was about to be told off for some misdemeanor. Once he was inside, seeing Neil's face while he explained the situation didn't make him feel any better.

"So can I expect the press to be hanging around the gates?" Neil asked irritably.

"Possibly, if they find out who I am. I'm sorry. We were going to tell the press officially next week. That's why I wanted to let you know in advance."

"I have to say, Iestyn, this isn't really what the school needs at the moment. You know we could get the call from Estyn at any time. I can just imagine the inspectors' attitude to having the press camped out on the doorstep. I know you have the right to a personal life but this is going to impact on your working life as well. Dan Morgan is big news. I'll have to let the governors know as well and warn the office to expect the calls. Are you going to Twickenham?"

"I was, but not now. Anyway, thanks, Neil. With any luck, it'll just be a flash in the pan."

He got on with the rest of the day. None of the kids linked him with the story, and in some ways, Iestyn felt hurt that he obviously wasn't considered good enough to be the boyfriend of the new Welsh captain.

Iestyn was relieved to find there wasn't a pack of reporters camped out in his garden when he arrived home. He picked up the phone to find a message from Graeme Starr, telling him to sit tight and say nothing. Iestyn wanted desperately to speak to Dan but all his calls got 'I'm not available to take your call. Please leave a message after the tone.' He'd left so many messages he doubted that Dan even knew what had happened, because surely the management of the team would want them focused on training.

Iestyn didn't eat much. He went to bed early, wanting sleep, but it mostly eluded him, and when he did sleep, his dreams were filled with images of faces, all asking him questions.

In the morning, he looked like death. He examined the dark circles under his eyes. He needed a shower and copious amounts of tea. Once dressed, he went downstairs into the kitchen, made tea and toast, and opened his laptop to check the news.

"Fucking hell!" he shouted, almost knocking the tea over his computer. His face stared back at him from the screen. True, it was a much younger version of his face, but it was him under the heading — *Gay Welsh Rugby Player's Boyfriend Revealed!* He read the story. So far, they had his name and that he was a teacher and not much else, except a bit about his university background. There was an appeal for more information and anyone who had a story to tell. He got up and pulled back the curtain slightly. Stood at his gate was a pack of people with cameras slung around their necks. *Shit! What the hell am I going to do?*

His phone rang.

"Iestyn, it's Neil. Sorry to call you but have you seen the headline? They know who you are."

"Yes, Neil, I've seen it. I have the press outside my house. I don't know what to do."

"Look, Iestyn, I think you should stay home for now."

Iestyn interrupted him. "But I haven't done anything wrong, Neil. Are you suspending me?"

"No, of course not. I know you haven't done anything wrong but if you're not here, the press will leave us alone. You know you have my complete support. Although you're *out* at school, not all our parents are going to be so supportive. Sit tight for now and I'd suggest you don't go out, if you don't have to."

"This is just wrong, Neil. I've never hidden the fact that I'm gay and I'm not starting now."

"No one is asking you to. Just let me handle this. I'll talk to the governors. Try not to worry. These things tend to blow over."

Iestyn had to trust him. Neil had always been fair but he felt like a caged tiger. He paced the floor and drank too much tea. He wanted to talk to Dan, even for a few seconds, just to hear his voice reassuring him that everything would be all right.

His phone rang again.

He listened as the ringing stopped then pressed the message button. It was the newspaper. So they had his number now, too. It rang again so he took it off the hook. His mobile sang out the Welsh national anthem. It was his mam.

"Oh, Iestyn, you're on the news. Are you all right?"

"Neil's told me to stay at home."

"But you've done nothing wrong!" his mother said angrily.

"I know, but he can't have press at the school and some parents won't be pleased that the school has a gay teacher in the news!"

"That's an old picture of you in the paper."

"I know, Mam. I think it's the one on Friendsreunited from university. Someone must have looked me up once they found out my name. Or perhaps it was someone from university who spotted me. Or maybe it was one of the taxi drivers who took me to see Dan. I don't know. I'm just worried about what else they'll dig up."

"Well, you haven't done anything illegal, have you? You've not taken drugs or anything."

"No, Mam, but there have been other men in my life, especially when I was at university. I'm not sure there's that much to kiss and tell, though."

"Look, love, why don't you get out of there? I'll get the car and check the back lane. I can pick you up. I'll ring you to let you know the coast is clear. You can stay with me for a bit."

Iestyn sighed but he knew that it was a good idea. He left the lights on in the front room so they'd think that he was still there. Once at his mother's house, he sank into the sofa and threw his head back to stare at the ceiling. His mam returned from the kitchen with tea and biscuits. She pulled a chair and sat in front of her youngest son.

"I don't know what to do, Mam. I haven't been able to speak to Dan and I really need to. I hate being cut off from him. I don't know what he's thinking. Hell, I don't know if he even knows he and I are headline news. He might be in trouble for it."

His mother put her hand on his arm. "I know, *cariad*. I know what it's like to need to talk to someone when you can't."

Iestyn looked at his mother and realized who she meant. He immediately felt guilty. "Oh God, Mam, I'm sorry. I didn't mean to…"

She squeezed his arm.

"It's all right, Iessie. I just miss him at times like this. He was always so calm and centered, unlike me. He'd have told you to either live with it or decide it wasn't for you."

Tears stung his eyes and rolled down his cheeks.

His mother put her arms around him. "Oh, Iessie, I hope he's worth all of this."

"I'm so useless at the moment. Look at me. I'm over thirty years old and my mam is hugging me because I'm crying. How pathetic is that!"

She looked at him. "Iessie, you're still my baby boy and I will always try to make it better. Now wasn't this Graeme Starr supposed to be ringing you? I think it's time he earned his money."

Chapter Twenty-Four

Iestyn learned very little from the phone call with Graeme Starr. Apparently, Dan hadn't been told about the news as they weren't allowed access to their phones whilst at the training camp. It seemed the media was banned as well and all they did was play and sleep. Starr reminded him that this was the most important game in Dan's career and the management were none too pleased about the headlines. Iestyn was told to sit tight and say nothing, regardless of what they printed, and that made Iestyn even more worried.

"Look," he said. "I've got kids I need to teach and you sound as if you know more than you're saying. What else do they have? There is something else, isn't there?"

Starr muttered incoherently and said that he had to go.

Iestyn returned to biting his nails, wondering what the hell else the papers could print. After the initial revelation of his name, nothing much had been published, except some more photos of Dan and his ex and a quote saying that he hoped Dan was happy. More worryingly, there was a quote from the school, advising that he was off sick and asking the press not to contact the school or pester the children. However, that hadn't stopped Josh giving his opinion.

'Mr Jones is a great teacher. We were there when he met Dan Morgan, skating. It was obvious that he fancied Mr Jones 'cos he gave him his card. We all know sir is gay. So what? Good for him pulling a rugby player. I hope we win on Saturday.'

Iestyn pulled the lid down on his laptop. At least the press hadn't turned up at his mother's house yet, but it was only a matter of time. He took out some essays and started to mark them. He had to get back to school sometime, surely? After the game, they'd do their interviews together and things would settle down. The international rugby season would end for a bit and he'd be able to get back to a normal life, wouldn't he?

* * * *

The calls and texts arrived in earnest on Friday morning, waking him from his slumber and warning about the papers. His mum took the car to buy the so-called 'exclusive'. When she returned, all the color had drained from her face.

"Mam, what the hell have they said?" He couldn't imagine what could be so bad. He turned over the paper. His face, next to Dan's, looked back at him under the headline – *Revealed – The Sex Games of Rugby Player's Boyfriend!*

The story hinted at wild nights while he was at university, of orgies and sex in unusual places and in unusual ways. There was some speculation over whether Dan would have indulged in these fantasies and did sir like to give him six of the best? It promised more revelations on Sunday.

"Shit," he said over and over.

"Iessie, is this true?" his mother asked calmly. "Because if it is, we'll deal…"

"What!" he said. "No, of course not. They're implying Dan and me play kinky games with each other. I've never done anything like that. Okay, once I got drunk and there was an incident in a bus stop, but orgies? I should be so lucky!"

"So there's no truth in any of this? They must have got it somewhere. Are you sure, Iessie? I know I'm your mother but I am a woman of the world."

Iestyn squirmed in his seat. For Christ's sake, this was his mother!

"Tell me everything, Iessie."

He stared up at her. If his mother thought it could be true then everyone else would as well. He knew he was in real trouble. He needed her to believe him.

"What? You think this pensioner hasn't ever done anything a bit naughty in her time?"

Now he really did want the floor to open up and swallow him. "It's nothing, Mam, just that Steve did like me to tie him to the bed occasionally. That's all, and I can't imagine him telling that story to the press. I've never got off on hitting someone like they're implying. Shit! If Neil sees this — and the kids — I could lose my job. You know people will think there's no smoke without fire."

They heard a key in the door. Before he could focus on who it was, he was surrounded by a warm body hugging him. Rhian pulled away and looked at him. "Bloody hell, Iessie, is it true? I never thought!"

"No, I'm not like that!" Now he was explaining his sex life to his sister! "Dan and I only had sex for the first time on that holiday." It wasn't true but he didn't want to explain the ins and outs of his sex life to his mother and sister. "We've hardly had any time together, because of the internationals. They're making both of us out to be perverts. I don't know where the hell this is all coming from but someone is making money. I'm going to phone the paper."

"No," his mother and sister said in unison. "You need legal advice first," his sister continued. "If this isn't true, you need to sue."

"Sis, what d'you mean *if*? Of course it's not true!"

"It says they'll name their source and have more revelations on Sunday. What more can they have?"

"I don't know," Iestyn said. "But this is a bloody disaster."

* * * *

The press arrived at lunchtime, just as Rhian left. She drove through them as their flashbulbs went off and questions were shouted at her car, asking her about Iestyn and who she was to him. Iestyn found it impossible to stay still. He paced the floor in front of the window like a caged animal, occasionally peeking through the net curtains, worried in case reporters invaded the drive trying to get a better picture. The local news talked about more revelations and there was a discussion about how this story could affect the big game, which had suddenly become one of the most important in the history of Welsh rugby. He wanted to take to his bed and pull the duvet over his head but it appeared as if the whole country was waiting for him to speak, to give his side, and, at times, he was tempted.

The phone rang non-stop. He wanted to take it off the hook, but his mother insisted it might be family calling, so they waited until the message had been left before listening. At seven, it rang again. Iestyn listened for yet another huge offer to print his side of the story.

"Iessie, it's me. Call me back."

Iestyn dashed to the phone. Surely this meant that Dan knew what had happened. His fingers shook as he pressed the numbers. When Dan said his name, Iestyn thought he'd never been so pleased to hear someone speak in his whole life.

"It's me. It's so good to hear you," he said. "Everyone else has been trying to help. Matt and Julie have offered to put me up. Even Gareth has emerged from underneath a soil pipe, but the only person I wanted to talk to was you." He realized he was gabbling and also that Dan hadn't said anything.

"Dan, are you all right? Did they tell you what's happened?"

"Someone at the hotel left today's paper in my bedroom. I got to it before Mac." His voice sounded cold and distant.

"Dan, I know it's not great and most of what they've hinted at isn't true. You know that. Once the game is over, we can sort this out, surely?" Iestyn heard the sharp intake of breath and Dan's next words cut through him like a knife.

"I'm not playing tomorrow. The coaches have decided there'll be too much pressure on me to do my job and that the English crowd may be less than supportive. They're going to say my shoulder is still causing me problems, though no one will believe that. They'll think I'm running scared and have something to hide. I can't win either way. I've been told to tell you not to speak to the press. They didn't even want me to speak to you with all that stuff about phone tapping going on."

Iestyn didn't know how to react. He knew Dan would be devastated. If Wales won, he might not even be allowed to celebrate with the team and lift the trophy. Somehow everything had gone wrong. His mother looked at him from across the room, concern etched in every feature of her face.

"I'm so sorry, Dan. Couldn't you persuade them to change their minds? You don't deserve this."

"No, I don't," Dan replied curtly.

"I don't either," Iestyn said quietly. "Those things they've printed are nonsense."

"So you've never…?"

"No! For fuck's sake, Dan. What? You think I get off on hitting people? You know me better than that. I don't do that sort of thing. The kinkiest I've ever got is a bit of bondage. You were the one who told me you'd worn a lace corset and stockings and got off on it!"

"Iestyn, just say nothing—and especially not that!"

Iestyn heard the worry in Dan's voice.

"I need some time. I'm not used to this either. I'd been with Aron for so long we didn't get this sort of publicity."

Iestyn stiffened at the mention of Dan's ex-partner. He couldn't help himself.

"Ah, the amazing Aron Roberts, who loved you so much he buggered off to America and got himself a brand new boyfriend!" He stopped. "I'm sorry, Dan. I know you're hurt about tomorrow, but it's not my fault," he pleaded. This was all going wrong. He'd hoped that Dan would be sympathetic and supportive but this coldness was reaching right through to Iestyn's bones to his very core.

"Look, Iestyn, I've got to go. I'll talk to you on Sunday."

The phone clicked off.

"I gather that didn't go too well," his mother said.

"No, it didn't," he said simply. "They've dropped him from the team for tomorrow. Mam, if Wales lose, the whole country will blame me, and I've no idea what they're going to print on Sunday."

She put an arm around him and he leaned his head on her shoulder.

"Oh, Iessie, let's face it. You've only known him a few months. Perhaps it's best to get out before you're in too deep. It's not like you've declared undying love to each other, is it? It's going to be very hard for him to cope with this."

"It's going to be hard for me too, Mam. He's not the only one to have his job taken away from him. They could suspend me officially, Mam. The governors are meeting to discuss my future and that's without Sunday's news. I don't know what the hell I'm going to do and now it seems like it may all have been for nothing anyway. I'm sorry, but everything is just so fucked up and I don't know what to do about it."

Chapter Twenty-Five

"I don't know why you split up with Aron in the first place," Mac said out of nowhere on the morning of the game. "There was never any of this while you two were together."

Dan looked up from where he sat staring out of the hotel window onto the grounds stretching northward. "There is the little matter of an ocean and half a continent between us," he answered. "And it was his choice, not mine. He said we'd outgrown each other and that our lives were too different. He also said we'd get bored of each other, as we hadn't been with anyone else. I think he meant he was bored with me, really. And now he's doing well in the US and has a new boyfriend, who looks like he should model Calvin Klein underwear for a living. I was trying to move on too. I like Iestyn — I like him a lot. He's funny and unassuming. He shares my passion for history and the arts." He saw Mac smirk. "Yes, I know I'm supposed to be just a thick rugby player but he never treated me like that, and he's bloody good in bed!"

"According to the papers, he seems to like other things too and it looks like he won't just be bending you over to have his wicked way with you."

Heat warmed his face. Mac was his best friend but Dan couldn't help feeling embarrassed. "He says it's all nonsense. You spoke to Julie last night. Isn't she coming to the game today?"

"Yep," Mack replied smugly. "She's sitting in the players' family section for the first time now that Iestyn won't be with her. She says he hasn't been out of his mother's house or said anything to the press, who are still camped out on the doorstep. Look, at least you'll be at the match today and your injury gives you an excuse for not playing. If we win, you'll still be part of it and the press can't exactly get to you in the middle of the pitch, now, can they?"

Dan shrugged. "But I won't be leading you lot out and I won't be lifting the trophy first. It's not the same and it's absolutely ridiculous. All I want is someone to share my life with and this happens, despite the fact that I'm already out. No wonder all those footballers are practically living in Narnia. They'll never come out of the closet when this is what happens to me. Am I supposed to live like a celibate hermit for the rest of my life?" Full of despondency, he picked up his bag. "We'd better go. The coach has just pulled up downstairs."

No one from the team knew what to say to him on the journey. He put on his headphones and closed his eyes to try to block out anything else. He knew he'd hurt Iestyn and had taken out his anger on him unfairly. None of this was really his boyfriend's fault, unless the stories were true, of course. He wanted to believe him. He *did* believe him. To be honest, he wouldn't care if Iestyn had been a bit naughty in the past. It almost seemed fashionable these days, although such things didn't really interest him. He had no problem with a bit of playful spanking but that's about as far as he went. Iestyn made him feel good but he couldn't help resenting the fact that he would be hiding on the bench, just watching the others, when he should be leading his team to victory.

It didn't take long to get to Twickenham. There was a large press pack, much bigger than usual. He pulled up his hood and ignored the shouts.

"Is it true you're not playing, Dan?"

"How d'you feel about being dropped?"

"Is it true you like kinky sex?"

"Have you ever been beaten by your boyfriend?"

"Is it true there's a sex tape of the two of you?"

Mac placed his hand on his back, pushing Dan forward, and Dan stumbled a fraction. A little while later, sitting in the corner of the changing room, he felt lost. He couldn't bear it any longer and went outside. Leaning on the wall, he desperately tried to stop the tears from coming. This was supposed to have been the culmination of his dream, to captain Wales to the Grand Slam, to defeat England, and now he was just going to be a spectator. Now he knew why footballer Zac McKenzie, the Scottish team captain, had retired early and returned to Scotland when he'd been threatened with being outed. He'd felt sorry for the man who'd poured out his woes over far too much alcohol. Dan had thought that his being out already had changed things for the better and made it easier for sportsmen to be gay, but as he took his place with the rest of the team subs and coaches, he heard the taunts from some of the crowd and realized that perhaps he'd been living in cloud cuckoo land after all.

* * * *

Iestyn could hardly bear to watch but something compelled him to. This time he wouldn't be sitting in the pub with a pint. He hadn't been out of the house in days and was beginning to feel like a prisoner in his old home. The TV had reported the shocking news that Dan wasn't playing. No one seemed to believe the bad shoulder story. Iestyn heard his name mentioned over and over, though at least there was some support for Dan and himself. When it was announced that *Panorama* would once again be investigating homosexuality in sport and why there were so few openly gay sportsmen, he wondered if he and Dan might be asked to speak—if there was even a 'he and Dan' now.

The camera swept over the place where Dan was sitting, head bowed. Iestyn longed to hold him. Until he did, he couldn't even begin to imagine how they were going to get over this. He knew that whoever had given the information to the press was certainly no fan of Welsh rugby. Had the instigator planned to disrupt the game deliberately? He watched as the team was led out by the fullback Luke Hathaway. The crowd roared and somehow the Welsh managed to out-sing the English for the anthems, even though they were away from home.

All at once, it began, and the ball was kicked to start the game. No one would have called it pretty. It was tough with no quarter given. Mistakes cost both sides penalties and by half-time England were leading nine to six. The discussion at half-time again centered on Dan not being there and the effect that had to be having on morale in the Welsh team. When their scrum-half got sin-binned soon after the beginning of the second half, everyone believed it was only a matter of time, as England pulled further ahead to make it twelve to six. But somehow, Wales managed to pull the game level with four minutes to go.

Iestyn, like the rest of Wales, sat on the edge of his seat as their team threw everything they could at the English defense. They managed to string a few passes together and the ball ended up in Mac's hands on the twenty-second yard line. He ran, dodging two attempted tackles, to put the ball down in the corner and give Wales the lead. The crowd and commentators went mad. Iestyn could even hear the press outside cheering. With the conversion, the whistle was blown and Wales had won nineteen to twelve. Mac was held aloft and carried around the pitch. When the team put him down, he ran to where Dan was sitting and attempted to drag him onto the pitch to join in the celebrations. Reluctantly, Dan moved to join his friend in the line-up to receive their medals and the trophy. As they waited, the camera panned to where the family supporters stood. Iestyn saw Julie in the group standing and cheering as the team went up to collect their medals, until finally the cup was handed to Luke Hathaway and raised aloft. Gradually it was passed around the team until it reached Dan. Iestyn tried to lip-read what he said but, as the champagne flowed, Dan's grim expression didn't change.

"Come on. We won," he saw Mac say, but Dan just looked lost amongst the celebrations and completely out of place.

Later, Mac was asked about it in an interview.

"Dan was glad to be there," Mac said. "He was devastated not to be able to play but his shoulder wasn't recovered enough. I think I'm speaking on behalf of the whole team when I say that he inspired us to this victory and that his leadership got us to this position in the first place. The rugby world needs to remember the role he's played."

"What about the recent newspaper stories? Did you know about the new boyfriend? How serious are they?"

"I'm not going to comment on the stories in the papers and, yes, I have met Iestyn. Dan is my best friend and I'm pleased he's found someone to care about. They should just be left alone to get on with their lives."

Iestyn waited all night for Dan to call. He'd tried his phone several times but it was obviously switched off. In the end, unable to wait any longer, he phoned Julie. He could hardly hear her above the noise.

"Is he all right?" he asked.

"He went back to his room earlier. Mac couldn't persuade him to stay. Dan said he had a lot to think about and that he didn't feel right joining in the celebrations, despite what the others said. At least we won, Iessie — they won't be about to blame you now — but it's going to take a bit of time for him to get over this. He'll need you."

"I'm not sure about that, Julie. And I've no idea what'll be in the papers tomorrow."

* * * *

In his room, Dan stared at the ceiling. Sleep evaded him so he relived the match and tried to work out what on earth he was going to say to Iestyn when he saw him. The management had made their views about the situation very clear and had told him what to do. The last time he'd cried had been when his mother died but hot tears ran down his face and onto his pillow. Now he wondered if they'd ever stop.

* * * *

The headline read—*More Sexy Secrets of Gay Rugby Player's Boyfriend!*

Iestyn read the story and finally had a name to put to it. He recognized the announcement as the bloke he'd met at that party at university. Apparently now he was between jobs, as the paper put it. There was one piece of truth in the whole story—that he had given Iestyn a blow job in a bus shelter. He'd been drunk as a lord that night and it had seemed like a fun idea to do something so risqué but as for the rest... Iestyn shook his head as he read what he was supposed to have done. The article said he liked to tie up his partners and beat them before they had sex— that this turned him on. There were hints about him taking part in drink-and-drug-fueled gay orgies, and even though this was a long time ago, Iestyn knew that it wouldn't matter—mud sticks. The killer blow came when the author linked Iestyn to persuading him to take drugs that had ruined his life. He had no idea how to respond. Iestyn handed the paper to his mother, got up and went into the kitchen. He stared out of the window into the garden, quietly watching the birds eating the seeds his mother had put out that morning. He knew he needed to deny the article but he couldn't say anything before seeing Dan.

His phone beeped.

Meet me at Julie's at four today.

That was it. There were no declarations of love or concern for his welfare. Dan didn't ask how he was. Iestyn simply replied, 'OK'. He spent the rest of the day sitting in his father's chair, trying to work out what he was going to say to Dan. Tomorrow he was also going to school to talk about his future. He had believed that Dan was worth it, but now he wasn't so sure. He needed Dan to support him and believe him. He knew he must be hurting, but surely he'd get the captaincy back in the future.

"I'll ring you when I'm on my way back," he said to his mother. He pulled up his hood, opened the door and quickly got into his car. At least he was able to do this out of sight. The flashbulbs started as soon as he appeared at the gate. The crowd shouted questions but he drove through them as carefully and as swiftly as he could. He looked behind, grateful that no one appeared to be following him.

Forty minutes later, he pulled up at the back of Julie's house and let himself into the backyard. Julie smiled at him through the kitchen window before coming out and pulling him into a hug. Drawing back he said, "Is Dan here?"

"Yes, he's in the living room. He's seen the report, Iessie."

"It's not true but I don't know what to do about it. It's my word against his, although he won't find anyone else to back up the orgies story — or to say that I bought drugs from them, but it doesn't matter, really, as most people will think there's no smoke without fire."

"You knew him, then?" she asked.

"Yes, but not very well. The story about the bus stop is true but that's all. I've never taken drugs in my life. You do believe me, don't you?"

"Of course I do, Iessie, but Dan is hurting as well."

Iestyn cast her one last look before walking into the living room.

Chapter Twenty-Six

Dan stood looking out of the window when Iestyn entered the room. Only the rugby player's outline could be seen in the dim light coming from the table lamp. Iestyn's stomach lurched and his legs shook. He suddenly realized he had no idea what to say to the man he loved. Dan turned around and tried to smile but he made no attempt to move toward Iestyn, who also stood his ground.

"I'm sorry I took my being dropped as captain out on you," Dan began. "I know none of this is your fault."

"No," Iestyn said simply.

"And I know the stories in today's press aren't true. Somehow, I can't see you as some sort of Dom with me as your sub. I don't think anyone would believe that."

Iestyn snickered slightly at the irony of that statement. "I think there are a few things people would find hard to believe about the truth behind the ever-so-macho rugby player image you present to the world, but I'm fair game, I suppose. Heaven forbid your reputation should suffer in all this!" Iestyn tried to control the anger bubbling up to the surface. "You do realize I could lose my job over these stories? I've got a meeting before the governors tomorrow." Fighting a losing battle to keep his temper, he didn't even try to hide his hurt and anger.

Dan sank onto the sofa. "Oh, Iessie, I'm so sorry. I never imagined it would be this bad. I thought we'd just announce it and have a few photos taken and that interest would die away. Did you know this bloke who wrote the story?"

Iestyn retained his position next to the kitchen door. He didn't dare join Dan on the sofa. "Only briefly. We met at a party. I got a bit pissed and allowed him to give me a blow job in a bus stop. I thought I was being ever so risqué. He offered me drugs but I wouldn't take them. At that time, I already knew I wanted to teach. It's all I have ever wanted to do and I wasn't going to risk getting caught doing something that stupid. That's never been me anyway. I like being in control too much to take something. I haven't ever drunk that much at a party since. Well, not enough to do something that foolish and have to be told about it in the morning."

"The management wants me to finish with you. It's the drugs angle they're worried about—not that we're in a relationship. Even if it isn't true—which I know it isn't—they think all the negative publicity hasn't done me any good. I feel like I'm being torn in two, Iessie. I've worked so hard to achieve acceptance in this sport. I'm a role model, so I've got to be squeaky clean and so has my boyfriend. Please try to understand."

Iestyn swallowed, his mouth completely dry, and he clutched the back of a nearby chair to steady himself. This was it, then. "So you're finishing with me? You do realize everyone will think you believe the stories?" Iestyn couldn't believe how quickly things had changed between them. He'd thought that Dan loved him, but it appeared that love wasn't strong enough to fight for.

"Don't worry. I'll tell them none of it is true," Dan assured him. "Graeme's got a statement ready for the press. He needs to know what you're going to tell them."

"So we've come to this, have we? I thought we were building something together but obviously, I was wrong. I feel sorry for you not being able to live an ordinary life. You can tell Graeme that I'll tell the press the truth and hope they will leave us alone." His voice was shaking as well now. Tears pricked his eyes, but he wouldn't allow them to flow. He cleared his throat. "You'd better go."

"I don't know what to say. I did have feelings for you — do have feelings. I'm sorry I've done this to you and your family but you're better off without me. Find someone ordinary, Iestyn. Whoever that person is will be lucky to get someone as special as you are. Hopefully the press will leave you alone now. I'll contact the school and tell them it's all nonsense. Some of the lads are going there to coach in a couple of weeks. You won't lose your job. I promise."

"That's big of you. I'd tell you where to stick your help but I need it, so I won't. I don't know how we ended up like this. The world is a strange place that treats its stars like this, just because they like cock, not pussy. Sport really is in the Dark Ages, so I guess this means you'll have to go back to looking in closets to find someone to love."

Dan shrugged, got up and moved toward Iestyn.

"Can I give you one last hug?" he asked, reaching out.

Every part of Iestyn's body screamed out for that contact. Dan was only inches away from him but his pride and hurt stood in the way. "I don't think that would be a good idea. Please, just go. I'm sure Julie will hug me if I ask nicely." Iestyn took a step back. "I'll say goodbye for you."

Dan trudged to the front door then turned to face him. His whole body seemed smaller. He hugged himself as if he was trying to stop himself falling apart. He cleared his throat as a single tear escaped and rolled down his cheek. "It was good, Iessie. It was so nearly everything I ever wanted. I want you to know that. You're a very special person."

"Yeah, but just not special enough," Iestyn replied. "Not special *enough*." He watched as Dan closed the front door behind him then sank onto the sofa. He let the tears come until Julie slipped her arms around him.

"Let it all out," she said.

He sobbed into her shoulder, his whole body shaking. He wasn't sure he would ever stop.

"Perhaps it's for the best," Julie said a little while later.

"Best for him maybe, because he won't be embarrassed anymore. I suppose it was good I found out now, not when I'd *really* fallen for him." He wasn't sure who he was trying to kid.

"Well, if you didn't love him, you just have to put it down to experience, as your dad would have said."

Iestyn turned to face her. "But that's just it, isn't it? No one seems to realize that I do love him—so much. I wanted him to stand up for me, but he didn't, and now I'm left with nothing but a nice set of photos and some lovely memories of our brief time together. How the hell will I find someone else when all I'll do is compare the person with him?"

"I don't know, Iessie, but for now, you need to work out what you're going to say to the press then the governors tomorrow. After that, you just have to get on with your life and forget him. I know that sounds harsh but there's no point in ignoring facts, is there?"

"No, I suppose not. I'm going to go to Mam's and write something. I'm sure they'll still all be there." He hugged Julie again. "Just don't let this split you and Mac up. He makes you happy, I can see that."

"Me and Mac are doing fine. Don't worry about us. I'll make a brew. There's nothing like tea to put things into perspective."

Iestyn watched her head to the kitchen, doubtful that he'd ever feel better again.

* * * *

A few hours later, Iestyn found himself in front of the press at his mother's front gate. When the flashbulbs stopped, he took out the speech he'd written.

"Good evening, everyone. I have a statement for you. As you have discovered, my name is Iestyn Jones. Until last week, I was just a teacher in a comprehensive school doing my job pretty well. Now I'm not even sure I have a job thanks to the unfair and untrue stories that have been written about me in the newspapers. A few months ago, I met Dan Morgan and we started a relationship. When I met him, I had no idea who he was. I'd never really been interested in rugby beyond being happy whenever Wales won. Suddenly, I found myself going out with the most eligible gay sportsman in Britain, a man brave enough to admit his sexuality, despite the reluctance of others in professional sports to do the same.

"Dan was everything I ever could have wanted in a boyfriend, both intelligent and handsome. We'd intended to go public after the Six Nations but someone, who no doubt wanted to affect Wales' game against England, leaked a photograph, which led to the lies that have been printed about me. And, with the exception of the incident in the bus stop, which can be put down to student drunkenness, everything that this person has told you is a lie. Although I can't prove it, I do know that no one else will corroborate his story.

"I have never taken illegal drugs in my life, not even when I was a student. I always knew I wanted to teach and there was no way I was ever going to jeopardize that. I love my job and I hope to keep it. However, I do have to tell you that my relationship with Dan Morgan is over. I cannot live with this level of scrutiny in my life. Perhaps I was naïve even to think we could be like any other couple. Now I would ask you to leave my family and me alone and let me regain the ordinary life I once had. I believe a statement will be made by Dan Morgan in the near future.

"Thank you. I will not be answering any questions."

The shouts followed him back into the house, where his mother waited to enfold him in her arms. They watched as the crowd finally began to move away.

Iestyn returned home once the horde had dispersed. His house seemed dark and lonely and he found himself wishing he had a pet. He sat on the sofa and looked around the living space. His gaze alighted on the photo he'd taken of himself and Dan on his mobile as they'd laughed on the bed, cuddled together for warmth in that luxury hut. He got up, shoved it into a drawer then dragged himself upstairs to bed.

He didn't sleep.

* * * *

Dan issued his statement on Monday morning. It was similar to the one Iestyn had read to the crowd at his mother's. Dan did at least say that he didn't believe any of the reports in the papers and that he thought the reporter should have investigated the veracity of his sources. Iestyn agreed with him.

His sister rang. "So it's all over then," she said.

"Yep, that was my fifteen minutes of fame," Iestyn replied. "Now all I've got to do is face the governors at work and try to keep my job. Then, if I manage to do that, face the kids, so nothing much."

"Oh, Iessie, you really liked him, didn't you? I'm so sorry. Why don't you come over and have dinner with us tonight? Playing doting uncle will take your mind off things and we don't see you enough."

"Yeah, I'd like that. But if it's bad news, I might just stay home and stew. I'll let you know, okay, sis?"

* * * *

A few hours later, Iestyn stood outside the meeting room and knocked on the door. He'd seen Neil briefly, who had told him not to worry, which of course made him worry even more, like the football manager told that he had the full confidence of the board only to be sacked soon afterward. He pushed open the door. Four governors and Neil were sitting around the table.

"Ah, Iestyn, I think you know everyone here. Take a seat. Now, gentlemen, shall we begin?"

Chapter Twenty-Seven

Four months later

"How long have you known about this?" Iestyn said, slamming the newspaper cutting down on the keyboard.

Julie looked up at him. "A while, but..."

"No buts, Julie. You're supposed to be my best friend but there you are with them stood next to you and Mac. You should have told me they were back together!"

"Why? Why would you be bothered that his ex is back? I didn't think you'd be interested. After all, you and Dan split up months ago and you were the one who said it was for the best."

"That was different. Look at them, Julie. They look so at ease with each other and I bet no one's going to be writing stories about him that will nearly cost him his job. Anyway, I thought he was working in the US and had a new boyfriend."

"He decided to set up his own company over here," she explained.

"So are they back together properly? Is he living with Dan?"

"I think they're seeing each other again but Mac says Dan doesn't want to rush back into things, so they're just dating again at the moment. Still, I think it's only a matter of time. Aron seems really nice. You'd like him."

"So they're fucking, then," Iestyn snarled, looking around, wanting to find something to punch. He realized he was as jealous as hell and that came as a bit of a surprise to him.

"I wouldn't know about that, but if you really want to know, I could ask Mac to ask him."

"No," Iestyn said emphatically. "It's all right." He tried to get a hold of himself and his temper. The tension in his body subsided and he inhaled and exhaled several times in an effort to regain control over his emotions. "I don't really want to know," he lied. "I'm sorry. I shouldn't have shouted at you. It was just a surprise to see them with you and Mac. That's a nice dress you're wearing, by the way." It was then that he finally noticed what Julie had been attempting to show him since he'd stormed in.

"Bloody hell, that's an engagement ring you're wearing, isn't it?"

"Finally, he gets his head out of his own arse and notices," she replied in an exasperated tone. "Mac asked me yesterday and I said yes." She stopped for a moment and smiled. "There's more. I'm pregnant. So we're not going to wait for very long."

"What! Bloody hell! You don't believe in doing things by halves, do you? Oh, my God, Julie, you're having a baby!" He grabbed her and hugged her tightly.

"We're keeping it quiet for a while so don't say anything, all right? I haven't told any of the others yet. Kate and Sian are so bound up with themselves and Matt is such a blabbermouth. No doubt he'd make some crass comment anyway. I'm not due until January next year. I'll tell Neil in a couple of weeks, before we finish for the summer holidays. We're hoping they'll have a slot so we can get married then. I want you there. In fact, I want you to give me away. You're my oldest friend, Iessie, and as Dad is no longer with us, I've no one else. It's either that or you're my chief bridesmaid. D'you fancy wearing a dress?"

Iestyn's emotions ran away with him again. Overwhelmed by her request, he said, "Anything for you, my angel, and I would be honored to give you away. Well, at least something good has come out of the debacle known as my love life." He stopped for a moment. "Shit, they're going to be there, aren't they? And I'm going to be going on my own." He sat on the desk.

"You might meet someone by then," Julie replied encouragingly. "What about that bloke Gareth was on about? You know the bloke whose central heating system he replaced. He seemed interested when Gareth told him about his good-looking gay friend. The thing is that Dan will be Mac's best man so you'll have to talk to him."

"Oh, well, I'm sure I'll manage but I'll pass on a blind date with Gareth's gay customer. I'd better get going."

* * * *

At break, Iestyn looked at the online news of the Welsh Sports Awards Ceremony. The Welsh team had won Team of the Year and this time Dan had received the trophy. He was pictured shaking hands with Gareth Edwards, the great Welsh scrum half of the 1970s. Iestyn had tried not to think about Dan over the previous four months but he had to admit that Dan had come through for him with the school board, even though, in the end, it hadn't helped.

At first, the governors had suspended Iestyn, despite Neil's and the union's support. However, the investigation carried out by *Panorama* had shown that the report about Iestyn's past was a catalog of lies fueled by the need for Danny Phillips to get money to support his habit. This had finally been admitted by the papers and an apology had been printed a couple of weeks later. His experience became part of the wider story about press intrusion into the private lives of individuals. There was also an out-of-court settlement, which had allowed Iestyn to pay off his mortgage. He'd returned to work with his head held high.

Strangely, he got more sympathy than comments when the kids found that his romance with Dan Morgan was over. He tried to bury himself in his work, thinking up new and inventive ways to engage the kids. Often, he'd worked himself to the point of exhaustion to make sure he was too tired to think about anything else but work.

During the weekends, he'd spent more time with his family, especially his niece and nephews. As the weather improved, he'd begun to take the twins out to museums and parks and also to the beach going as far as Longleat.

On Friday nights, he went out with the usual crowd. Kate and Sian were now out as a couple and Iestyn found himself looking at their ease with each other in public with envy, especially when they touched each other if one was going to the bar or the toilet—those little touches that he'd never been allowed to have with Dan, and certainly not in public.

* * * *

"I see your old boyfriend was out on the town with our Julie," Gareth said the next Friday as tactfully as ever. "Is he back with his ex, then?"

Iestyn sighed and swallowed more beer. "It would appear so," he confirmed grudgingly.

"You must be gutted," Gareth continued.

Somehow, Gareth always seemed to say what the others only thought. Even Matt had said nothing.

"He's a bit different to you, isn't he?" Gareth continued. "I mean, physically. Nothing personal, but I couldn't see why Dan went out with you in the first place. Apparently, this bloke is some sort of genius and likely to be on his way to being a self-made millionaire soon, and let's face it, someone built like Dan Morgan would go for someone like this Aron."

Now Iestyn couldn't help himself. "So, are you saying Dan is a money-grabber? He's paid a decent wage and you haven't seen where he lives." Iestyn hesitated before his curiosity got the better of him. "And not only that, but you think he should have a type? I'm intrigued. What makes Aron Roberts a better fit than me, then?" He couldn't help laughing when he saw their stunned faces. "Go on," he goaded.

Never one to cut his losses and run, Gareth continued his explanation. "Well, Dan is a big, fit bloke, isn't he? And you're not exactly small, especially considering you've put on more weight lately."

Iestyn attempted to pull his stomach in. He knew he'd been comfort eating and drinking, and there'd been far too many takeaways late at night. He decided he needed to do something about that if he was going to give Julie away and get into a morning suit.

"Gareth!" Julie said.

"What? It's true and, well, this Aron is smaller, leaner and more likely to let Dan... Well, you know. Do I have to spell it out to you?"

Now Iestyn did smile. "So, if I'm right, what you're saying is Dan must be a total top, because he's such a big bloke, and because Aron is smaller, he must be a bottom. You do realize it doesn't work like that, don't you? Some men don't fuck at all and some are happy switching." Iestyn laughed to himself. "I can't believe I'm trying to educate someone about gay sex!"

"So," Matt interrupted. "Dan isn't a top, then." He raised his eyebrows suggestively and smirked before drinking his beer.

Iestyn kept his eyes down before replying, "Not entirely."

The others looked at each other, then one by one they began laughing. Gareth slapped Iestyn on the back. In the end, even Iestyn had to smile and reality hit him. In a month or so, he'd be in the same room with Dan. He knew what Dan needed in bed and he suspected it wasn't what Aron Roberts was prepared to offer him. All at once he knew what he wanted—he wanted Dan back—and somehow he was going to do that. But he was going to go a step further. He was going to get Dan Morgan to *want* him back.

Chapter Twenty-Eight

Iestyn sat at the restaurant's bar wishing he hadn't agreed to this date after all. In the end, it had been easier to give in rather than listen to Gareth saying how hot this guy was and that he'd totally do him if that was his thing, not to mention Matt telling Iestyn that he needed to get back on the horse all the time. In the end, Julie had sat him down and given him a good talking to.

"It's been months, Iestyn, and you need to see if there is anyone else out there worth looking at. You wanted to split with Dan, didn't you? He let you down, so there's no point in mooning over him anymore, is there? And this guy is supposed to be totally hot."

So, here he was, vodka tonic in hand, perched on a stool, trying to look cool and checking out every person who came through the door. He was trying to forget that the last first date he'd had was with Dan. The next person through the door came in by himself and scanned the room. Iestyn held his breath as he looked at the walking cliché. Shit! If this guy really was a firefighter he hoped the local brigade had done one of those naked calendars for charity, because Gareth had not been lying.

The man wore a black suit and a white shirt, left open at the neck. His short hair boasted gray in a most distinguished way. He reminded him of an actor he couldn't quite put a name to. No doubt it would come back to him at some point. Iestyn thought his date was probably older than he was but it was hard to tell, and he seemed to be about the same height. Then he smiled. Wow! Iestyn instinctively covered his groin. Well, his body appeared interested. Mr Handsome walked toward him and held out his hand.

"You must be Iestyn," he said. "I'm Jake, Jake Williams."

"Yes, I'm Iestyn. How did you know it was me?"

"Gareth gave me a pretty good description. Can I get you another drink?"

"Yes, a vodka tonic, please." The waiter signaled to Iestyn. "I think our table is ready."

"Great, I'm starving. It's been a long day. Did you see the news about the fire in a vegetable warehouse this morning? We had to call in engines from all over the place to get it under control. I swear I've washed five times and I can still smell baked potatoes." He leaned toward Iestyn. "You can't smell it, can you?"

Iestyn obligingly sniffed the other man's neck and thought that it was a good ploy. "No, you smell pretty good to me. Calvin Klein, isn't it?"

"Yes, good call. Have you been to this place before?" he asked. "I've never had Turkish food. It seems kind of familiar as well."

They sat at their table in the window. The restaurant gave a good view into Cardiff Bay. "Do you watch

Doctor Who? This was the place they used in one of the episodes."

"Of course! I should have known, as I've watched every episode. You often see them filming around here."

Iestyn breathed a sigh of relief, shifted in his seat and fiddled with his glasses. "Sorry, I always worry about letting my inner geek show. You're right. A lot of *Doctor Who* and *Torchwood* is filmed around here."

Jake flashed his gorgeous smile once more. Iestyn realized he was staring. Heat flushed through his face and he hastily looked down at the table in an effort to restore his composure. A finger lifted his chin. There was that smile again. Iestyn glanced in several directions but no one else had seemed to notice.

"Don't worry," Jake said, his deep blue eyes twinkling more than the sky on a clear summer's night. "I have to admit I'm a big fan myself. I get a lot of stick at work for being gay *and* a sci-fi fan. I daren't tell them about my love for *Merlin* as well. My sister bought me the calendar and I have to keep it in my bedroom so none of the other guys see it if they come round!" He winked as he spoke. "Of course, that's the only reason I'd keep pictures of Knights of the Round Table in my bedroom!"

Iestyn laughed. "You know the shrine for Ianto Jones is just below here? It should be light enough for us to see it when we leave. Even though I've lived in Cardiff all this time, I've never actually been," he said.

"Looking at the menu, I'll need a walk after this, so perhaps we can go for a stroll around the Bay?"

Iestyn found himself relaxing as they made their orders and talked more about the TV and film they liked. Jake fixed him with a wicked grin. "Can I help it if I'm a bit of a sucker for the dark, brooding types who need fixing?" Iestyn smirked.

"I can see I'm going to have trouble with you, if that's your level of innuendo." Jake put his hand briefly on Iestyn's as someone walked past. The couple took their seats at a table behind Iestyn as their food arrived.

"This steak is really good," Jake said a few minutes later. "I wonder what herbs they put on it. What's yours called again?"

"Meyvali Tavuk," Iestyn replied. "It's chicken with fruit and it's really good."

Jake put his cutlery down for a moment. "Don't look around but there's a guy over there that keeps staring over here, and he doesn't look friendly."

"He could be an ex pupil," Iestyn mused, "although I usually don't have any problems that way."

"Could be he didn't know you were gay and he's surprised seeing you out with another man."

"No, I've always been out at work. I'll go to the loo when I've finished this and see if I recognize him."

"Have you always been out? In your job I guess that can be a problem."

"I decided I wasn't going to keep it a secret. Things have improved for teachers generally, but yes, it can still cause problems." Iestyn wondered whether to tell Jake what had happened with Dan but for now, he kept it to himself. "What about you? I imagine being a gay firefighter can have its drawbacks."

"You could say that. It hasn't always been easy, and there are still some homophobes in the service, but my crew is pretty tight. We know we have to have each other's backs, so we had a big chat and thrashed some things out over a lot of booze and things have been okay since. We even have a woman on our team we're so progressive! You know, he's staring again."

"I'll go now," Iestyn said. He recognized the man as soon as he got up but had no idea whether he should say anything to him, as he'd only met him once. Their gazes locked but Iestyn hurried into the toilet. When he came back, he sat as quickly as he could, without looking.

"Well, who is he? You must be feeling his eyes boring into your back and if looks could kill you'd be dead."

"His name is Luke Hathaway. I guess you're not a rugby fan."

"No, I'm more of a footie fan," Jake explained.

"He plays fullback for Glamorgan Giants and Wales. That's his wife with him, I think."

"So come on, is he a closet gay you had a one-night stand with and he's afraid you'll tell his wife, or what?"

"Definitely or what. I met him once at a party being hosted by my ex-boyfriend."

"Ah, is this the mystery man Gareth wouldn't tell me about? The one who broke your heart?"

Iestyn took a deep breath. "Yes, his name is Dan Morgan. I don't know if that means anything to you. He's the only current out gay rugby player and he was captain of Wales before they dropped him for the last match in the Six Nations." Iestyn watched as the cogs turned in Jake's brain.

"Oh, my God, you're him, aren't you? The one the stories were about in the papers? Shit! They wrote some really cruel stuff about you then had to apologize, didn't they? That must have been tough."

"Tough is one word for it. Dan lost the captaincy because of those stories, and I was suspended from work. We ended up splitting over it. He couldn't be associated with me since he's a role model, and I couldn't face living in the limelight. I thought it was best at the time. I imagine Luke is nursing a little anger as he is a close friend of Dan's and, although he did get the captaincy, there was a lot in the papers about how it should have been Dan lifting the trophy. It was a bad few weeks in my life."

Iestyn looked out over the Bay toward the Cardiff Eye. The sun was beginning to go down over the Channel, creating lovely colors in the water. Although it was a beautiful, warm evening, Iestyn's head was back in that dreadful time in March. He had to get his emotions under control.

"I guess you liked him a lot. And from the look on your face, you still do," Jake said, putting his hand once again on Iestyn's.

"I thought we had something special but, when push came to shove, it went wrong and now he's back with his ex. I have to go to a wedding over the summer where Dan is going to be the best man and I'm giving away the bride, who is my best friend. She met her husband-to-be through Dan. He's Dan's best friend. I've no idea how I'm going to cope with seeing him in the flesh again."

"Look," Jake said. "D'you wanna get out of here? I can live without the coffee. I expect there's somewhere we could get one out there. "

Iestyn bought coffee from a little café on their way down to the place where people had left memorials to the fictional character Ianto Jones. They spent a few minutes looking at the myriad of messages and drawings. Iestyn had to admit that it was impressive.

"I'm surprised they haven't taken this down," Jake said, laughing. "All that paper must be a fire hazard! Got to admit, though, he was a handsome bastard."

"That's what his brother-in-law called him," Iestyn replied, surprised that Jake had used that exact phrase.

Jake winked. "I know. I couldn't believe it when they killed him."

"You bastard, you *are* a fan, aren't you?" Iestyn punched his arm.

"Come on, what did you expect? It's filmed in Cardiff and has the omnisexual Captain Jack Harkness as the lead character. I have all the box sets and I'm word perfect on many scenes."

"Bloody hell, you'll be telling me you read slash fanfiction next!"

Jake looked at the floor and shuffled from foot to foot. "I may have read one or two stories," he admitted, grinning. He gazed out across the water. "It's nice here, isn't it?"

They watched as the sun set, sending tendrils of red and orange across the sky and sea. The lights of Cardiff began coming on behind them. Steady numbers of people still appeared to look at the shrine.

"That's why they keep it," Iestyn said. "It's a tourist spot now." Just as he spoke, a group of girls appeared and added another message to the wall. "See what I mean? There would be an outcry if they removed it now. Come on. We've talked enough about me. What happened to split you up with your ex?"

"Simple, really. Too many hours working and not enough time spent together. There was also the complication that he wasn't truly out at work with everyone or his family. I'm not a full-time firefighter, I'm what you call retained, which means I get called out whenever there's a shout. The rest of the time, I'm a health and safety advisor in the chemical industry. There are a few plants along the coast at Barry, so I mostly work there, but I travel all over the South Wales coast. I act as the expert in chemical fires and also help investigate what has caused them. It can be interesting work but the hours are a little uncertain. Michael mostly does traffic. It's how we met—at an accident on the M4 when a tanker overturned."

"How long were you together?" Iestyn asked.

"Eight years, on and off, then I suggested that he come out properly and we have a civil partnership. He just panicked and ran three months ago and I haven't heard from him since. I hear he's a mess, according to his best mate."

"You two really need to talk by the sound of it."

"Duh, you reckon? I could say the same about you and Dan. God, we're sad bastards, aren't we? Both sat here, watching the sun go down over the bay, next to a shrine to a fictional character from a show we're fans of, still loving the men we've split from."

"When you put it like that," Iestyn replied, smiling, "you may have a point. So what are we going to do about it?"

"How d'you think your guy would feel if you turned up to the wedding with me on your arm?"

"I've no idea but I suppose he might be a tad jealous. Only one way to find out if his getting back with Aron is serious or not and that's to test it. But that won't get you back with your Michael, will it? Is he the jealous type?"

"Usually he's as possessive as hell."

A somewhat dreamy look crossed Jake's face, causing Iestyn to laugh and wonder about handcuffs and their uses.

"Well, we'll have to see if we can make him jealous then, as long as he's not the sort to attack me with his truncheon!"

Both of them burst out laughing.

"Okay, a pact then." Iestyn pressed his coffee cup to Jake's. "To getting our men back — by fair means or foul!"

Chapter Twenty-Nine

Dan heard the alarm and reached out, trying to find the snooze button. He failed. He opened one eye experimentally and remembered that he'd deliberately moved the clock to the other side of the room so that he couldn't find the snooze button. Then he heard movement in the corridor and the door opening.

"You're up, then," Mac said.

Dan put his head under the pillow. They were going to the final fittings for their wedding outfits with Mac's brother and father. He dragged his legs around to sit on the edge of the bed when his phone beeped at him. He looked at it and sighed. July twenty-first, Iestyn's birthday. He imagined there would be some sort of party with his family or friends or both. He removed the reminder and padded to the bathroom. No doubt Iestyn's brother and sister would be there, too, with their families. Ben would have his phone glued to his fingers and might acknowledge that other people were there. He would be starting secondary school after the holidays. Dan wondered how much bigger the twins were now. They'd be at school full-time as well in September. He felt sorry for the teacher trying to tell the redheads apart. Megs would probably be talking in sentences now, as well as still dancing. They'd all be shouting over each other, arguing and telling stories about embarrassing events with Mary running around after them.

As he toweled his hair dry and tried to get it under control, he looked in the mirror. He'd been such a fool. He could be there today, embraced by all those people and part of a family, a family he'd longed for all his life.

"Coffee's up," Mac shouted. "Get a move on."

Dan got dressed in jeans and T-shirt then attempted to control his hair yet again and, as usual, gave up. Mac sat watching the news on morning TV when he wandered into the kitchen. Dan absent-mindedly poured himself some muesli, added sugar, then milk and sat at the table.

"You look like you've lost a pound and found a penny. What's the matter? Look, I know this is a pain but once we've got the fitting out of the way, we can go for a drink."

Dan looked up at his best friend. He was the only one he could say this to. "Today is Iestyn's birthday. He's thirty-five. I bet the whole family will be at his mum's. I was just thinking the kids will be all over him. Julie said he's been spending a lot of time with them, being good old Uncle Iessie. He's wonderful with kids and would make a great dad."

"You *both* would," Mac said deliberately. "Have you and Aron not thought about it? If others can do it, why not you?"

"He doesn't want to. He says I'm away too often on tour and that he'd end up having to be around for them. He doesn't want the responsibility, especially now he's trying to get the business set up. That's where he is at the moment—in Strasbourg—talking to people about this new bit of technology he's developed. He's tried to explain it to me but I don't get what it's supposed to do. I've hardly seen him over the last couple of weeks. He's not even sure he's going to make it to your wedding."

Mac moved to the table opposite his friend, seemingly determined to find out what was really going on in his head. "Are you and Aron okay? It's just that you don't seem to be very happy and after what you just said about Iestyn, I can't help wondering about you, buddy."

Dan stirred the muesli, moving it about in the bowl without purpose. "I don't know," he said. "We hardly talk at the moment and that's different for us. We've always been honest with each other, even if we didn't want to hear what the other one said, but he's so focused on his new company I haven't wanted to distract him. The thing is, I'm worried I've gone back with him because there's no story in it, and after what happened with Iestyn, you can't blame me for not wanting to get some other poor bastard involved with me and the nonsense that surrounds me."

"So you got back together, even though you're not sure it's what you want? You're twenty-four, Dan, and that's too early to settle for familiarity and safety. You're young, good-looking, and not without a few bob. You could be out fucking a different bloke every night."

"Yeah, until they sold their stories to the papers. With Aron and me, there's nothing to write about, not anymore, although there has been a little bit about him being back. It's easy to understand why other people keep being gay to themselves. You have to have a thick skin to survive in sport and the ability to ignore comments from the crowd, even when you'd just like to punch people in the face or dive in and kick them like that footballer did. The world just seems to be full of people willing to sell their souls for a fast buck. Aron isn't news, so it's easier and I do love him, but..."

"You don't fuck like rabbits anymore?" Mac interrupted.

"We hardly do anything at all and if we do, it's just a quick in and out." Dan stared into space for a moment. There was no way he was going to explain to Mac that he missed being on the bottom or that he missed Iestyn's strength and size or the way they'd laughed together and talked about everything—books, films, TV. He remembered them watching *Spartacus* and giving every gladiator a mark out of ten based on criteria they'd established. Iestyn had even brought some Roman artefacts home and they'd planned to re-enact a few special scenes—but their split had stopped that.

"This may be getting a bit too detailed for me now," Mac admitted, smiling. "Come on, we'll go and get these outfits fitted and then get pissed."

* * * *

Iestyn had been woken that morning by the parcel postman knocking on the door. He'd stumbled downstairs, discovered that the postman was gay if the way he'd looked him up and down said anything then after he'd left, Iestyn excitedly opened the parcel. This was his birthday present to himself and would complete his set of *Avengers* models. Now that he had Thor and Loki, he had a full set of the characters who'd gathered together in the recent film. He took them through to the cabinet in the front room and placed them next to Captain America, Iron Man and The Incredible Hulk. The phone rang.

"Iestyn, it's me. Just checking when you'll get here."

"Hi, Mam. I'll be over before lunchtime, all right?"

"Perfect. Everyone will be here by then."

"Oh, good. I'm really looking forward to having the whole family together." His mother sighed heavily.

"I know, Mam. It'll be strange with Dad not being there. I'll see you soon and I'll pick up the drink supplies on my way."

He put the phone down and looked at the photograph of his parents on the mantelpiece. This would be his first birthday without the steady presence of his father and the first time the whole family, including his brother-in-law Gareth, had really been together since the funeral. He was the baby of the family and it was the weekend, so everyone could come. In some ways, he was dreading it as well as looking forward to it.

* * * *

He found his mother and sister in the kitchen when he arrived. Through the window, he saw Huw, Gareth and the twins kicking a football around.

"Susan is upstairs with Megs," Rhian explained.

Iestyn went back into the living room. Ben, sat on the sofa, nodded to acknowledge his presence before returning to his game. Iestyn thought he'd grown again and was likely to be as tall as his own father, who was well over six feet.

He felt Megs before he saw her wrap her small arms around his legs.

"Uncle Iessie, Uncle Iessie, look."

"You'll have to let me go, sweetheart, or I'm going to fall over."

The arms withdrew, and he turned to see Gareth knelt next to his niece.

Iestyn joined him on his knees. "So what is it you want to show me, Megs?"

"Puppy," she said, pointing at Gareth.

Iestyn noticed the small white bundle of fur in Gareth's arms and the frown on his sister-in-law's face. "You got a dog," he said. "I thought you were dead set against it."

The twins came in and started to smooth the puppy.

"Mummy got us a puppy, Uncle Iestyn. He's called Bobby," Lloyd explained.

"We've got to learn how to look after him and he's going to keep Mummy company when we go to school all day," Lewis continued.

Susan watched her daughter try to smooth the puppy with her cousins. "Trouble is now Megs wants one but we can't, as we're out all day."

"I've got an idea," Iestyn said. "I'll just go and see if I can find it." He scooted upstairs, opened the door to the attic and pulled down the ladder. Somewhere in that space he expected to find what he was looking for and hoped it would be something that might keep Megs amused. The attic was stuffed with things, but his father, always extremely organized, had kept the children's things to one side. Really, they needed to have a thorough look at what was there.

It didn't take long to find what he was looking for. He smiled—the poor thing was a bit bent but he'd dragged it everywhere. White with brown spots and a red collar and lead, it was hard to tell what breed the toy dog was supposed to be. Megs would be able to pull it along and pet it. Susan would probably want to give it a wash first and check that it was safe.

Back downstairs, he found his niece licking the chocolate sauce off a spoon in the kitchen. "I thought this might be all right for her," he said to Susan who was sitting at the table. He carried the dog into the kitchen.

"My goodness," his mother said. "Where on earth did you find him?"

"Up in the attic. You know Dad. He had a place for everything and I was up there a little while ago and remembered that Spotty was still there."

His mother lifted Megs down from the work surface.

"Puppy," she said.

Iestyn gave her the lead and she tugged it happily around the kitchen then petted it. They watched as she took it into the garden.

"Thanks," Susan said. "That should help. We really couldn't have a puppy with me working. We were wondering about getting a cat but wanted Megs to be old enough not to annoy one." They watched as Megs pretended to walk the toy dog around the garden with the puppy dancing around as well.

Huw came into the kitchen. "Is that your old dog?" he asked. "You took that thing everywhere. We've got the barbie heated up, so Gareth and I are going to get started. The table and chairs are out there already, so it's present-opening time for the birthday boy here. My baby brother is thirty-five."

"And you're only five years from fifty," Iestyn replied. "And Rhian is forty next month, although she says she's staying at thirty-nine for now."

"Certainly am," Rhian said, coming into the room.

Mary looked at her children. "Your father would be so proud of the three of you," she said. "Come on, let's get this party started."

* * * *

The next couple of hours were spent eating, drinking and laughing. They told stories, mostly about their father and about Iestyn—who was trouble with being the youngest. No one mentioned what had happened with Dan but Iestyn found himself wishing he was there, just like Susan and Gareth were, in the bosom of a family who loved each other and enjoyed being together. His presents had been typical of his family. His mother had bought him a couple of T-shirts.

"How did you get these, Mum? They're signed." He held up the Captain America and Iron Man shirts.

"I have a friend in California who went to the Con and got them for you. I thought, knowing you, you'd frame them, so I bought you a couple of frames as well."

Huw and Susan bought him the latest *Doctor Who* releases on DVD and Rhian and Gareth got him the Owain Glyn Dwr book he'd bought for Dan.

"You haven't got it, have you?" Rhian asked, suddenly concerned.

"No, I haven't. Thanks everyone."

Megs was given a parcel and held it up. "My present, Uncle Iessie."

"Thanks, Megs." He took the parcel from her.

"It's from all the kids," Susan said. "We thought you could distract yourself from marking with it." He opened it to find a small red Dalek that would roam around his desk shouting 'Exterminate'. He set it going on the table, causing the puppy to bark at it excitedly. He switched it off again.

Rhian looked at the twins, who had begun to yawn. "Time for us to be off, I think. These two are dropping and I have something to finish for a client they need by Monday. These due diligence cases need thorough research to make sure the companies haven't employed someone with something to hide. Luckily, I think this one is going to be pretty straightforward."

Rhian and Iestyn scooped up a twin each and took them inside. Gareth grabbed the lead and Bobby followed on happily.

"I'll help you wash up, Mary," Susan said, gathering plates from the table. Megs sat on Huw's lap, going to sleep.

"Are you really all right?" Huw asked. "You know, after all that stuff with Dan. I know it's been a few months but we haven't really spoken and I am your big brother."

Iestyn smiled. "Oh, yeah, I remember how you loved to take care of me. Sit, shut up and eat the chocolate. And yes, I'm okay. I'm going to see him for the first time since…you know, at Julie's wedding."

"Are you worried you'll be a sad single while he's there back with his ex?"

"You know about that, then?"

"Yeah, I saw the pictures in the papers and Mam mentioned to me that you might be a bit fed up. The other guy's nothing like you, is he? He's a lot smaller and thinner than you."

"Thanks, bro, you're not the first person to point that out, and, for your information, I won't be a sad single at the wedding." Iestyn tried to look smug. "I'm taking a fireman as my date."

Huw looked at him. "What? You have a new man in your life? You kept that quiet and hey, I know something Rhian doesn't. She'll be so pissed off about that. So, come on, spill, Iessie. When did all this happen?"

Iestyn thought a moment then decided to be honest. He needed to talk to someone about what he'd planned. "His name is Jake Williams, and Gareth — you know, my friend the plumber — set us up on a blind date. He turned out to be drop-dead gorgeous. He's about ten years older than me, tall and looks good in a suit."

"And a fireman. Isn't that every gay man's wet dream?"

"Ha bloody ha! He's actually a retained fireman. His day job is as a health and safety officer for the chemical industry and, although we got on really well, he realized he's still madly in love with his ex, who is in the police and not really out."

"That must have been a bit of a punch in the gut. So how come he's going to the wedding, then?"

Iestyn could almost see the cogs turning behind his eyes.

"Oh, hang on. I get it. You've persuaded him to go to make Dan jealous, haven't you? Why the hell would he do that if he's still not over this copper? And I thought you were over Dan. For God's sake, are you serious? You really think being there with this Jake guy will show Dan what he's missing? I thought you were pissed off with him for letting you down after all the stuff in the papers. You're on really dodgy ground, Iessie. This could go so wrong and you could get hurt all over again. I thought he was back with his ex-partner, so why would he care that you're there with someone else?"

"I was pissed off with him, and in some ways I still am, but when I saw that photo of him with Aron, I realized I was jealous as hell and still want him. I love him, Huw. It doesn't matter how often I tell myself to get over it. I can't. I have to know one way or the other if there's any hope for us but I can't exactly go up to him and ask, can I? Hopefully, he'll say something to Mac, who'll tell Julie, who'll then tell me, and I'll know more about where I stand."

"And then what? You skip off happily ever after? Have you forgotten why you split in the first place?"

"No, of course not, but we won't be in the middle of the Six Nations this time and the papers ended up looking so stupid the last time that hopefully they'll leave us alone now. We were so good together, Huw, and I've never felt that way about anyone, ever. He wanted me and he had no desire to change me into something I'm not. He's also bloody good in bed and not what people expect him to be. I don't think he was happy with Aron in the end but it's easier for him— and safe. It's bloody hard being him, facing the abuse he gets from people in the crowd every match, not to mention some of the opposition players. Mac told me some things Dan has had to deal with, so it's no wonder rugby and football players don't come out.

"Well, on your head be it, little brother. I really hope this little plan of yours works out, and thanks for taking Ben for the next few days. You'll be lucky if you can prise him away from his games."

"Not going to even try. We have two days of tournament planned and I'm also going to teach him how to play chess properly."

"I'll drop him at nine tomorrow morning."

"I look forward to it. At least I'll get a couple of hours' lie-in, and it gave me an excuse not to go for my fitting. You know we're all in Scottish dress because of Mac, and Julie thought we'd look cute. I'm going to her wedding dress fitting on Wednesday. Kate and Sian are coming too then we're having lunch."

Huw laughed.

"Yeah, I know, very *Sex and the City* but hey, I'm gay, so I'm allowed."

When Susan came to the door, Huw got up, holding Megs in his arms.

"See you tomorrow, big bro, and thanks for listening."

"That's what big brothers are for." Huw put his spare arm around his brother. "Happy birthday, Iessie."

Chapter Thirty

"You've lost weight, Mr Jones. I'm having to tighten the buckles further than the original measurements suggested."

Iestyn turned and looked at himself in the mirror. The kilt skimmed his knees, revealing a little flesh above the hose, as the dresser had insisted on calling the socks. The shoes laced up over the socks in an intricate pattern. He was told there was a video online that would show him how to do that for himself. He knew he would need it. He ran his finger around the collar of the white shirt, hoping he could wear the bow tie more loosely on the day. It would look kind of cool just hung around his neck.

"Hands up, sir. Let's get this sporran around you. I'll need to pull this in, too. I have to say you really look the part. You can carry this much red with your coloring. At least you don't need anything out of the ordinary, unlike the best man. My goodness, he has a pair of shoulders, not to mention those thighs. My wife was quite envious that I'd been able to dress him."

Iestyn shut his eyes for a moment, remembering those thighs gripping him as he pushed into Dan's willing body, urging him on, but it wasn't really the time to get an erection, not whilst a man was fitting his sporran.

"Yes, I understand the best man is a rugby player," he said, trying to keep his voice in neutral.

"Welsh captain no less, despite the fact that he's gay." Iestyn wondered what was coming next.

"Good for him, I say. It's ridiculous that there aren't more gay people in sport willing to come out. Mind you, after what happened with his boyfriend, I'm not surprised."

Iestyn needed to head this conversation off at the pass. "Can we try the waistcoat and jacket now?"

"Certainly, sir." He held up the rest of the outfit.

Iestyn put his arms in and did up the buttons.

"There now, don't you look smart? I think the bride would like to see you before we pack the clothes away. Try not to lose any more weight in your shoulders, sir. It's more complicated if we have to take the jacket in."

Iestyn eased his way out of the changing room to the viewing area. Julie, Kate and Sian were sipping what looked like Buck's Fizz. From the way they were giggling, looking at catalogues, he didn't think it was their first. Just as well he was the designated driver today. Julie saw him first.

"Bloody hell, Iessie! You look gorgeous! You should wear that at the teaching awards. You'd certainly make an impression, and after all the work you've done this year, you really deserve to win."

"I think I'll just stick to the suit," he answered. "I'm sure I'm just there to make up the numbers."

"Don't be so hard on yourself." She paused for a moment, staring into the distance as if she was thinking of something. She shook her head. "Anyway, having five of you in kilts is going to be fabulous. I'm going to have matching tartan ribbons in my bouquet and Kate and Sian will have tartan sashes over their dresses. Luckily, cranberry is an in color this year and we've chosen the styles of our dresses already. Today we get to try them on for hopefully the final time. If they don't fit, we've two weeks to get them altered." She looked excitedly at them all. "I'm getting married in two weeks and this time I know I've made the right decision. I'm so glad you three are going to be there with me. Shall we go and try the dresses on, ladies?"

They got up.

As she went past Iestyn, she whispered, "Don't worry. Mine just has a dash of champagne but we may have to carry those two out. I wouldn't be surprised if they're the next people getting married, the way they are with each other."

For a few minutes, Iestyn stood just enjoying listening to his female friends chattering to one another.

"I can't remember the last time I got to dress up in a posh dress," Kate said. "I'm not sure it's me, really."

"You'll look lovely," Sian assured her. "And they've got little sleeves because neither of us wanted to wear one of those off the shoulder things."

"I haven't got anything to hold a strapless dress up with," Kate said.

"We can always get you some chicken fillets," Julie said. "Or you could borrow some of mine. At this rate, my boobs are going to be through the door before me. Good job its only two weeks to go and my dress gives me a bit of room."

"I love the design you chose. With all that lace, you're going to look stunning. The dress is really beautiful. Your red hair will look amazing as well. I wish mine wasn't so mousey but I refuse to get into dyeing it all the time. Kate, d'you think I should dye it just for the wedding? Yours is so long and dark."

Iestyn smiled at their talk as the assistant went in bringing the tartan sashes that would be worn around the waists of the dresses. A few minutes later, Kate and Sian stepped out into the bigger viewing area and twirled around.

"You two look wonderful," Iestyn said. Neither of them was very tall but they had very different shapes. Somehow, the dresses managed to suit both of them.

"I hope I can get up the aisle in these shoes," Kate said, looking at her feet. "Still, they do mean I reach a willowy five foot five."

"So where's the bride, then?" he asked.

At that moment, Julie stepped through the curtain. The dress she had chosen looked perfect with its lace sleeves and shoulders, lace that then covered the bodice and wide skirt that spread from below the bust line. On the day she'd have a bouquet and similar flowers and ribbons decorating her dark red hair. Iestyn got up and stretched out his hands to take hers. He turned her to look in the mirror.

"You will be the most beautiful bride," he said. "I will be so proud to walk you down that aisle. Mac is a very lucky man and I hope he appreciates that."

"He does," she said simply. "You are going to be all right on the day, aren't you? You know, with Dan and everything. This guy you're bringing?"

"He's called Jake," Iestyn reminded her.

"So do we get to meet Jake before the big day? Mac and the lads are going to Paris for his stag party at the weekend, so I'm just having our usual gang for my hen party at the pub then all back to my place. You could bring Jake then, couldn't you? I'd like to meet him. Gee says he's nice, and very good-looking."

"He is good-looking and he's nice as well. It's early days, as he's only recently broken up with his boyfriend, but I'll ask him if he feels like coming out for a drink. Of course, it depends on if he's working or not, and he could always be called out if there's an incident."

"Okay. We'd better get these dresses off. I see the assistant hovering, just in case we damage them. You are both all right with the dresses, aren't you? I think they look wonderful. If we'd had more time, Dan's friend Hayley said that she'd have designed something for us, but I think we've made great choices." She smiled to herself.

"What?" Kate asked.

"I was just thinking that at least I won't have to worry about the best man trying to get into the bridesmaids' knickers at my wedding."

"No," Iestyn agreed. "This must be one of the gayest weddings ever, which is amazing considering that it's a rugby player getting married. Is Mac's family all right with it?"

"Yeah, they've known Dan for ages. They've been really nice every time I've met them and they're made up that we're going to have a baby, as it's their first grandchild. His mum is already knitting like mad. I'm expecting lots of Fair Isle, as she's brilliant apparently, but I've said no pink. Chances are this little one will get the red hair gene that Mac dodged but that went to his brother, especially with my hair. I also found out what his real name is. You know he always insists on being Mac on every program."

"So come on, then. Spill the beans. It's not that terrible, is it?" Iestyn asked.

"His real name is Angus Gordon MacDonald."

Iestyn snickered. "I know I can't talk with my name, but that is bad. No wonder he keeps it quiet."

"Gordon is his grandfather's name and Angus is where the family came from in Scotland. It's like trying to work out your porn name from your first pet and the street you lived on when you were born. We'd share the same surname. I'd be Goldie Sinclair after my goldfish and you'd be…"

"Buffy Sinclair, after the dog we had when I was little. Both of them sound all right, actually. Come on, let's go and get some lunch. I'm totally starving and could demolish a family-size pizza on my own."

* * * *

When Friday night came, Iestyn was really nervous about introducing Jake to his friends. He knew they wouldn't expect him to be all lovey-dovey this quickly, but they had to appear interested in each other, and there was no doubt in his mind that Julie would do her version of the Spanish Inquisition. She'd already asked him a lot of questions when they'd been out to lunch with Kate and Sian. She would also try not to worry about what Mac and the others were up to in Paris and no doubt would be checking her phone every five minutes. Iestyn had tried to reassure her that Dan would take care of him.

She'd replied, "Duh, they're rugby players. Have you seen how much they can put away?"

Iestyn knew these men could drink. "Perhaps Dan'll take them to a gay club. At least they'll be safe there from women throwing themselves at them—or a stripper appearing."

He pulled up his black jeans, pleased that he could get into them once more. Letting loose his inner geek, which he knew that Jake would appreciate, he added a *Star Wars* T-shirt displaying the Millennium Falcon. The humid, sticky weather would make for a hot evening at the pub. He was looking forward to some cold beers to slake his thirst. His mouth was dry with nervous anticipation.

They were going to their usual watering hole, only a ten-minute walk from his house. He planned to meet Jake outside so they could go in together. He was there when Iestyn arrived, leaning nonchalantly against a silver-gray BMW. Jake had dressed in jeans and a shirt that showed that blue was *definitely* his color.

"You didn't bottle out, then," Iestyn said.

"No, I said I'd help, so here I am. How exactly do you want me to play this? I mean, I could be all over you," he said, pulling Iestyn into a hug. "Or I could just say it's early days every time you go to the bar, or the loo, and I get interrogated by your friends."

"Perhaps something in between, whatever that may be. I don't know, the occasional brush of hand on thigh would probably be all right. Julie will be the one who wants to find out all about you. Matt will want to know how you cope with being gay in the fire brigade and if you've ever had sex on top of an engine. Kate and Sian will ask you about art and politics, and Gee will buy you a pint and ask after your new central heating system, if he hasn't been called out."

Jake smiled as they headed for the door. "Well, I've never had any complaints about my plumbing in the past."

Iestyn looked at him as he opened the door. "No, I don't suppose you have," he said, raising an eyebrow. "Ready?"

"Ready—at least I hope I am."

The others were all sitting, drinks in front of them, in their usual place when Iestyn and Jake walked into the lounge bar of the pub. It was a place they'd been coming to on a Friday night for two years.

Gareth got up as they approached. "I didn't get anything in because I wasn't sure what you'd want to drink, Jake. I'm assuming the usual for you, Iestyn."

"Yeah, a pint for me, please. I need something cold. It's so sticky out that I won't be surprised if we have a storm. Jake, what d'you want?"

"Just a fizzy water for me. I'm not supposed to be on call, but you never know when there might be an emergency. Ice and lemon as well, please."

While Gareth got their drinks, they sat and Iestyn introduced Jake to the group.

"A fireman," Matt said. "Wow, you've finally hit the jackpot and scored every gay man's fantasy!"

Iestyn glared at him. "I've no idea why I put up with you," he said.

"My natural charm," Matt replied, grinning widely. "And obviously the fact that you've never got in my pants, therefore you let me hang around in the hopes that I might give in to your constant pleading."

Jake gave Iestyn a look that asked, 'Is he for real?'

"Ignore him. He knows there's no way I'd want to get into his pants, as there's nothing in them worth the bother. His arse is so bony I'd cut myself if I went anywhere near it."

Matt went to utter another witty retort, but Julie placed her hand over his mouth.

"Shut up, Matt." She turned back to the newcomer. "So, Jake, tell us about yourself."

Iestyn sat as his pretend boyfriend answered all of Julie's many questions as best as he could. He had to admit that Jake did pretty well. They really did have a lot in common. He also kept stroking Iestyn's thigh every so often, just for added effect—so much so that it was beginning to have an added effect.

"I told you he'd be perfect for you," Gareth said proudly. "I should set myself up a dating service for gay men. I bet there's a market for it." He paused as if he was already planning the website.

After a few rounds, they adjourned to Iestyn's house, as it was nearer than Julie's, and ordered Chinese. Iestyn took Jake into his front room to look at his collection of geekery, as Matt called it.

"How am I doing?" Jake asked.

"Brilliantly. So good, in fact, even I believe you."

Jake kissed him then winked when Iestyn looked concerned.

"Just for the act," he said. "But if we weren't doing this for pretend, I think we'd make a good couple and I'd get to sit and watch old *Doctor Who* episodes without being moaned at."

They all sat around talking, drinking and eating Chinese food. Jake made his excuses and got up to leave at ten thirty.

"I'm away early tomorrow on an inspection up in Runcorn, so I don't want to be out too late. It's been good to meet you all and I'll see you in just over a week for the wedding."

They all said their goodbyes and Iestyn waited with him for the taxi. He kissed him goodbye and waved him off, knowing that as soon as he went back inside, the questions would begin again.

"I like him," Julie announced when he went back in.

"You have a lot in common," Sian added. "He's really good-looking with that gray hair and tan."

Matt sniggered and Sian reached over and punched him on the arm.

"Jeez, you really are a pillock, Catlow," Sian stated. "Just because I'm gay doesn't make me blind. I do teach art for a living and I've drawn enough naked men to appreciate what looks good."

"One day some woman is going to absolutely fascinate you and I really hope I'm there to see you being led by the nose and kept in your place," Kate added in support of her girlfriend.

"Never gonna happen," Matt assured them.

"True. They'd have to be completely mad," Julie said.

Iestyn could see this was going downhill fast. "Coffee, everyone? Now, let's get my new machine working."

* * * *

The stag party attendees were in a nightclub dancing and drinking the night away. Mac sat next to his best friend, watching the others out on the floor shaking their stuff with a group of locals they'd met in the club.

"It's a pity Aron couldn't come on this weekend. It would have been good for both of you to have some fun together."

Dan, somewhat worse for wear, merely nodded. He'd tried to persuade Aron to come but something had come up and, as usual, it wasn't anything interesting. They'd spent more time apart than they had together recently but Aron had assured him that he would be at the wedding.

Mac put his hands on his best friend's shoulders to steady himself, their noses practically touching as if Mac was going in for a kiss. He heard a wolf whistle from one of the others.

"Sod off, Hathaway," he said cheerfully. "Look, Dan, I've known you for eight years now. We started at the Giants together then for Wales. I've seen you when you're happy and when you're not, and I know that there is something seriously wrong with you at the moment. I don't know what's going on with you and Aron but I think you might just be afraid of starting over again, so you've run back to where you feel safe."

Dan went to open his mouth but Mac put a finger to his friend's lips.

"No, you're going to listen to me, you great lump. You let someone you love slip away because you were upset and selfish. He did nothing wrong and you acted like a kid who'd had his favorite toy taken away, because they stripped you of the captaincy and you didn't get to hold up the trophy instead of that sad dad-dancing bastard over there. You loved Aron once, but in your heart of hearts you know you don't love him now, don't you? You'd both moved on, but you're back with him now because it's easier. Face it, Dan, you're just making do. You're twenty-four years old, an international sportsman and celebrity, and you are making do, because you're not brave enough to admit that you've been a selfish prick."

Dan looked at him, his eyes suddenly widening with understanding. "Shit, you're right—that's exactly it, Mac! I am just making do, but what the hell am I going to *do* about it?"

Chapter Thirty-One

When Iestyn got to Julie's house, Sian and Kate were already there and all three were getting the full works—hair, nails and faces. Iestyn was glad he didn't have to put up with any of that palaver. It was going to be hard enough just putting on his outfit. He'd emailed himself the video page so he could see how to do up the laces on his shoes properly. He hoped it would be easy to follow come the big day

"I'll just stay out of the way while you three are pampered," he told them.

"Your clothes are in the back bedroom, and the button holes are in the fridge. Can you ring Mac and check that everything arrived at his flat?"

Iestyn got a surprise when he heard his former lover's voice on the end of the phone. "Umm, hi, Dan. Is Mac there? Julie wanted to check that the buttonholes had been delivered," he said, trying to keep the quaver out of his voice. If he was this bad just hearing those lovely deep Welsh tones, how the hell was he going to cope with seeing his ex in person?

"Yes, they've all arrived, Iestyn. We're trying to remember how to tie the laces here."

"There's a video on YouTube. I can send you the address if you want."

"That would be great, then we can all look the same. Congratulations on the teaching nomination, by the way. Julie told us about it. Are you looking forward to the ceremony?"

"I'm not sure, really. I don't think for a minute I'll win, but I'm taking Mum with me and she'll enjoy it. I can hear Julie calling me. I expect I'll see you later."

"I am a bit difficult to miss and I will be at the front with you, after all."

"Yeah, of course. I guess I'm a bit nervous. I've never given anyone away before."

"You'll be fine. Later, then."

Iestyn put the phone down then sat, breathing heavily. His hands shook. *Shit! I need to get my act together before I see the man.*

Jake was meeting him at the club. He would sit with Gareth and Matt during the ceremony. Iestyn's mam was coming to the ceremony and his siblings would be at the reception afterward. It was a pity about Julie's sister but the wedding had been arranged at the last minute and a cruise in the Caribbean was costly to cancel.

He looked at his watch. Ninety minutes to go. It would only take twenty minutes to get to the stadium from here but he decided to get ready now. Upstairs, he used his phone to email the website address to Dan. It seemed strange doing so after all that had happened between them.

Then he turned his attention to his wedding clothes. They'd all had strict instructions to wear underwear under their kilts. Apparently, real Clansmen had worn their kilts between their legs and over their shoulders to make up for the lack of undergarments and the idea that nothing was worn under the kilt was a modern one. Iestyn for one was glad to be covered. He didn't particularly want to reveal himself during a Highland fling.

One by one, he put on every piece of clothing. It was going to be warm wearing the full regalia but at least the day was cooler than it had been recently. Just so long as it stayed dry to take the photos on the middle of the pitch. He managed to lace the shoes up but had trouble with his sporran. He was going to have to get one of the others to tighten the buckles properly, as he didn't want it to slip down then find himself tripping over it as they processed up the makeshift aisle.

He knocked on the bedroom door before entering. Julie told him to come in and that they were all decent. He took in the scene before him.

"Wow, you three look amazing!"

Julie stood. He'd seen her in the dress but not with her hair done.

"You are beautiful," he said. "Your dad would be so proud to walk you down the aisle, just as I am." He poured four glasses of non-alcoholic wine and lifted his own. "To my wonderful best friend. I hope you'll be very happy and that Mac realizes just how lucky he is."

All four raised their glasses.

"To Julie and Mac." Iestyn pulled out his phone and filmed them all.

"You two look good as well," he said to Kate and Sian. "The tartan sashes really work with that color. Could you just buckle me up a bit tighter so my sporran doesn't fall? I'd hate there to be an incident. Then we'd better get downstairs to wait for the cars."

Kate and Sian went down before them to give them a little time alone. "I'm so glad you're here… You look fabulous in the kilt. I see you've added a little Welshness to your sporran." Iestyn had placed a Welsh dragon brooch onto the leather.

"I've got a bit of Welshness for you too." He gave her the box.

"Oh, Iessie, these are lovely. I'll put them on now." Iestyn put the necklace with the dragon pendant around Julie's neck while she fixed the dragon earrings.

"Something new," he said. "I assume you have the usual blue garter."

"Yes, and your mother lent me this silver band for my hair, so that covers old and borrowed. She said it belonged to your grandmother, another redhead."

The photographer was waiting for them when the cars arrived at the stadium.

"He turned up, then?" Julie asked him as they posed in a variety of positions outside the building.

"Oh yes, and he looks very handsome. I've filmed and taken photos of everyone," the photographer assured her.

"We'd better get this show on the road." She turned to Kate and Sian. "Will you make sure my train is off the floor going up the stairs?"

"Are you ready for this?" Iestyn said as they reached the door to the wedding venue. "Now is sort of the last time you could run."

"I'm ready," Julie said. She turned to Kate and Sian behind her and said, in a shaking voice full of emotion, "And one day I hope I'll be able to attend your marriage ceremony."

Kate and Sian looked at each other with uncertainty then smiled.

"Perhaps," Kate said, taking Sian's hand to walk behind the bride.

"Okay then, let's do this." Apprehensive, Iestyn pushed the door open.

Inside, around fifty guests were seated on either side of the aisle. As they waited for the music to start, Iestyn touched Jake's shoulder and was rewarded with a warm smile. At the first note, Mac and Dan turned around. The gasps were audible even from the back. Dan looked amazing in his outfit, like a man-mountain that Iestyn longed to climb and explore. He was thankful for the room his kilt afforded him as part of his body attempted to rise in salute.

Slowly they walked the small distance to the front of the room. Julie took her place next to Mac and Iestyn stood at her side. For the first time in months, he stood three feet away from Dan. He could have almost reached out and touched him. Out of the corner of his eye, he spotted Aron sitting in the front row. The press photographs hadn't revealed just how much smaller and slighter Aron was from Iestyn's former lover. Dan must be a good eight inches taller and five stone heavier than his boyfriend. Iestyn idly speculated about how they managed the difference in bed, as surely Dan's physique would overwhelm someone so much smaller. Then again, he suspected that the other man was quite athletic, unlike himself. He allowed himself to daydream for a moment, remembering their week away in Cornwall and the times they'd made love in that hut. Dan lying on his back as he pushed into him over and over again until the smell of sex and the sound of their groans filled the air.

"Iestyn," Julie said, interrupting that favorite memory. "Are you okay?"

"Yes, sorry, miles away. Did I miss anything?"

She smiled somewhat indulgently as if she could guess where his mind had gone. "No, nothing important, just my wedding vows. We need to sign the register now." Iestyn had forgotten that the ceremony for a registry office wedding was quite short.

"Oh yeah, of course." He waited next to Dan, as they were both witnesses.

"You suit a kilt," Dan said.

Iestyn looked him up and down and said, "You too."

"Julie said you were bringing someone with you."

Inordinately pleased that Jake had come, Iestyn grinned. Perhaps Dan was a little bit jealous after all. "Yes, Jake. He's at the back there between Matt and my mam. I see Aron managed to come. Julie said he's been working hard to get his business off the ground."

"Yeah, he's flying to Hong Kong tomorrow."

"Shame you can't go too but I know you hate to fly. What are you going to do about going to Australia for the World Cup?"

"Same as usual — take tranquilizers and sleep for as long as possible."

They signed the certificate side by side. Dan's aftershave tantalized Iestyn and it was all he could do not to just reach out and lightly caress Dan, just so he could touch him again. In his head, he imagined Dan bent over. He could see himself pushing up the kilt to reveal that Dan was just wearing his rugby jockstrap. He almost felt himself leaning over to run his hand over those firm arse cheeks before he fell to his knees and pushed them apart and began to lick… Abruptly he was brought back to reality when the music began and the wedding party headed out to have pictures taken on the pitch. At that moment, he was so glad he was wearing a kilt.

Iestyn only managed a few words with Jake, who looked good in his gray suit. "I hope you dance," he said, "because I intend to dance with you later."

Jake kissed him deliberately, knowing that Dan was watching. He also fiddled with his bow tie—an intimate gesture and Iestyn knew it.

"He's watching," Jake said. "And yes, I do dance. I had lessons and I can even tango if required. That might be fun and shock a few people."

"Oh God, can you imagine if we did that?"

"We'd have to decide who was going to lead. You're the one wearing the skirt, so I guess it'll have to be me!"

Once everyone was back in the room and seated, Iestyn stood to give his father-of-the-bride speech—the moment he'd been dreading.

"I'm not unaccustomed to public speaking but usually my audience is a little younger. I'm here because, sadly, Julie's dad passed away a few years back. I know he would have been immensely proud to be standing here. I've known Julie nearly as long as he did. We grew up on the same street and attended the same schools. Now Julie teaches at the same school as me. She is as talented as she is beautiful and, if you ever get a chance, make her play for you because she is fantastic." Iestyn paused, scanning the faces in the room. He wished he could see Dan sitting to Mac's side but he couldn't turn around without making it obvious. A sharp pain in his ankle brought him back to the task in hand. "Sorry," he said, looking at Mac. "Now, what else can I say about my best friend? Well, firstly the red hair truly does indicate that she has a bit of a temper but she only gets annoyed with you if she likes you, so be warned, Mac. I also have Julie to thank for helping me decide on something really important. Julie and I, on my thirteenth birthday, had an experimental snog." Someone thumped on his behind. "See, she still can't resist me, but, sadly for her, it was that kiss that confirmed that I was really gay. So I have Julie to thank for helping me with that. Seriously, though, Julie is a wonderful human being and Mac is a lucky man. So raise your glasses to Julie and Mac — long life and happiness always!"

Iestyn sat, happy to have finished his speech. He knew Dan was next and he could tell the rugby player was nervous, as the paper shook in his hand.

"Unlike Iestyn, I don't often make public speeches but I have told Mac what to do more than once. However, my instruction usually consists of 'get hold of the ball and run as fast as you can'. This may not be the best advice now."

Some minutes later, after several stories of overseas tours and an incident with a kangaroo that had the audience crying with laughter, Dan finished with his own toast to the happy couple.

Finally, Mac stood up to make his speech. "I'd like to thank a few people but I'll try not to keep you for too long. Firstly, I'd like to thank my family for all the support they've given me over the years. Mum, you look lovely, and, Dad and Alex, thanks for wearing the kilts without protesting too much. Thanks to Iestyn, for giving away my beautiful bride and for being gay. Otherwise, things could have turned out very differently after that kiss. I also need to say to Kate and Sian that you're both stunning and Julie and I have a couple of little gifts for you to say thank you. To Dan, my bestest best man, thanks for listening to me go on and on about this gorgeous woman and for being the reason why we met. Lastly," he said, taking Julie's hand, "I'd like to say that I am obviously the luckiest man in the world because I am now married to you. So, everyone, please raise your glasses to my wife Julie then the fun can begin!"

Once the meal was finished, it was time to hit the bar and get the party started. Iestyn watched with pride as Mac led his best friend onto the floor for their first dance. The opening bars of *Waiting for a Girl Like You* rang out and Iestyn had to brush away a tear. Slowly the rest of the party joined in.

"D'you want to dance?" Jake put out his hand and pulled Iestyn into the swaying throng of people. He leaned in close, tucking his head on Iestyn's shoulder and resting his hand in the crook of his back.

They danced slowly together, a couple just like all those around them. Iestyn couldn't help but notice that Dan was standing at the bar, looking their way. He hoped he hadn't made a mistake involving Jake, as he didn't want Dan to assume there could never be anything between them again. He guessed he should feel guilty even attempting to make Dan jealous but, if he really was over him and back with Aron, then it wouldn't matter, would it? And if he wasn't, it would be better if Aron knew that, wouldn't it?

As the evening progressed, Iestyn danced with Julie, Kate, Sian then his mother. She might be in her seventies but she missed nothing.

"Jake seems very nice," she observed.

"Yes, he is."

"I hope he knows what you're doing tonight."

"Sorry?"

"Oh, come on, Iessie, I know my son. Jake is gorgeous, but you're not really into him, are you? He's your target audience," she said, nodding at Dan, who was dancing with Julie. "Every so often you sneak a look at him and his eyes have hardly left you all day. You've never stopped loving him, have you?"

"No, Mam. I did try, but from not knowing who he was, I now see him everywhere. I can't get him out of my head. I want him to see me here. I want him to want me back."

"What about his boyfriend?"

"I don't know. Julie has dropped a few hints about their relationship not being what it was."

"But you want him to come back to you. Pride can cause all sorts of problems, you know."

"Is it so wrong? If he cares for me then he will, won't he? And if he doesn't, then I'll have to get over it."

"Oh, Iessie, you don't make life easy for yourself, do you?" She hugged him.

"If I'd always chosen the easy path I wouldn't be a teacher, I wouldn't be gay and I wouldn't have fallen in love with him, but you know, Mam, nobody does it like me!"

The music changed and *Crazy Right Now* blasted out.

"Too fast for me," his mother said.

Iestyn was about to sit when Jake moved behind him.

"Show time," Jake said, grinding his groin into Iestyn's arse. "I think it's time to show the straights how to do it." For the next few minutes, they twisted and ground into each other as if their futures depended on it. And perhaps, for Iestyn, it did. Jake slid his hands around Iestyn's waist. He took hold of Jake's hands, pushing back against Jake's now more than obvious erection.

Friction can do that.

They moved in total harmony together. He saw Matt to one side of him, dancing with a woman dressed from head to toe in a vivid green dress that hugged every contour. Her hair whirled around as they spun again and again. How she stood in those heels he had no idea, but she had Matt by the nose and was leading him, pulling him closer, and Matt, like an obedient puppy, was following her lead.

He wondered if Dan was watching. He'd never actually seen the rugby player dance and very few people had ever seen Iestyn let go as he was now. He felt wonderful and freer than he'd done in ages, losing himself in the music and the feel of another body next to his. He had to admit that Jake was amazing. He truly hoped that somehow this man's boyfriend would come to his senses and realize what he was missing. When the music was over, they fell back down in their seats.

"God, I'm getting too old to do this," Jake said between breaths. "I need a lie-down." He picked up his drink and finished it in one gulp. "I also need another drink."

"Just a fizzy water for me," Iestyn said. "I'm not getting drunk tonight." He watched Jake get up.

"So, little brother, how's the plan going?"

Huw and Susan had arrived and sat next to him. Iestyn looked at Dan, who was now dancing with Mac and Julie. He had to admit that what Dan lacked in technique, he made up for in enthusiasm and that kilt was certainly revealing his assets. Iestyn got lost for a moment, remembering those strong thighs clasped around him. Susan brought him back to the room.

"I have to say I've never seen you dance like that before and that Jake is so hot."

"Are you supposed to say that, Sue, with your husband sitting there?" Iestyn asked.

"Oh, Huw agrees with me."

Iestyn laughed.

His brother pretended to look shocked. "What!" Huw said. "Paraphrasing a comment you often use — I'm straight, not blind! He's good value for a pretend boyfriend."

"Yes, he is. I think I've found a good friend. Mam, Rhian and Gareth are around somewhere."

"We spoke to them when we arrived. We're late because Megs wanted her usual stories. She was asking about you again. Uncle Iessie can do no wrong."

"I'll take her out at the weekend. We can go and feed the ducks again and she can run around the park."

Jake came back and handed him his drink. "Jake, this is my brother, Huw, who fancies you, and my sister-in-law, Susan, who does as well."

"Is this a family thing? I'm not sure I'm up for a threesome!"

Huw, who'd just spluttered into his pint, did so again. "I was just — "

"Shut up, Huw!"

Iestyn waved to the rest of his family. Together everyone sat talking and people-watching.

"Are we still going to do this tango if the right music comes on?" Jake asked.

"I'm game if you are, although I suppose I'll have to let you lead, as you're wearing the trousers."

"You tango?" Susan said breathily. "I think I may have to leave my husband for you. He can't dance at all. I actually think he's got three left feet. Have you ever considered changing sides?"

"Not since Damien Hughes gave me a blow job in the school showers when I was fifteen," Jake replied.

Iestyn leaned in. "Oh yes, tell me more."

Jake whispered in his ear and once again Iestyn caught Dan looking toward them.

"Bloody hell," he said, putting his arm around Jake. "Was he that good?"

"Absolutely! He did this thing with his tongue. I thought I'd died and gone to heaven. And was the story about Julie true?"

"Yep, I kissed her and realized I'd much rather snog Jason Evans from the sixth form."

The music changed and finally the right tune came on for their tango. "Shall we?" Jake said.

Iestyn's whole family looked at him expectantly.

His stomach fluttered as a frisson of excitement swept over him. "Yeah, let's do it!"

The floor had emptied a bit as they took their positions and began. It was strange, as memory kicked in and Iestyn managed to follow Jake's lead with every step, every turn and every staccato head movement, only fluffing occasionally. Hand in hand, hip to hip and groin to groin they moved around the floor. Jake had such grace and strength and Iestyn wondered why on earth Jake's boyfriend had ever let him go. It was beautiful, and gradually the floor cleared as everyone stopped to watch until the final flourish when Jake bent Iestyn over, holding him until they both collapsed into a laughing heap on the dance floor. The room exploded into applause as Jake got up and put out his hand to pull Iestyn up. They took their bows and returned to their seats, flushed with success.

"Wow, that was brilliant," Iestyn said, "and much sexier than dancing with a girl!" Out of the corner of his eye, he saw Aron say something to Dan then move off toward the toilets. Iestyn thought that Dan looked wistful and a little sad.

By the end of the evening, Iestyn was exhausted but sober, unlike Dan, who he saw swaying a little as Mac and Luke helped Aron to get him outside. Gradually, people began to drift away after saying their goodbyes to the bride and groom. Jake and Iestyn made their way to the car park. The taxi pulled up soon afterward. He let Jake get in first then looked around. It surprised him to see Dan and Aron sitting on a bench, farther along from the entrance, observing their departure. He deliberately took Jake's outstretched hand and got in the car. After the evening he'd had, he could only hope that, with a little help from his friends, Dan might realize exactly what he'd lost and what he still might gain.

Chapter Thirty-Two

The next morning, Dan slowly opened one eye to the daylight coming through his bedroom window and groaned. The effects of the copious amount of alcohol he'd consumed were playing out a samba beat somewhere behind his eyes. Reluctantly, he pulled back the sheet and swung his legs so he was sitting on the edge of the bed. He waited for the room to stop spinning and grabbed the glass of water Aron had left by his bed. The painkillers were already in it. Gratefully, Dan swallowed it down and stood up, throwing on a T-shirt to go with his underpants.

When he emerged from the bedroom and entered the kitchen, he found Aron sitting at the table, clutching a mug of coffee. These days it wasn't unusual for him to be up, logged on to his computer, talking to businesses in Japan, China or India, but this morning he was just staring into space. Dan thought he looked worried and sad at the same time, his eyes ringed with red as though he hadn't slept or had spent some time in tears. Dan had slept like the dead, despite all the things competing for attention in his head, but that was the effect of drinking — to forget how happy the man he loved looked dancing with another. No, that was wrong. Aron was the man he was supposed to love, wasn't he? Guilt hit Dan all over again. He knew he'd made such a pig's ear of everything.

He went over to the coffee machine, the one Iestyn had taught him to use. The sun shined brightly through the windows. It looked like it was going to be another hot day. Usually he had tea in the morning but instead he made a double espresso, in the hopes it would wake him up, and opened the doors to the terrace.

"Why don't we have breakfast out here?" he asked, staring out toward the Bay. "It's too good a morning to waste and I could use the fresh air."

"Dan, sit a minute. I need to talk to you. *We* need to talk."

"That never sounds good," Dan replied, placing his mug on the table and taking the adjacent seat. "The last time you said we had to talk you told me you were leaving me. You're not leaving me, are you?"

Aron didn't reply immediately but instead took Dan's hand. Dan withdrew it as if he'd been scalded.

"Shit, you *are* leaving me, aren't you?" Although this was what Dan wanted and he knew it was cowardly to admit that this would be easier, a part of him was still sad to hear the words Aron was about to say.

"Dan, you must know things aren't right between us. I should never have come back and just moved in as though nothing had happened. We'd both moved on and we couldn't ever go back to how we were. You know that's true, Dan. You don't love me."

Dan began to protest but Aron stopped him.

"No, you *don't* love me, not like you should. You're not in love with me anymore and I'm not in love with you. Dan, we were sixteen when we got together, all hormones and dicks, in more ways than one. Neither of us had any real idea what we really wanted or needed in a relationship."

"But we were happy, weren't we?" Dan said sorrowfully. "I didn't imagine that. You weren't pretending, were you?"

"No, come on, Dan. Look at you. I was and am so proud of you. You stayed true to yourself in a world that didn't entertain homosexuality. You put up with all the abuse from the stands and from the other players but you got through it all, no matter how much it hurt you. D'you think I didn't know how much pain you were in when you cried in my arms in the dark?"

Dan saw him struggling to hold back his tears as Aron drew a couple of breaths then looked straight at him and took his hand. "There is no man on this planet I admire more than you but we're not really alike enough, are we? Well, are we?"

Dan shrugged and shook his head. He didn't know what to say.

In a quiet voice, Aron continued, "I watched you last night as you watched him. Sometimes you watched him for minutes as he danced with that Jake bloke. Your eyes followed them around the room last night, just like they'd followed him all day. I saw so much longing and regret. You're totally in love with him, not me. He fascinates you. All night you talked about him, without even realizing, to anyone who would listen, including me—how clever he is, that he plays chess online and tried to teach you, and that he knows so much about history you could talk about your favorite Owain Glyn Dwr. You were lit up, excited. I make technology for a living. I don't think you've ever asked me about it. I also play chess."

"Oh, hell. I'm sorry. I didn't mean to hurt you and I know I have. I know you're really clever, Az but you've never even tried to teach me how to play chess, and he did. I guess it's what he does — he teaches."

Aron shook his head and smiled. "You never could remember to call me Aron, could you? And we won't even visit your teacher fetish! I was never going to be able to compete with that. Shit! Now I sound like a jealous prick, which I am a bit, but if you don't try to get back with him, you're a complete fool."

"But how do I do that? I let him down and he has Jake now. Did you see him? Bloody hell! And he's a fireman!"

"And you're an international rugby player and model, over six foot tall, shoulders like a tallboy, blond hair, blue eyes and a cock you know what to do with. He may have been there with Jake, but I didn't see anything to indicate they were really into each other, even during that dance, hot as it was. In fact, he kept sneaking looks at you. You need to talk to him, Dan. You know his friends, so there must be a way." He stopped for a moment as if he'd just thought of something.

"You okay?" Dan asked.

"Yeah, so what are you going to do to sort this mess out?"

"I don't know. I can't just turn up on his doorstep and with Mac and Julie being on honeymoon, I can't speak to her. I need some way to see him on neutral ground." *Of course he'll be there.* In his mind, he began to make plans.

A voice interrupted his thoughts.

"Dan, I'm going now. I've packed a few things for my flight in a few hours. I'll be back in a couple of days. I'll collect the rest of my stuff when I've found a place to rent."

"I'm sorry, Aron." It still felt wrong to call him that. "You can stay here in the spare room for as long as you want, you know," Dan said.

"No, we need to do this properly. I'm going to go." Aron got up and put his mug into the sink as usual. Dan followed him and wrapped his arms around the smaller man. For a moment, Aron stayed that way then turned around. They kissed a kiss that was full of love, but without passion or need. To Dan it was comfortable and familiar but not enough for either of them anymore.

Breaking apart, Dan looked down at the person who'd changed his life eight years ago. "There's someone out there for you, Az. I know there is and he'll be a very lucky man."

Chapter Thirty-Three

Iestyn sat in his car for a few minutes. Nothing had changed since the wedding. There'd been no call from Dan to tell him he'd made a huge mistake and wanted him back. He was lonely and fed up so when he'd picked up the phone and received an invitation to lunch from Aztec, his online chess opponent who was visiting Britain, he'd accepted, welcoming the distraction. Iestyn was looking forward to meeting the person he'd played chess with for over a year. He'd brought a chessboard just in case Aztec fancied a game after lunch. His mobile rang.

"Hello," he said, pressing the loudspeaker button.

"Hi, Iestyn," Jake said.

"Jake, good to hear from you. How are things?"

"That's why I'm phoning. Things are good. In fact, things are great."

"Do I get the feeling a certain traffic cop is back on the scene?"

"He is. He saw the photo in the paper. We were both at the same shout at a factory down on the docks and, after a little persuasion from me that I was just helping you out, we got to talking again. One thing led to another and now we're back together."

"You sound happy."

"I am. How are things going at your end?"

"Not sure. Nothing from Dan yet but I'm trying to be positive. I'm just going to have lunch with someone I play chess with online. He's over from America. I'd better get going actually or I'll be late. We must keep in touch. You know if…."

"Yeah, I know. I enjoyed our dates and if things had been different, it would have been fun getting to know you better, Iestyn Jones."

"You too. I'll ring you soon. You never know…perhaps we could go on a double date some time! Gotta go."

"Bye, Iestyn, and good luck."

He picked up his chess set, exited the car and wandered over to the entrance. He'd never been to this pub before. The Llandaff Inn appeared to be part of a chain and had a sign declaring it was now under new management. The entrance led straight to the bar. He looked around but no one waved at him so he went to the bar to ask if anyone had left a message. Perhaps Aztec hadn't arrived yet.

"What can I get you, sir?" The girl smiled in greeting.

"Um, I'm here to meet someone. My name's Iestyn Jones."

"Oh yes, sir. Your lunch date is over in the farthest booth, if you'd like to take a seat."

A tickle of doubt made the hairs stand up on the back of his neck and it struck him that he had no idea who this man was. He hadn't even asked for his real name. He almost turned around wondering if it might be some newspaper reporter. Then again, perhaps it was Dan—after all, he knew the name his opponent had used. He made his way slowly to the booth. He knew it wasn't Dan when he saw the size of the man and his dark hair. When he turned round Iestyn couldn't believe his eyes. He halted, riveted to the spot, unsure of what to do next.

"What the hell are you doing here?"

Aron got up and put a hand on his arm. "I know this is a bit of a shock …"

"You're telling me. I was expecting a strange chess player, not you."

"I'm Aztec," Aron explained simply. "I've been playing chess against you for over a year. You're pretty good."

"But, but…" Iestyn couldn't quite get his head around what he was hearing.

"Yes, I know. Sit, Iestyn. We need to talk."

Unable to think of anything else to do, and somewhat intrigued, Iestyn slid into the seat opposite.

"I thought you might have caught on that it was me. Aztec as in Aztechnologies. It's not a great leap."

Iestyn shook his head, unable to speak, mostly because he didn't know what to say. He'd been expecting some geeky American visitor, not the boyfriend of the man he still loved. It was awkward, to say the least, especially after the wedding last week. Iestyn hadn't been able to help but notice Dan looking toward him during the evening. Their gazes had met across the room on more than one occasion. So was he now about to face an angry boyfriend here to tell him to back off? The strange thing was, Aron didn't look angry.

"D'you want to order some food?" Aron asked. "I did invite you to lunch, after all, and I believe the chef here is good. There are a few things we need to discuss."

Iestyn thought he may as well. "Okay, thanks. I suppose it won't do me any harm."

He picked up two menus and handed one to Aron. The waitress hurried over and took their orders.

"Is Joe cooking today?" Aron asked.

Iestyn wondered who Joe was.

"Sorry, I'm new here. I don't know anyone called Joe," the girl answered. "The chef's name is Simon. I'll ask, if you want."

Aron nodded.

Iestyn couldn't help but notice a look of disappointment cross Aron's face before he turned back to Iestyn.

"I suppose you're curious as to why we're here," he said matter-of-factly.

"Just a little. You were the last person I imagined would be here. I was expecting some nerdy American who'd want to discuss chess moves. I even brought a travel set just in case you wanted to play but I imagine this meeting isn't about chess."

"No, it isn't. Although I did mean what I said. You are good."

"Thanks, I've enjoyed the games we've played." Iestyn decided to take the bull by the horns. "I suppose we're here about Dan, as he's the only other thing we have in common."

"We split up the day after the wedding."

Iestyn stared at the other man for a moment, unsure what to say. Before he could answer, the waitress brought their meals. He looked at his steak sandwich and chips then across at Aron's salmon with no dressing and salad. The man was slight enough already. He couldn't imagine, knowing how much

Dan had to eat to maintain his weight, how Aron managed to keep his figure, but obviously he was more disciplined about what he ate. Iestyn picked up a few chips and chewed slowly, trying to process Aron's last statement and what it might mean about why he was here.

"It was amicable," Aron said into the silence. "I've known for a little while I was wrong to come back and the wedding just confirmed it for me."

Warmth spread across his face but he wasn't about to admit what he'd done. He bit into his sandwich.

"I saw him looking at you all night and you sneaking looks at him. Anyone could tell you and Jake weren't together, really—or anyone who was looking as closely as I was. You were so busy trying hard to be casual that it was obvious. You're still in love with Dan, aren't you?"

All right, now there was no point denying it. "Yes, I don't think I've ever not been in love with him, almost since we first met. Did he ever tell you I landed at his feet at an ice rink and he pulled me up? The kids with me just stared at him. I didn't really watch rugby so I had no idea who he was. I just knew he was gorgeous, but getting an erection during a school trip because you're hand in hand with an Adonis probably isn't the thing to do."

Aron laughed. "No, I can see that would be a problem. Mac told me Dan had been watching you for a while that day and was really impressed by how you were with the kids. Dan doesn't make a habit of handing out his number. He must have thought you were someone special. You know Dan has a thing for teachers, don't you?"

"Thankfully. We're not usually the subject of fantasy, but I know there were two teachers in particular who helped him deal with being gay—and you, of course. He told me a bit about how you two got together."

"I always knew I was gay. Dan never cared. I studied at Cardiff University so we could stay together, even though I had offers from all over. He was playing for Glamorgan Giants and it was obvious he'd be picked for Wales. He never made a secret of the fact that he was gay from then onwards, and I admired him so much for that. He took so much stick from the crowd and from some other players, even the press at times, but he told the Giants' coach he was gay when he signed for them then played everyone else off the field. No one could stop him in full flight and he proved himself over and over again. His teammates were always great, especially Mac, and that helped, but it wasn't easy.

"When they offered me the job in America after my doctorate, I really didn't know what to do but we'd been drifting apart for a while. There was nothing obvious but it wasn't the same. I knew he wanted different things from me and I was bound up in my work, even obsessed by it. He'd gone on tour when I was finishing my PhD and there were days when we didn't speak to each other. In the end, I took the job and Dan suggested a break to see where we were— and that was that. I'll always love him but I'm not *in* love with him anymore and he's not in love with me. He loves you and I think you love him, but you're afraid after what happened."

"He let me down," Iestyn agreed. "When all that rubbish appeared in the papers, he let me down."

"He knows that, but he was under tremendous pressure from his coaches. You know what sport is like about drugs and any connection to them. He was the captain of Wales and a role model for so many and he let that win. Remember, he'd only known you a few months. It hurt him so much not to lift that trophy because he may never get that chance again. It's the World Cup over in Australia in September and he is desperate to be captain for that. Wales has a great chance. After winning the Grand Slam, they're confident about taking on the All Blacks and the Wallabies."

"Look, Aron, this trip down memory lane is all well and good but I need to know he means it this time. This has to come from him. I know it's stupid and a bit needy, but I need some sort of —"

"Romantic gesture to sweep you off your feet. Well, you do have a bit of history for that, don't you?"

Iestyn laughed. "I suppose so. Are you going to tell him we've had this conversation?"

"No, but don't give up on him yet. We talked about you and his feelings, and I know he can be quite resourceful when he wants to be."

A little flicker of hope appeared in Iestyn's mind and he envisaged opening up his front door to find Dan there with that shy smile on his face. Either that or he'd send his nan round or try to get to him through his mother.

"What are you going to do?" he asked Aron.

"Build my company up. I'll base myself here because it's home for me. America was exciting but I missed Wales. I have a few flats to look at and I'll be spending time traveling, developing new ideas and raising finances. I'm going to be busy. I hope we can be friends and keep up the chess. I believe you tried to teach Dan to play. You must have the patience of a saint is all I can say. I could never get him to sit still for that long."

"I found that strip chess concentrated his mind quite well," Iestyn replied. "Especially when achieving checkmate produced a much more interesting climax to the game."

He laughed at that and Aron joined him. Their conversation turned to the game they both loved until Iestyn suggested he get the board out after all.

A few hours later, Iestyn told him goodbye in the car park.

"It's a shame that chef wasn't there anymore. He obviously made an impression on you when your car broke down on the motorway."

"Yeah, his baby will have been born by now, so perhaps he's moved on. They seemed a bit odd about it in there but I suppose you don't give out personal information to some complete stranger. Well, it's been good meeting you, OwainGlynDwr. Oh, and that was the way I worked out who you were. Dan showed me the book you bought him and suddenly everything slotted into place."

Iestyn smiled. "That may be the best twenty quid I've ever spent. It was good to meet you too, Aztec. I hope everything goes well for you."

"And he will sort this out, you know. I've known him for fifteen years. Somehow, he'll find a way to make that gesture. Just don't play too hard to get, will you?"

"I'm not stupid," Iestyn replied. "And perhaps now I'm a little less naïve. It's been good this afternoon. I'm glad we had this talk. I'd better be off. I'm collecting my niece from the nursery." He got in his car, brought the window down and waved.

It certainly had been an interesting afternoon, which is why, two weeks later, when it was announced that Dan Morgan would be presenting the award for secondary school teacher of the year, Iestyn wondered if the event was going to be when Dan intended to make that longed-for gesture.

* * * *

As he stood on the stage in St David's Hall, ready to introduce the winner of the next category, Dan hoped he was finally going to get his chance to put things right. He clutched the envelope, already knowing who the winner was.

"Anyone who knows me or has been to these awards in the past is aware of my admiration for the teaching profession," Dan began his introductory speech. "When I was a teenager, I went through a difficult time and it was my school, and especially two particular teachers, who helped me deal with being gay and my mother having cancer. They showed me that being gay shouldn't stop me doing what I wanted to do with my life, that I didn't have to hide from anyone, so I decided I was going to be myself.

"The person who has won this prize is also someone who has remained true to himself. I have personally saw how hard he works with the students in his school when I helped to coach their rugby team. He was nominated for this prize by one of the boys in his form, who also plays rugby, and this young man told me how much he loves studying history with this teacher. Here are some people to tell us more."

Dan looked up at the screen as staff and pupils explained why they thought the winner should receive this award. Dan wasn't sure he'd ever felt so happy to make an announcement in the whole of his life.

"The winner of Welsh Secondary School Teacher of the Year is Iestyn Jones of St Illtyd's High School, Cardiff."

All sorts of thoughts assailed Iestyn when he heard his name, so many that he had difficulty pinning them down. He'd won and that was hard enough to comprehend, but even more wonderful was the fact that Dan was standing on the stage, waiting to give him the award. It took him a little while to get up.

His mother nudged him. "They're waiting for you, Iessie."

A minute later, Iestyn stood behind the podium, looking out over the assembled crowd in St David's Hall. When Dan had stepped out to announce the winner, his stomach had filled with butterflies and his heart with hope. Had Dan planned to seek him out because he knew he was here? Now, when he was standing just behind him, perhaps they had a chance to sort things out between them, but first he had a speech to make. He looked at the trophy.

"It's funny how you spend much of your professional life talking to groups then suddenly you're faced with something different and your throat goes dry. Anyway, I need to say thank you to a few people. Firstly, to the students I teach who cooperate with a teacher who provides them with shovels and wood to build a trench then turns a hose on them. Secondly, I'd like to thank my colleagues. Although we face the classes ourselves, none of us could do our job without the wonderful teaching assistants we have and the other teachers who provide a sounding board for mad ideas, and usually tell me—don't do that. Finally, I'd like to thank two people—my mum, who is over there crying, for inspiring my love of learning, and my dad, who died earlier this year. He would have been as proud of my achieving this as I am to be his son. So this is dedicated to my father, Geraint Jones."

The audience clapped as he left the stage with Dan. They found themselves in a foyer where a helper tried to direct them back to the auditorium, but Dan took Iestyn's hand and they faced each other.

"I'm sorry. I was stupid," Dan said. "Please give me another chance. I've missed you so much."

Iestyn looked at him for a moment before replying. "Yes, you were stupid, but so was I. I need to know you *really* mean this."

"D'you know how many strings I had to pull to be able to give this to you? I always present one of the prizes but I asked who'd won this prize and switched so I could present it. You deserve this so much. I loved the trench warfare re-enactment on the field, especially soaking them with the hose."

Iestyn grabbed Dan's lapels and pulled him forward into a kiss he wanted to last forever.

When they finally broke contact, Dan looked at him with concern on his face. "Bugger, what about Jake?"

"It's all right, you idiot. I love you too and I was only doing Jake a favor to make his ex-boyfriend jealous."

Dan sighed and said, "I did wonder a bit about that."

Just to the side was a leather sofa, so they sat on it together.

"I missed you too," Iestyn said. "I missed seeing that unruly blond mop of yours lying on my chest, feeling your breath on my skin and having my arms around you."

Dan gripped Iestyn's hand once more before he answered. "I missed the fun we had, the laughter and how you took care of me, but most of all I missed talking to you. I'd see something in the news and wonder what you would think. I read that book you gave me but then I couldn't talk to you about it." He leaned in and lowered his voice. "I also missed the sex and how you made me feel. I thought I'd lost you, Iessie, because I was such an idiot. I'd rather never play rugby again than not have you."

Iestyn looked at him, stunned by that statement and all it meant for Dan to have made it. He realized it was exactly what he'd needed to hear.

"Aron came to see me, you know. He told me you'd split up…"

"He did?"

"Yeah, he really cares for you," Iestyn said.

"I know he does. We talked," Dan said, clutching Iestyn's hand even tighter. "So, are you ready for all the madness?" he asked.

"I'm ready for you. Everything else, as Shakespeare might say, is meaningless persiflage."

Dan got up and pulled him toward the press area. "You know I love it when you talk clever and use those long words." He pushed through the door.

Iestyn leaned in to whisper in his ear, "I know you do, *cariad*."

The fact that they were holding hands was not lost on the local press when they stood in the hotel lobby and the cameras flashed.

Dan put his hand up to stop any questions. "Gentlemen, I have an announcement to make."

Epilogue

Some months later

"Here, taste this." Dan opened his mouth for Iestyn and let the food melt on his tongue. "God, that's so good it's positively orgasmic! This guy can really cook. We were lucky to get him at such short notice."

"His brother says he's only just started to work for himself. Try another one."

"Are you trying to fill me up?" Dan asked before he opened his mouth once more for Iestyn to place the canapé on his tongue. He moaned then used his finger to brush the crumbs into his mouth. Deliberately he sucked on it and watched as Iestyn squirmed in his seat.

"Well, you're always telling me you have to keep up your calorie intake because of all the exercise you do to keep this body of yours in such perfect condition. As for filling you up now, maybe I'm planning to do that later on this evening. It will be our wedding night, after all, and I believe it's a tradition."

Dan's eyes widened and Iestyn grinned when he saw the twinkle.

He leaned toward him and whispered into his ear. "You love it when I talk dirty, don't you?" At the same time, he ran his hand up Dan's thigh, causing Dan to shiver.

"Couldn't we just go now? Everyone is happy. There's plenty of food and drink. We could just slip away."

Iestyn looked around the room that contained all their family and friends. Julie was dancing with Mac. She was still on maternity leave, having given birth to Carys a few months before. Kate and Sian danced next to them, still bound up in each other. On the other side of the room, he could see Hayley with Matt. He was still following her around like a puppy. She could have put a collar and lead on him and he wouldn't have cared. Iestyn had never seen his friend like this before.

His family had danced as well but Huw still had three left feet, despite the ballroom classes his wife had insisted on him attending. Sitting just apart from them, he could see Jake and his boyfriend. Iestyn was glad his friend was happy. He knew Michael was still adjusting to being out but they were working through it. He smiled. All of these people had helped them get to this point. Only one person was missing. He knew Dan had wanted Aron there, because he was his oldest friend, but Iestyn had understood when Aron had phoned them to say he had to go abroad at the last moment. Business was business, after all.

He took Dan's hand. "Come on, then. We'll need to get a taxi, as we're both over the limit. Mac will take care of everyone, I'm sure. You go and let him know what we're doing and I'll make the call. I'll meet you downstairs. Don't be long." He reached and pulled Dan toward him, bringing their lips together. It felt so good to be able to do this with everyone around them.

"God, I need you inside me," Dan said. "The things you do to me!"

* * * *

It took a little while to get to their new house on the coast, not far from Iestyn's childhood home. They'd only moved in recently after Huw's firm had done the necessary renovations. Dan loved it. He and Iestyn often sat out on the patio, staring over the lawn toward the sea.

Iestyn pushed Dan against the inside of the front door as soon as it was closed, and began to remove his jacket.

"Have I told you how sexy you've looked in this suit today?" he whispered only centimetres from Dan's lips. "But you're going to look even sexier out of it."

Dan couldn't breathe. He hoped Iestyn would still think he was sexy when he made his great reveal. He loved it when Iestyn was like this, controlling, powerful. Being well over six feet, it took a big man to make him give up control. Iestyn kissed him while reaching down to Dan's arse and pulling their groins together. They ground against each other.

"If we don't get upstairs, I'm going to come here in my pants and I don't want to ruin my trousers," Dan managed to say in between kisses.

Iestyn was now paying attention to his ear and biting it gently.

"Oh shit, Iessie, please, I'm going to come if you keep doing that."

Iestyn pulled back and took Dan's hand.

They took the stairs two at a time. Dan found himself pushed back onto their bed as Iestyn fell on top of him. He needed to stop this for a little while. He had his own plans regarding what should come next. He began undoing Iestyn's shirt and kissed his exposed chest, working his way down until he reached his trousers. He undid the button and pulled down the zip. Seeing the damp spot forming on Iestyn's briefs, he rolled him onto his back, slipped down onto his knees then began to nudge the bulge with his mouth.

"Get undressed," he said. "I've just got something I need to do in the bathroom. I won't be long, I promise. Lie on your back and wait for me."

Iestyn looked up at him. "Okay, but don't take all night or I might start without you."

Dan reached into the drawer next to their bed. "I've got something I want you to wear." He pulled out the blindfold.

Iestyn's eyes widened.

"Just go with me," Dan said. "I'll shout and tell you to put it on, okay?"

"You're not going to drop hot wax on me or anything, are you?" Iestyn asked.

Dan could hear the tremble in his voice.

"No, nothing like that. You'll see."

He threw the blindfold over to Iestyn, who ran the black silk through his hands.

"Okay, I'm game."

Ten minutes later, Dan shouted he was ready from the en suite. Iestyn chose his pose carefully and lay naked on his back, blindfolded and gently stroking himself. He couldn't help hearing Dan gasp loudly when he came back into the bedroom.

"Gone all shy on me, have you?" Iestyn asked.

It was weird not being able to see what Dan was doing. Weird, but also strangely exciting. He heard Dan walk in the direction of the bed then the bed dipped as Dan moved up it toward him. Dan took hold of his cock in one hand and Iestyn heard the sound of a tube being squeezed. Dan spread lube up and down Iestyn's cock then seconds later, the full weight of the powerful rugby player sat astride him. He guessed Dan was directing his cock and he felt himself pushing at Dan's entrance. He loved that there was nothing between them now. The first time they'd gone bareback had been an experience Iestyn knew he would never forget. For him it was the first time ever, the first time he'd trusted anyone enough. It had been magical as they'd taken it in turns to fuck each other just so they could both share the feeling.

Slowly, heat engulfed his cock as Dan lowered himself and allowed his arse to be filled.

Iestyn groaned. He needed to see Dan. "Please, let me take this off. I want to watch you ride my cock." He heard the bathrobe hit the floor.

"Okay, you can take it off now," Dan said.

Iestyn opened his eyes and gasped at the sight above him. His hips thrust up in an effort to get even further into the other man. "Oh, my God! How? When? What the…?" He could see Dan's concerned face. "You look so fucking hot."

Dan wore a red corset edged with black lace and small black bows. His legs were encased in black stockings. He held his own cock, stroking himself gently.

"D'you like it?" he asked.

Iestyn stared at him. When Dan had told him about the outfit he'd worn in the past, Iestyn had never really envisioned what he would look like. "I love it!" he whispered. "Please, Dan, move."

He raised his hips to meet Dan as he slowly glided up and down. Iestyn watched his Adonis rise and fall, engulfing him again and again in his heat. He looked simply magnificent with his blond mop of hair and sparkling blue eyes totally dilated, his body framed by the corset. His wide shoulders above and his narrower hips below with the suspenders stretching as he moved. The stockings almost covered his strong thighs, just leaving the stripe of bare flesh at the top. Iestyn hadn't ever thought he'd find this as overwhelmingly sexy as he did. He reached out to touch Dan, taking his beautiful cock into his hand.

"Please," Dan moaned as he threw his head back.

Iestyn's orgasm gathered. He knew he wouldn't be able to hold it back much longer and he wanted Dan to come with him, wanted Dan to come all over him. He thrust up again and again. The sound of their bodies meeting filled the room along with their groans.

"I'm going to come," Iestyn said. "Come with me,"

Dan's arse contracted around him. Dan put his hand over Iestyn's and stroked himself. Finally, he came, sending ribbons of hot liquid over Iestyn's chest until he couldn't hold himself up any longer. Dan fell down over him and kissed him as Iestyn's cock slipped out. His cum now coated both their chests.

"You're going to get stains on that beautiful corset," Iestyn warned. Dan rolled off him to one side, still breathing heavily. Iestyn turned and tucked himself under Dan's arm. He ran his fingers over the silk and lace. "This is truly beautiful," he said. "You look magnificent. That was the perfect wedding present."

"I wasn't sure," Dan said. "Hayley made it just for me so it would fit perfectly. It had to be red, of course. As captain of the Welsh rugby team, I couldn't wear any other color. Now she's thinking of designing a line of corsets for men."

"Well, you can tell her you won't be modeling for them. You are all mine, Dan Morgan, all mine." He wrapped his arm around Dan. "This has been the best day of my life. I love you so much."

"And I love you too. Sleepy now. I'd better get this off."

He got up and turned around. Seeing the way the suspenders striped Dan's arse gave Iestyn's cock more ideas.

Dan must have heard him groan. "Like the view, do you?"

"Oh yeah, maybe next time we could try that with you doing a reverse cowboy?"

Dan looked over his shoulder as he undid the suspenders and rolled the stockings slowly down his legs. He undid the hooks at the front of the corset then returned to the bed.

"Maybe," he said.

Iestyn turned over and Dan spooned behind him, which let their bodies meet in as many places as possible. Surrounded by the scent and touch of the man he loved, Iestyn knew he had everything he'd ever wanted—a job he loved, a family who loved and accepted him, and a man who adored him. He needed nothing more and it was the best feeling in the world.

About the Author

Originally from South Wales, Alexa has lived for over thirty years in the North West of England. Now retired, after a long career in teaching, she devotes her time to her obsessions.

Alexa began writing when her favourite character was killed in her favourite show. After producing a lot of fanfiction she ventured into original writing.

She is currently owned by a mad cat and spends her time writing about the men in her head, watching her favourite television programmes and usually crying over her favourite football team.

Alexa Milne loves to hear from readers. You can find her contact information, website details and author profile page at http://www.totallybound.com.

Totally Bound Publishing